EXILED

K.N. NGUYEN

It's been ten years since I've first come to Corinth.

Ten wonderful years.

Now, onto adventure.

I

L EN WRINKLED HIS NOSE as the man next to him lit a pipe. He knew the smell all too well - bad opium and piss weak ale. The sharp, sour smell stung his eyes. His forearm stuck to the bar as he leaned forward, its surface two shades darker with drink, sweat, and gods knows what. Ignoring the way the smoke made his chest tighten, Len took a sip of his drink. The rancid taste of the drink, an insult calling it ale, sent a wave of nausea through him, causing him to blink slowly as he fought to keep his stomach from revolting. The Lián Huā, the Lotus, used to be a fine establishment fifteen years ago, but once Henrei took over things had gone downhill quickly.

The five men that Len was with, members of the notorious pirate captain Kayna's crew, milled about the smoky room. Three sat at a table with two other men, a pile of coins sitting in between them and a stack of cards next to a surly looking man named Jolly. A pipe dangled from Jolly's mouth, his own wisps of smoke mixing in with that of the tavern's. The remaining two members of Len's makeshift crew sat at another table in the corner, a pint of something in front of each man.

Apart from his crew, the Lián Huā was still fairly crowded. Five out of the six tables were full, as was every seat at the bar. General chatter created a blanket of noise that filled the room. Occasionally, a bark of laughter or a curse broke over the general hum of conversation, punctuating the atmosphere of the tavern.

Picking up his flagon, Len spun around on his stool and leaned back against the sticky wood. His keen eye scanned the crowd, searching for signs of danger out of habit. As a powerful warrior and member of the Qu'ari elite back in his homeland of Xan, Len spent the last two decades traveling the Eastern Seas with Kayna's crew as her personal mercenary. Using his skills as a world-class warrior, Len often traveled out to investigate rumors of bandits, pirates, and rogues causing trouble. Many times, just his presence was enough to quell the scalawags, but on the rare case that it wasn't enough, Len reveled in introducing them to the edge of his blade.

For the most part, the men inside the Lotus were minding their own business. A shout from a couple men who joined his crew playing cards caught Len's attention. Len's eyes were drawn to a burly man, the many scars covering his upper arm accentuated against his leathery skin like the deep scratches gauged into the bar's surface. The man pounded his fist into the table, the force of his actions making the flagons rattle and the coins dance in their little pile, their clinking almost melodic against the rowdy din. Unperturbed, the three members of Len's crew ignored the outburst with a laugh, dealing more cards as the pile disappeared into the slender hands of Flint. The burly man, must not have been too upset as he didn't say anything more.

Len hid a smirk behind his mug under the pretense of taking another sip. The warm ale touched his lips, but didn't enter his mouth. He just couldn't bring himself to drink anymore today. At least, not anymore of this swill. Flint's beady eyes glinted in with wan light of the dust-smeared windows, his thin lips hidden behind his cards. More coins thumped onto the table. Len noted how Flint shared a glance with Jolly and Callum seated on either side of him.

Tearing his attention from the trio, Len scanned the rest of the tavern once more. No one seemed to bat an eye as a slender man dressed in dark clothes entered. Instead, most recoiled as the blinding light of the outside world penetrated their darkened hole. Several cries to close the door rang out, which the newcomer obliged without a word – not even an apology.

The tavern was once again plunged into semi-darkness. Len blinked as his eyes readjusted to the dingy room. No one said a word, and Len took note of the man's silent indifference. It wasn't normal. Len tracked the man as he crossed the tavern and sat in one of the few remaining empty chairs. Locke and Dipper, the two men secluded in the darkest corner, pulled their flagons closer. They were watching the newcomer just like Len. Dipper leaned forward, resting his elbows on the table, and whispered something into Locke's ear. Len's gaze lingered on the pair for a moment longer before turning back to face the bar.

"We don't see many of your kind often," Henrei remarked, coming up behind Aigu'o, the barkeep.

Not meeting the owner's face, Len brought his tankard to his lips once more. He hated pretending to drink. The stuff was absolutely awful and a waste of money.

"I've been coming here for years," Len mumbled over the din. "I don't know why we have this same conversation every time."

Pushing Aigu'o to the other side of the bar, Henrei sidled over until he stood in front of Len. A sour smell poorly masked by mint hit Len as Henrei breathed on him.

"We don't like outsiders," Henrei said simply. "We prefer our own."

Not letting the words sting him, Len met Rozin's gaze. The owner leaned against the bar, his elbows uncomfortably perched atop the ancient, stained wood. He stood a good head shorter than Len. Even if he were taller, Len would not have been intimidated. As the former Great Heart of Xan, a title bestowed to the leader of the six clans within Xan, Len spent the duration of his reign working with the other clan heads in preparation for his conquest against the other nations of Corinth. A pompous fool like Henrei didn't even faze Len.

"My money has always been good," Len said evenly. "As has my men. Perhaps you'd prefer we didn't purchase your piss water and just take up the empty chairs that your non-existent patrons sit in?"

Something flashed in Rozin's eye and his jaw clenched. Len worked hard to hide the smirk that wanted so desperately to play on his lips.

"Or perhaps you'd rather I didn't offer my services and keep the undesirables away from your shite tavern? There are others out here that beg Lady Kayna for my services, but for some reason, she has a soft spot for the Lotus and Aigu'o."

Len tilted his head in the barkeep's direction. To his credit, Aigu'o acted as though he didn't hear his name and continued to clean up behind the bar, though Len was fairly certain that the older barkeep strained his ears to pick up what was being said. Beside him, one man lay slumped over the bar, his mouth hanging open as he slept, while the other few patrons wobbled in their stools, slurring their words as they spoke to each other.

"We were here before you," Len continued. "Remember that."

The former Great Heart let his words hang in the air. Henrei always proved to be more slippery than a snake and a pain in Len's side. Fighting down his contempt, Len kept his face neutral, letting the implication of his words do the talking for him.

To his credit, Henrei did not back down. The Lián Huā's owner continued to clench his jaw, gnashing his teeth together so hard Len briefly wondered if they would be ground down to a fine powder. Before Henrei could respond, another shout broke out from the center of the room, followed quickly by the sound of chair or table legs scraping against the dilapidated wood floor. Spinning around to face the commotion, Len saw Flint and Jolly on their feet, Callum slipping their collection of coins into his pouch while the other two men faced a third man – the slender man dressed in dark clothes.

In the back corner, Dipper and Locke also stood, their movements unnoticed by the rest of the tavern as all eyes appeared to be securely locked onto the table of gamblers. Len's hand went to his hip, resting on the hilt of his scimitar, and waited.

A dagger flashed in Flint's hand, the skeletal man's eyes darkening as his brows knit together. The two nameless gamblers faced the lone man, their own blades drawn. Bodies closed in, unaffected by the exposed weapons. An uncomfortable silence fell upon the tavern.

"What seems to be the problem?" Aigu'o asked.

Out of the corner of his eye, Len noticed that the barkeep continued to wipe the glass in his hand. Henrei slipped up beside the older man and placed his own dagger on the bar. No one else seemed to notice the owner's actions.

Without turning to address the barkeep, the lone man took a quiet step back. "It's all just a misunderstanding."

His words came out low and gravely, like the rumble of thunder. Len noticed a hint of an accent that he hadn't heard before. An accent possibly from the lands beyond the Eastern Isles.

"Trying to pocket our money like we wouldn't notice is no misunderstanding," Callum replied.

Flint continued to glower at the man, his dagger arm resting at his side. The two unnamed gamblers shared a glance before giving the members of Len's crew and the lone man a wider berth. They sheathed their weapons, their stake in the disagreement having disappeared, and pressed themselves between the passed-out drunks at the bar.

"I think it's time you leave," Henrei said, picking up his dagger.

Rozin's head turned to face Len, requiring the Xanan to take his eyes off of the stranger and address the owner of the Lotus. The two shared a glance, Henrei nodding his head with finality before facing the lone man once more.

Freyna's mercy, Len swore to himself. *What is this piece of shite doing?*

Removing his hand from his hip, Len began walking towards the tavern door. He trusted his men would not escalate the situation further. The sound of boots against the wood sounded behind him. Multiple boots. Pushing the door open, Len did not expect the lone man to be the first out of the Lotus. He didn't expect the man to leave at all. As the man tugged at his cloak, his loose sleeve fell down to his elbow, revealing a mixture of smooth, rounded markings mixed with some darker, jagged patterns, and completed with thin, spiraling marks, wispy and ethereal, going up his arm.

God-blessed.

Len's body tensed, his hand dropping to the hilt of his scimitar. It had been a long time since the former Great Heart had seen one of the rare magi who had been blessed by the goddess Aria. He had never seen a god-blessed this far out in the Eastern Isles. Acquiring the magical gifts carried a risk of losing one's mind if they were rejected, or if they were blessed with one of the cursed styles like Wind. Len racked his mind, trying to remember any hint of magi going missing, a sign that their blood was being used for draughting – a way to bypass the Blood Ceremony and to acquire the holy blood and magical gifts. He couldn't recall anything.

Damn, he swore to himself. *If we're not careful, this will end badly. He looks like a Stream mixed with a Spark or Tempest?*

Despite being surrounded by hostile people, the man didn't spare a glance at Len or his men. He seemed completely nonchalant about the whole ordeal. That combined with the unidentified markings only served to increase Len's now rising agitation. Wiping the light sheen of sweat that coated the palms of his hands, Len waited, letting the situation play out.

Callum and the others didn't seem to notice the markings on the man's arm. They gathered around the tavern door one-by-one, waiting for Len's word. Locke and Dipper spoke to Flint softly, their voices not carrying far. Flint continued to glare at the retreating figure of the lone man.

Len wondered if he had been mistaken. There were no god-blessed this far out in the east, but plenty had familiar markings, not unlike Len's people in Xan or the barbarians in the frozen north. There was no reason to think that the practice of tattooing the family line was only common in Corinth. Len mentally chided himself for letting his imagination get the better of him. Still, he found himself watching the direction the man had disappeared.

Something doesn't feel right.

A soft gust of wind pulled at Len's tunic, pushing him towards the traveler as though it were beckoning him to follow the man. He took a step forward, trusting the Ayr to guide him in the right direction.

"What do you think?"

Callum's question broke the spell, bringing Len's attention back to his crew.

Ignoring Len's hesitation, Callum continued on with his train of thought. "I think Kayna ought to know. She may want to deal with Henrei herself."

"Yes," Len replied. "We should head back. Although, I might just make a special visit to Henrei myself later on."

"Be careful not to get Aigo'u in trouble," Jolly warned.

"Aye," Flint agreed. "He's one of the good ones. But what about that one?" Flint gestured in the direction the lone man had been walking. "He's trouble, I'd bet my last coin on that."

"Leave him," Len said. "For now. Keep your ears open. If you hear anything, come to me. This one is one I'd like to handle without bothering Kayna, or the Scourge."

The five acknowledged his request. Emotions having finally settled down now that they were outside in the warm sun, it was as though a pall had been removed and level-heads managed to prevail. Flint and Callum no longer appeared agitated. Even Locke and Dipper resumed their usual, stoic affect.

The six made their way back to their ship, the Lián Huā becoming a tiny speck in the horizon. Callum and Jolly joked about how much they'd managed to win from the two men at the bar. The clink of coins in their pouches attesting to their profitable venture. Locke and Dipper were locked in conversation with Flint, the three following the other two. Len trailed behind the group, his mind replaying the moment he saw the strangely familiar markings on the man's arm. They looked like a combination of Stream, Tempest, and Spark, but the man had been composed and lucid, not the wild-eyed type like most with the erratic wind abilities.

How would someone out here get access to the blood? Len wondered. *People in this area don't travel to Corinth unless they have business. Draughting? That seems improbable too. I think I've seen one god-blessed since moving out to the Bone Coast. God-blessed don't take up the sea life.*

Len's brow furrowed, his mouth drawing into a tight line. Nothing was adding up.

I could be wrong, he admitted to himself. *I'll have to consult the bones when I get back to the Coast. Maybe I will need to take some time away from the ship. I haven't been on my own for a while. It might be a nice change of pace.*

Unsure of what to believe, the Xanan continued making his way back to his ship. Inside his chest, he felt something stir. A yearning that he hadn't experienced since he decided to give up his title as the Great Heart and leader of Xan to move to the Bone Coast and live a life of piracy. Gradually, it morphed into a tingling, a thrill of adventure. Len would find the man and learn his secrets.

Len would discover if there was truly a god-blessed out in the Eastern Realms.

II

GULLS CRIED OVERHEAD as the warm sea breeze filled the sails of *Death's Rose*. The heavy fabric of the mainsails snapped as they tugged against their ropes. Above the crow's nest, the *Rose*'s flag whipped wildly in the air. It was a warm day, the kind of day where men remained below deck to avoid heat exhaustion when they weren't on duty. The perfect day for Deylan to wander around. The wide brim of his hat protected his pale skin from the ravages of the sun and afforded his amber eyes the same. His silver hair tickled his face with each gust. Nobody paid him any mind as he wove between the few who worked on-deck. The *Rose* couldn't function without her skilled and faithful crew. And neither could Deylan.

A dip of his head earned Deylan a grunt from those nearby. *Death's Rose* didn't have many who liked to talk. Talking got you killed. To break the silence, he began to whistle. A jaunty melody flew from his lips like a bird's chorus in the forest. The gentle swaying of the ship aided Deylan in his wanderings, allowing him to weave on the deck without a care. He liked it that way. It made his job easier.

After making a full circle around the *Rose*, Deylan began another. The few crewmen who had been working above deck retreated below, leaving only those in the crow's nest to scan the horizon. Craning his neck, Deylan waved at the duo, earning himself an unsavory gesture and scowl from the pair. The corners of Deylan's mouth twitched up, bemused.

Lazy bastards, Deylan mused. *Can't even bother to put up a pretense of politeness.*

The young man's hand traced along the top of the hull as he made another lap. His little shanty floated in the air amid the slapping of the waves. One of the men in the crow's nest shouted out a curse in broken Ro'thre. It wasn't the first time he was mistaken for one of the Northerners. Feigning embarrassment, Deylan stopped whistling.

As he neared the end of his second lap, Deylan stopped and looked out to sea. His hands rested lightly on the edge of the hull, and a pleasant breeze caressed his face. Graak really blessed their journey with calm seas and favorable winds. Closing his eyes, Deylan let out a sigh of contentment. It had been a long time since he'd been home. His work had taken him further and further away, but the rewards justified it every time.

Azure water sparkled in the light of the sun. The white froth from the spray topped the waves like cream on a cake – light and foamy. Even from where he stood, Deylan could make out the extraordinarily delicate bubbles. In the distance, a porpoise breached the water, its body moving in a graceful arc as it slipped through the ocean's surface.

Maybe I should go home this time. Gods know it's been a while.

Four years to be exact. Deylan regretted not visiting his mother and five siblings during that time. His father's death had devastated him, leaving him trying to fill that void. Not even the Trials could fix the mistakes of Deylan's past, however. The future was all he could hold onto, and pray that he was not called upon for Redemption once more.

More porpoises jumped through the air. A sign of good luck. The creatures played in the water, ignoring the incoming ship. Their streamline bodies broke the water with ease, barely making a splash unless they chose to spin through the air.

"Hey, jhafti!" one of the men in the crow's nest called out.

His partner leaned over the railing, a massive smirk filling his face. Deylan sighed, pulling his attention from the crystalline blue waters. He hated being known as a mainlander. He much preferred the Ro'thre curse. In the short period of time that his hands had been resting on the ledge exposed to the sun, his pale flesh carried a hint of pink.

"You hear me, jhafti?" the man called out again.

Laughter cracked from above. The pair leaned over the nest's edge, amusement flashing on their faces. Playing with the brim of his hat, Deylan took a moment before responding.

There was nothing he could do except take the taunting with good humor. Talking got you killed.

"How can I be of service to you?" Deylan replied. He dipped the front of his hat in lieu of a bow with a cheeky grin on his face. "My shift doesn't begin until nightfall."

A sneer crossed the first man's face. Deylan could almost picture his taunter's nose turning up in disgust. The image threatened to draw out more emotion from his carefully crafted nonchalant expression. Perhaps the porpoises were about to bring him some luck. This particular trip had been less than fruitful and Deylan really needed to avoid returning home empty-handed.

"Don't think you can talk your way out of this," the man growled. "You're lucky we brought a jhafti like you onboard."

"Oh come now," Deylan said, bringing his hand to his chest as though he were insulted at the vitriol spat at him. "How many jhafti do you know that can do what I do? I've sailed for years. Graak has blessed me on every journey, and therefore blessed those who I travel with."

The man wasn't impressed, though his partner raised a brow. The dislike appeared a bit one-sided – but nothing Deylan couldn't move to his favor.

"Besides," Deylan continued. "I managed to ingratiate myself with your beloved captain. Making that crusty barnacle tolerable is a true gift. You should be thanking me." Deylan couldn't help but emphasize the "me" as he held the man's gaze.

The man's partner nudged him with his elbow, rapidly mumbling something in his ear. Holding his expression as neutral as possible, Deylan waited for the second man to finish speaking before deciding his next move. He didn't have to wait long before being rewarded with an incoherent snarl from the first man as the pair returned to their duties in the crow's nest.

Deylan turned away from them back to his spot and raised a hand in farewell. He kept his hands under the shade of his hat this time, not wanting to actually burn them.

Healing sun salves were quite expensive since most who needed them were not seasoned sailors, but visiting merchants and self-important lordlings. Not many like him traveled this far. Not many like him traveled anywhere.

The porpoises were gone. He scanned the horizon, but they were nowhere in sight.

"Damn," he muttered.

Leaning forward, Deylan rested his arms on the ledge once more, and his chin on the back of his forearm, keeping his exposed flesh safe under the brim of his hat. It was a shame they'd moved on. On the horizon, he could make out a landmass. The Bone Coast was maybe a day or two away. He would have to act fast.

A bell rang aboard the ship. Mealtime. Another godsforsaken meal of stale biscuits and extra watered-down wine. The one silver lining to the end of this trip was that Deylan could finally get a decent meal once he returned home. His time on the *Death's Rose* had not been as successful as he'd hoped.

Dhruvasht was supposed to be a formidable pirate with good informants. Had he been misled?

I'll have to keep my eyes peeled. Dhruvasht is famous for a reason. He knows something about the Eastern lands that he's not sharing – even with his men. But Graak's mercy, I don't know how much longer I can take this shite. And this shite food.

The bell rang once more. It wouldn't ring again. If you missed dinner, you went hungry. Deylan had skipped more than his share of meals during this trip. As if on cue, his stomach rumbled in protest. He couldn't skip another meal no matter how bland it was. Pressing his palms into his face, Deylan let out a growl before straightening up.

"Graak's mercy," he swore. The pale grey of dusk before the vibrant oranges and pinks painted the heavens had begun to slowly creep into the rich blue of the sky. It wouldn't be dark for a few more hours. All at once, the emotion left his body, leaving Deylan deflated. "What in the seven hells have you gotten me into?" he muttered. "Gods' mercy."

Unconsciously, Deylan's hands went to his hat once more. His fingers played with the fabric for bit, shifting it minutely until it was just right before heading below deck. He had a role to fill, and he couldn't mess it up with only two days left.

III

DARKNESS BLANKETED *Death's Rose*, wrapping her gently in its velvety purple-blackness. A few torches dotted the ship, providing a small radius of light for the crew to see by. The crescent moon did not bathe the ship like a full moon had. The heavy cloud cover took away what little light Toron's moon could provide. Even the sparkling stars could not provide much light. The constellations were invisible. Not even the panther goddess, Maah-res, could be seen. Deylan walked by himself without a torch. His amber eyes glinted with speckles of silver in the faint starlight, allowing him to take in his surroundings better than his comrades.

Dinner had been a miserable affair. The biscuits were so stale, Deylan could have sworn they were rocks. The wine, if you could call it that, had been so watered down that one could barely taste it. Dhruvasht wasn't exactly known as a generous captain, but this was a new low even for the sourly man. Deylan had been on another voyage with *Death's Rose* and he didn't recall the meals being so grotesque. The only saving grace came when one of the crewmen pulled out the last vestiges of his dried meat to share with the crew. There wasn't even enough for a bite amongst them all, but the little morsel of salted meat was enough to remind Deylan and the others what food tasted like.

As Deylan continued his patrol, he prayed that no one found the small stash of dried fruit he kept inside his pillow. He'd learned long ago to not rely on the kindness of pirates and seafaring men to keep his belly full. The man who'd shared his dried meat was a gem amongst dull stones. Deylan would remember him.

Night patrol was lighter than day. Two men manned the crow's nest, and including Deylan, there were only three other men working night shift. Dhruvasht kept a small crew aboard the *Rose*. Deylan rather liked the intimate group. Made it more of a challenge to complete his duties, however. The jaunty shanty from the afternoon found its way past his lips as Deylan began whistling once more. Unlike his daytime counterparts, those on night shift welcomed the tune. In the distance, one of the bobbing lights started to sing the melody to Deylan's song. For a pirate, he had a lovely voice.

Maybe this isn't a wretched piece of shite after all, Deylan mused. *I should be able to find something to salvage this trip. Just a little longer.*

As night wore on, the waves became a little rougher. *Death's Rose* rocked back and forth on the choppy sea. The torches bounced and swayed with the ship.

"Probably a good thing we don't have the torches attached to the ship," Deylan noted as one of the crewmen passed by.

The man staggered, arms flailing, boots skidding across the slick deck as the waves slammed into the boat. He caught himself on the railing with a grunt. Even for a seasoned seaman it was difficult to maintain balance.

"Graak must be angry," the man said. "Wonder who displeased him?"

"And so close to home," Deylan agreed. "Is there something we could offer him to try to appease him?"

The pirate shook his head. "Nothing I can think. Damn! I haven't seen seas like this in quite a while."

Wave after wave battered *Death's Rose*, each one more vicious than the last. Some spilled over the rail, the icy water slapping the deck and drenching boots. Shouts rang out as the night patrol stumbled back, soaked to the bone. This wasn't the warm drift of the Eastern Seas, and no one had dressed for cold. Not even Deylan. Water drenched Deylan after another powerful wave hit the ship.

"Thuul's hells!" he cursed. He tried in vain to shake the water off of his body, his arms waving in the air. This chill bit to the bone. "Dammit, Graak! This was my nice shirt. And my boots! Damn!"

Through his profanity-laced rant, another voice called out from far away. At first, Deylan couldn't make out what was being said. Despite wanting to continue his grumbling tirade, Deylan stopped. His ears strained to listen, hoping to pick up what was being said. The bobbing torches converged, making their way over to where he stood.

"That's not normal," Deylan muttered.

The wind picked up, adding another layer to the cold. The voices picked up once more. It took Deylan a moment to realize they came from above. Craning his neck, Deylan tried to make out their words.

"What's going on?" the first torch-bearer asked.

"How could you hear that?" Deylan asked.

Incredulity colored his tone. The man had been on the opposite side of the ship and heard the call. Amidst the shaking of the ship and the howling of the wind, the message from the crow's nest struggled to break through.

"Graak is furious!" This voice came from the man Deylan spoke to earlier.

The fire light created deep shadows on the crew's faces, giving them gaunt, haggard appearances. Their eyes were wide as they strained to listen to what was being said. The third torch joined the group, confusion etched onto his face in the light.

"Storm approaching!"

The words broke through the howl of the wind at last. The sails whipped about, straining against the ropes that held them. Deylan's breath caught in his throat as the three pirates broke into concerned chatter. Graak was angry indeed.

"We must wake Dhruvasht," one man said.

"Tie everything down and wake the crew," a second added.

The third man, the one who joined the group last, stood rigid. Petrified. His hand grasped at a pendant hanging around his neck. In the light of the torch, Deylan could see that the color had drained from the man's face.

"This is what happens when you pray to heathen gods," the man said at last.

His words caught the attention of the other three.

"What?" the second man asked.

"Is this really the time for that?" the first added.

"Praying to jhafti gods like Graak have brought Maa'zhun's wrath. Her anger comes swiftly to take down those who displease her. We must pray that she spares us and the ship."

Deylan opened his mouth to reply, but before he could say anything, the third man spun on his heels and raced to the stairs leading below deck. The two other men stood in stunned silence next to Deylan. Through it all, the two from the crow's nest continued to yell out warnings to the three.

"What... waiting...?" The words were torn from the crow's nest and lost to the wind. Luckily, the basic meaning of the message could still be made out.

The rope from the nest dropped in front of the trio. Gusts of wind tugged at the rope, attempting to rip it away and throw it into the ocean. The second torch bearer grabbed the rope tightly. Deylan took up the remaining section of rope as the other man raced below deck to warn the crew. It wasn't long before the two in the crow's nest began to descend. Their bodies were tossed around in the gale despite Deylan and the other man's attempts to steady the rope. Heavy rain began falling, its drops stinging the flesh as it fell from the sky. The flame of the torch was snuffed out, plunging the four into total darkness.

Rain slicked Deylan's hands, the rope slipping through his grip. His waterlogged clothes clung heavy, on his body. As the lookouts descended, a wave slammed into the hull with bone-rattling force. Deylan stumbled back, his footing lost, and hit the deck hard. The other man crashed down on top of him. Water surged over them, cold as ice. Deylan gasped, breath punched from his lungs, as the sea drenched him again. Every time the water hit him, it was like a knife twisted into his chest, making it more difficult to breathe. Cries from the dangling men could be heard over the roar of the wind.

"Hang on!" Deylan called out. His voice was ripped from his throat and carried away. He wasn't sure the men even heard him.

Rolling the man off him, Deylan struggled to his feet. The rocking of the ship dropped him to his knee twice before he managed to finally regain his footing. By the time he stood up, the second man had as well. Labored breathing told Deylan that it was as much of a struggle for that man as it had been for him.

The cries for help from the look-outs dangling above became more frantic as the wind buffeted them against the mast. Their bodies bounced against the thick wooden beam.

With a shriek, the man closest to the crow's nest lost his grip and plummeted to the deck. In the darkness, no one saw his flailing arms. Only the man's death scream let them know he was there. Deylan's hands found the rope just as the falling man's body slammed into the deck. Wooden planks cracked as the impact created an ear-splitting crash.

"By the gods!" a shout came from beside Deylan.

The man dashed toward the fallen lookout, Deylan gripping the rope for the last man's descent. The wind hit him hard, almost ripping it from his hands. He held fast. The rope slid, burning across his palms, the fiber biting deep. His knuckles turned white, his arms trembling with strain, as every muscle screamed to maintain control of the rope. In the distance, he thought he heard a chorus of voices yelling over the storm, but it was too far to focus on.

Closer the man came to safety. Inch by inch, the man shimmied down the rope. Another body ran up behind Deylan and grabbed the excess length of rope behind him. Together the two held it steady as the look-out made the final bit of his descent onto the deck.

"Grab onto what you can!" Dhruvasht commanded as he rushed over to the helm from below deck. His deep bass rang over the howling squalls.

Deylan found himself placing his back onto the mast, maintaining his death-grip on the rope. The man behind him and the trembling look-out scrambled to find something secure to hold onto. In the darkness, Deylan saw indistinct figures tying up the last of the cargo in hopes of saving their waning supplies. Deylan wondered if he should help, but quickly dismissed the idea. He would only get in the way. Possibly even kill himself.

A crack of lightning illuminated the heavens. The bolt went all the way down, striking the tumultuous ocean. Men screamed, calling out to each other as another wave struck the side of the *Rose*. Deylan shielded his eyes, the sudden brilliance blinding him momentarily.

"I need more hands!" Dhruvasht's voice rang out. Panic filled every word of the seasoned pirate's plea.

Deylan watched as their captain struggled to hold the wheel steady. The waves rocked the boat mercilessly, nearly toppling her several times. Despite his call for help, no one moved to help him.

"To me!"

Dhruvasht's command penetrated the chaos of the storm once more. The mast was not too far from the wheel. Deylan took a step towards the captain, but his hands remained clenched around the rope. Still, no one came to their captain's aid. With a gulp, Deylan worked to release his death-hold on the rope. It was like he fought against Death himself.

"God dammit!" Deylan cried.

His yell was enough. Adrenaline helped Deylan release his hold on the rope. Without thinking, Deylan raced towards Dhruvasht. He zigzagged across the deck as the ship continued to be tossed about. Gale-force winds threatened to toss him like a ragdoll. It felt like an eternity.

Once he reached the wheel, he wrapped his hands around the handles and locked his arms. His legs were shoulder width apart to help Deylan create a sturdy base as he struggled to hold the wheel. He could feel the sea trying to rip the wheel out of his hands despite both Deylan and Dhruvasht clinging to it.

"We just have to hold out until morning," Dhruvasht said. His words disappeared into the maelstrom. "Storms like this don't last for days."

"Why would Graak curse us like this?" Deylan asked. He'd never been one to believe in the God of Storms before, but he couldn't turn down the possibility that someone had angered the god and earned his wrath. "The weather was clear just hours earlier."

"Stop asking stupid questions, boy. You need to save your energy. Now hold!"

A strong tug against the rudder nearly tore the wheel from Deylan's hands. His arms ached and his hands felt like they would permanently be stuck as claws, so the sudden jolt surprised him. A yell of frustration was torn from his lips as he readjusted his grip. Another flash of lightning lit up the sky. The bolt fell from the heavens and hit the mast. A thunderous crack rent the air as the sails went up in flames and the mast split in two. Men cried out as loose chunks of wood fell onto the ship. Dhruvasht let out a stream of curses as the fragments crashed onto the ship.

Lightning flashed once more. Squinting his eyes against the blinding agony, Deylan thought he saw the silhouette of a lone figure standing aboard a small ship. Waves exploded against the boat, spray kicking up and no doubt drenching the figure. However, he seemed unconcerned. It was only for a split second, but it seemed so vivid to Deylan. An extraordinary pain lanced through his head. Deylan's vision went white as a section of the mast landed on his head. Dhruvasht's voice babbled off in the distance.

Deylan's body crumpled as his vision went black. The wind pelting rain began to subside as the *Death's Rose* started listing to the right, sending Deylan's limp body towards the edge of the sloping ship. Further away, lightning flashed one final time.

IV

"ANOTHER SHIP HAS GONE MISSING, my lord." The hurried tone of the page well into his middle years caught Len's attention as he walked through the quiet streets of the upper west district.

The streets were peaceful in the warm afternoon sun. Young couples and families strolled about, finishing their shopping in the lower coast or setting their children free to run amok in the cobbled streets before heading down for an early dinner. The Xanan stuck out amongst the wanderers, the battleaxe on his back and scimitar on his hip sticking out just as much as his rich tawny skin. When he'd first moved to the Bone Coast, his appearance would draw stares, but after nearly two decades, what once was surprise and amazement turned to disinterest, and sometimes mistrust.

"That's seven in the last fortnight, and no sign of foul play." The page's voice cracked as he squeaked out his message.

"That's impossible," Baron Ciadpach hissed, dropping his voice noticeably. A short, soft-bellied man with slicked back hair, the oil causing his hair to glisten in the light. "And keep your tone down." The baron's last words struggled to get past his clenched teeth.

Taking advantage of the men's distress, Len slipped a piece of weathered parchment from his coin pouch, pretending to read the message he'd already memorized – a message from his wife eight years ago: *Another daughter of Xan. Arezou.*

Out of the corner of his eye, Len noticed the baron and his page glancing his direction. Wanting to dispel their concern, Len began muttering in his home tongue, scratching his head as though the message perplexed him. He was rewarded for his little show by the baron quickly turning to face his messenger and dropping his voice to just above a whisper.

"I'm sorry, my lord," the page squeaked out. "What should we do? The merchants are growing angry. They're hiring mercenaries and bootleggers, paying obscene amounts of money, and ships are still going missing."

Len held still, straining to listen. The streets had quieted down, the families having turned onto other streets or disappearing into shops or homes. Even the gulls stilled, as though they were waiting to hear what the baron had to say.

"Damn," Ciadpach spat. "What are those damned bootleggers good for if they can't keep ships from sinking? Have one of those mages gone rogue?"

Len's ears perked up. The strange man's markings flashed in his mind. It had been a month since the encounter at the Lotus, and Len hadn't heard a word of anything out in that area.

Could they be related? he wondered.

"No one knows, my lord," the page stuttered. "There's no sign that god-blessed are involved. Many are talking about Graak being displeased and sending rough waters that scupper the ships."

The baron snorted, slapping the page on the back of his head in the process. "Those damned fools. There's no man in the sky punishing people for not following superstition. Gods, these simpletons will believe anything."

Rubbing his head, the page glanced up at his lord. "But my lord." The page's voice caught in his throat. "That still doesn't explain what's going on with the ships? If it were an act, they wouldn't be disappearing either. Four men washed ashore after this last one. Captain Dhruvasht said that it was like no storm he'd ever seen. Surely, the fact that all but these four perished means that there's something afoot."

Ciadpach paused. Len observed how the baron rubbed his chin while the page watched the baron's hand anxiously, waiting to see if another smack was coming his way.

The messenger makes a good point, Len reluctantly agreed. *I don't think it's of Ayr, however. It may not be the man, but there's only one way to find out. We sail in three days for the East. I need to act fast.*

"Send word that no one is to leave the ports," Ciadpach said at last. "If merchants are being extorted and still not receiving protection, we must look into this scam. I don't trust those bootleggers anymore than I trust their kind."

Still staring at his parchment, Len noted how the baron openly gestured towards him, not even bothering to keep his voice down anymore. Len's pulse quickened as the baron continued to ramble on to the page, the two resuming their walk down the street.

"You miserable bastard," Len muttered in his native tongue. "When I return, I'll be keeping my eye out for you."

Folding the aged paper carefully, Len shoved it back into his coin pouch and turned towards the Scourge's tavern. His blood boiled. There was no honor in maligning others. It was not the way of the Brothers of Xan, and if Ciadpach wasn't careful, he would learn what happened to those who didn't hold their tongue.

V

IND ROARED IN DEYLAN'S EARS as he raced back home. In his mind, he could hear his little sisters crying. His pulse pounded in his ears. He had to save his mother. Her limp, bloodied body lay in the kitchen, unconscious. Thin tracks on her cheeks marked where her tears washed over the blood. Deylan had never seen his mother look so helpless.

Deylan remembered seeing Xi, his sisters' father and mother's husband, passed out at the front door, barring his mother's escape. As his home loomed ahead, Deylan's vision went red.

The local patrol said that he'd stabbed Xi twenty times that night. His hands ached as the thick ropes, their fibers digging into his wrists, were tied behind his back. The Guards mentioned something about reinforcements and keeping Deylan contained. He was only fifteen, and there were eight grown men. What could he possibly do? Some of the men tended to his mother who woke up after the attack while the remainder examined Xi's body. No one wanted to listen to Deylan.

He could either be put to death, or he would spend the rest of his life repaying Xi's family for his actions. Such was the judgement of the Trials. Deylan watched as his mother wept, her shoulders shaking silently. His sisters stared at him, eyes wide in disbelief, their cries ignored by the Crown. That night, Dzaria smuggled Deylan out of their little village in Ro'thre. It was the only way. Murder was not tolerated in Ro'thre.

<div align="center">~~~</div>

Head throbbing, Deylan groaned as the bright orange light of day shone through his closed eyelids. Gulls cried out and birdsong filled the air. The tangy scent of salt wafted in the air. Deylan tried to turn away from the sun, but a wave of pain lanced through his head. Nausea rolled over him. His empty stomach cramped as the sickness hit. Another groan escaped his lips. Forcing himself to move, Deylan found his body wrapped in blankets. A soft pillow swallowed the side of his head as he turned.

His heart ached. He hated dreaming about the Trials. A hiss escaped his lips as he pushed Xi's ugly face out of his mind. To this day, Deylan could only remember what Xi looked like when he lived. What the Guard claimed Deylan did was lost to a haze of red. The phantom ropes tied around his wrist slowly faded away as Deylan focused on his discomfort.

Gingerly, Deylan's hand went to his head. Thin strips of cloth wound around his forehead. He tried to remember what happened, but all he could remember was the storm. The storm, and that strange figure standing out in the middle of the sea as though he didn't have a care in the world.

"What in the seven hells happened?" he muttered, pushing himself up to a sitting position. Even talking was painful.

A few more strips of cloth wrapped around other parts of Deylan's otherwise unclothed body. Someone must have tended to him while he was unconscious. The thought of someone riffling through his things when he couldn't do anything to stop them left him feeling unsettled. On a chair near the bed, a pitcher of water and glass waited for him.

The images from his dream quickly faded away. The emotion tried to linger, but his pain brough back memories of the storm. Disjointed flashes of massive waves, merciless rain, and the howl of the wind played in rapid succession. He could almost hear the lightning crack as it struck the ship.

I wonder who survived. Deylan couldn't imagine *Death's Rose's* wreckage out in the middle of the Eastern Sea. They were still at least a day away from shore. Surely no one saw them. *The fact that I'm alive is a miracle. Wonder if Dhruvasht made it.*

The thought of the captain created a pit in Deylan's empty stomach. He still had business with the pirate.

First, food. I can't take too long, though. People like Dhruvasht don't wait around long even when their ship's destroyed.

Such was the allure of the sea. Deylan had felt her calling him on several occasions. Each time, he nearly gave in. But he couldn't. There was too much he needed to finish before he could settle down.

A soft knock on the door startled the young man. The roar of the wind and the crashing of the waves had consumed him, almost as though he relived the moment. They had drowned out everything – stealing the voice of countless men. Glancing over to the door, Deylan's eyes swiftly passed over the oaken writing desk underneath the window, the nib of the quill shining in the light as it rested on the table. Next to it, a pot of ink waited to be used.

"Excuse me," a sweet voice called out to him. The door opened a sliver and a deep brown eye peered at him through the door. "Are you awake?" Her voice was like an angel's. If only they existed.

"Aye." Deylan's reply came out in a croak.

Through the pain of his throbbing head, he managed to make his way to the chair and fill the cup with water. The room spun from the efforts of his exertion. Bringing the cup to his lips, Deylan took a sip. The cool liquid soothed his dry throat and refreshed him. He greedily finished the cup and poured himself a second by the time the young woman opened the door and squeezed into the room.

"I'm sorry to bother you," she began, "but I was asked to change your cloths. Would you like something to eat?"

Her gaze dropped as she took in Deylan's lithe frame. Years on the sea had strengthened his muscles. It also blessed him with a few scars – one on his right breast and another on his right bicep. Her tanned face flushed and her eyes darted upward as she noted Deylan's lack of pants.

At least she left me with something to cover myself, he mused. *Wonder how she managed to change me those other times?*

Trying not to embarrass the poor girl further, Deylan returned to his bed, cup in hand. The young woman sat on the bed next to him and began unwrapping the cloths on his body. Her fingers gently grazed his flesh several times, sending a tingly wave up his spine. She smelled lovely – of honeysuckle.

"How long have I been unconscious?" Deylan asked, breaking the awkward silence. He could have watched her work in peace, but he had so many questions.

"Three days. They found your ship two days ago. Or what was left of it, at least. The storm pushed her into the rocks not far from the harbor. We didn't think anyone would survive. Most of the ship was burning." She met his gaze properly for the first time. "Not many made it."

The pit in Deylan's stomach grew heavier. What if Dhruvasht didn't survive?

"Did the captain survive? Tall man. Personality of a plank of wood."

His words brought a soft smirk to her lips. "The captain and three other men returned alive. Most were lost at sea. Some in the fire." Her smile faded as she recalled the wreckage. "You were found half submerged in water. Your body was barely dangling on the rocks. They thought you were dead, but someone saw you breathing. They were ready to kick you into the ocean."

The news sent a shiver down Deylan's spine. He'd never wanted a burial at sea. The notion that he'd just barely escaped such a fate seemed to be the work of the gods.

"Graak must have blessed me then," Deylan said. "Shame more couldn't have shared his blessing."

The young woman hummed in agreement, nodding. Her fingers moved deftly and soon she was done tending to Deylan's wounds. Next, she fished into the little bag on her hip and pulled out a few leaves of featherfew.

"For your head," she said, holding them out for him.

With a word of thanks, Deylan popped the leaves into his mouth and began chewing. They tasted awful, but within a few minutes, he could feel the effects of the plant. The ache in his head hadn't subsided, but became a little more tolerable.

The two sat in silence once more as he chewed his featherfew. Now that he could tolerate the light of the sun, Deylan took in his surroundings. Next to the chair with the pitcher stood a lone table. His shirt and pants were neatly folded and rested on the table's surface. His boots and socks sat by the doorway. It appeared that his wide-brimmed hat had been lost to the sea. Pity, he rather liked that hat.

"Where are we?" Deylan asked. "And what is your name?"

"You're in the Lost Siren. We may not be the most famous tavern, but we are well known by... your type."

Deylan found himself a bit indignant at the insult. He was no pirate. Still, he remained quiet.

"My name is Nefeli."

"A beautiful name for a daughter of Ayr," Deylan said.

He reached out and gently took her face, caressing her cheek with his thumb. She was quite lovely. Her wavy brown hair flowed freely down her back, and her dark eyes were framed by thick lashes. Even the freckles that dotted her face seemed to be deliberately placed. Nefeli's face flushed once more and her eyes turned down, hidden by her lashes.

"You are too kind," she murmured.

Deylan sat across from Nefeli, still holding her face delicately in his hand. They remained this way for several seconds before she jumped.

"Your food!" she nearly yelped. "Please, let me bring it to you."

As she shot up from the bed and hurried towards the door, Deylan found himself wanting to follow. His head still hurt, but after chewing the featherfew, he felt strong enough to at least walk downstairs into the tavern proper. The injuries to his chest and arm didn't bother him enough to keep him confined to his bed. Now would be a good time to explore and see what everyone knew. Taverns like this could hold a wealth of information. But talking got you killed. He would have to be careful.

"I feel strong enough to make my way downstairs. May I take a table instead?"

"As you wish."

Without another word, Nefeli left. Deylan could hear her boots on the wooden stairs quickly disappearing. Taking a minute to gather his strength, Deylan got dressed. Hidden under his tunic, Deylan was pleased to find that his silver dagger was not lost or stolen. He strapped it to his hip and covered it with the bottom of his shirt that he'd pulled out from his trousers. While he got ready, he worked at finishing the water so that by the time he put on his boots, Deylan had emptied the jug.

Ignoring the throbbing of his head, Deylan made his way down the stairs and into the tavern proper. Despite it being what he could only imagine as mid-day, the room was quiet. He had been to a number of taverns over the years and none had ever been so devoid of patrons. It unnerved him.

"What in the seven hells...?" Deylan muttered.

A few tables held customers enjoying their lunch, but even those did not appear to be enjoying their meal. Deylan noted how their bodies were stiff and they did not talk much as they ate. Taking a table near the other filled ones, Deylan sat and waited for Nefeli. An empty pirate establishment did not bode well.

He sat in silence, attempting to gather information from the snippets of conversations that he managed to overhear. Nothing came to him. He needed to know what was going on. As if on cue, Nefeli returned with a pint of ale and a rice dish. Deylan's mouth watered as the aroma of the fragrant rice and spiced meat hit him. His stomach growled once more, begging for food. But it would have to wait.

Motioning to Nefeli to come closer, Deylan dropped his voice to a whisper. His lips nearly brushed her ear as he spoke, his hand delicately grasping her arm.

"What is this?" Deylan's words came out in earnest, his eyes darting around to see if anyone noticed they were talking. "*Death's Rose* was found crashed just off-shore, burning like a funeral pyre after being struck by lightning. All but four survived. How is it no one is speaking on this?"

Nefeli's breath caught in her throat and Deylan felt her body stiffen. He watched her intently as she began surveying the tavern as he had moments before. She body trembled, her breathing quickening and becoming ragged.

"I cannot say," she stammered. Her attention shifted to him, her eyes wide in panic. "Please, don't make me."

"Feli." Deylan took a chance by using a term of endearment. "Am I in danger? What happened to Dhruvasht?"

"Nefeli!" a man's voice rang into the dining room from the kitchen.

At the sound of her name, Nefeli placed her other arm on the table and pushed her breasts out towards Deylan. A coy smile played on her face as she leaned in closer to him. Her lips almost touched his. Her eyes, however, were still round in fear.

"Coming, love," she called back. Keeping her seductive posture, she said to Deylan, "I might be convinced for a little fun when I'm go on break, love. I can be talked into taking you to my room – if you can prove that you're worth my time." Honey dripped from her words, and at the very end, she leaned forward and pressed her lips against his. "Think about it. I usually take a walk to clear my head." The words came out as a whisper.

With a wink and a swish of her hips, Nefeli disappeared into the kitchen. Deylan watched her the whole way. He noted how her hand lingered on the barkeep's bicep, her big doe eyes meeting his. As she entered the back, the barkeep pinched her backside. Once Nefeli was gone, the barkeep's attention turned to Deylan. A dark scowl crossed the man's visage making Deylan's blood run cold. Something inside him screamed at him that he was not safe.

Dropping his gaze, Deylan turned to his meal. The lamb shank was more tender than he expected. The meat juices dripped down his chin and onto the rice. A moan escaped his lips as he ate. It had been a while since he'd had a hearty meal. The mead had a hint of blackberry to it that complemented the seasoned lamb perfectly. It didn't take long before the meal was completely consumed.

The tavern was empty by the time Deylan finished. He hadn't seen any other barmaids while he ate. None came out to interact with the other patrons, and Nefeli didn't come and check up on him. The only person who paid Deylan any mind was the man behind the bar. Not wanting to spend any more time with the surly barkeep, Deylan quickly made his way to the exit.

The streets were bustling. Gulls cried out as they picked at scraps of food tossed into the street. In the distance, calls from the merchants and other seafaring men in the harbor wafted into the main thoroughfare. A stray cat pounced down from a roof, scattering the gulls and stealing the partially devoured fish. Deylan scanned the crowd, wondering if Nefeli actually was going to be outside the Lost Siren. He got the feeling that she usually didn't just meet drifters.

He wandered about, taking in his surroundings. Deylan scanned the streets looking for Dhruvasht. He had so many questions for the man. Down the street, he knew he would find the Drunken Crossbow. The more high-end tavern was where Deylan preferred to frequent. Dhruvasht wasn't a classy man, but perhaps his tough exterior would help him blend in.

"Deylan!" Nefeli's honeyed voice called out to him as she raced down the street.

Deylan paused in his tracks, waiting for her to catch up to him. The closer she got, he noticed a bit of bruising on her cheek that hadn't been there before. He opened his mouth to ask her about hit once she stood in front of him, but she silenced him by collapsing into him.

"I'm glad I found you," she gasped. "I didn't think you would stay so close."

"What's going on?"

"The Scourge has been gone for too long and the Bone Coast is without a leader. Yours wasn't the first ship we found in such a state. Men have been going missing, lost to the sea, for the last year and a half. Only the most ruthless have managed to escape. When you and the others were found, people began talking – is it a curse from the gods, or something else?"

"I don't understand. Merchants have been traveling for decades. I have almost five years of travel alone. What could a bunch of merchants done to anger the gods?"

"The people are thinking it's not the merchants. The new baron has issued a decree that the Bone Coast is to be closed until we find a way to ensure our ships' safety."

Deylan raised a brow. Shutting down the harbors like that would devastate the local economy. Pirates needed a safe haven where they could replenish their stores and trade their plunder. The local taverns and inns would also suffer. No one could survive such a financial blow. To ban the pirates and merchants would spell death for the Bone Coast and the newly developing Thyllasis. Possible even all of Kalimba. The effects of such an order might even reach deeper into Corinth.

"How would they enforce that?" Deylan asked.

"He's hiring a pirate ship to monitor the harbor. There's already been so much fighting. If you go in deeper, you'll see the burnt buildings. Oh gods, so many people died in those fires. They're not even trying to leave the families out of their squabbles. The number of homeless has grown."

"And the Lost Siren is suffering because we washed ashore?"

Nefeli shook her head. "You were just the final straw. If none of you survived, they could have pretended that it never happened. But you and four others did."

Deylan pinched the bridge of his nose. His mind raced as he tried to weigh her words. Without Dhruvasht and the information he held, Deylan would most definitely be doomed and forced to atone for his sins through Redemption. No. He couldn't do that. Deylan needed to find the treasure of Xiashen.

The closer she got, he noticed a bit of bruising on her cheek that hadn't been there before. He opened his mouth to ask her about it once she stood in front of him, but she quickly silenced him by collapsing into him. Deylan touched her cheek with the tips of his fingers, gently caressing her soft flesh. With a gasp, Nefeli jerked away, her hand popping up to cover her injured face, her eyes hiding behind her thick lashes in shame.

"It's nothing. Don't worry about it," she mumbled.

"Is it because of me?" Deylan asked. His body tensed as he waited for her answer.

A solitary tear rolled down her sun-kissed cheek and her eyes dropped. That was enough for Deylan. Once more, his mind raced as he tried to find a solution to his problems.

"What if I took you with me," he offered. "I know some people further up the coast who could take you in and keep you safe."

"No, it's okay. I promise."

"That's not okay. Especially since it was from me."

"He's not usually like that," she mumbled. "It's the stress of knowing that his business could close any day now. Keets isn't exactly a model citizen. If his business goes down, he would lose all of his livelihood. I'm fine."

Deylan didn't believe her. Turning away, he scanned the streets once more. The carefree people he noticed walking through the streets earlier seemed more tense, their gait hurried as though they rushed to finish their business without being noticed. Stray dogs and cats roamed the thoroughfare, their ribs protruding as they looked for their next meal. Rough looking men and woman wandered the roads. They were the only ones who truly appeared relaxed.

Deylan's attention fell on a man who looked familiar. He appeared to be from Nem Pah, his bronzed flesh showing under his sheer tunic. Thick muscles stretched the seams of his outfit, and around his neck, a pendant hung from a silver chain. This man carried himself with an air of nonchalance, but Deylan could see how tense he was. The man was on high alert.

Shifting his gaze from side to side, the man seemed to be looking for something. Something, or someone. If this was who Deylan thought he was, Deylan knew that he needed to follow the man. This man, the religious man who condemned the

Death's Rose for worshipping a false god, would be Deylan's best chance at finding Dhruvasht.

Deylan's attention turned back to Nefeli. She remained silent as he followed the Nem Pahlan man, his head swiveling as the man moved through the streets. She watched Deylan and the man intently. He saw that she was making her own decisions. Deylan needed to act now before Nefeli changed her mind about helping him.

"I have some unfinished business," he began. "Can we meet up again when I return?"

It was now Nefeli's turn to raise her brow. "Why?" her question came out slowly.

There were many layers of emotion to the simple question. Possibly too many. Deylan feared that he'd lost her sympathy. Taking a chance, he took a deep breath and faced her.

"Because I trust you." He sounded exhausted, and he was. His normally composed and charismatic demeanor cracked. His head throbbed, his body still needed nutrients after so many days at sea without adequate food, and there still was so much to do. "You see things that others may not. I don't know. I feel as though we can help each other survive a little while longer."

Nefeli stood still. Deylan regretted his moment of honesty. If she did not share his sentiments, she could turn him in and get him hanged, or worse. He could become a target for rouge pirates or the ones chosen to watch the harbor. Too much could go wrong.

"Send any correspondence to my sister," Nefeli said after a lengthy pause. "She won't question much. You can pretend to be a love interest. I get a bunch of letters from the men downstairs. Comes with the territory, I guess." She met his gaze, her own turning to steel. "You won't betray me?"

"Never," he promised.

"I have to go," she said, finally breaking their connection. "If that man doesn't lead you to who you seek, you may try the tavern that is favored by Kayna and her crew. It's a nondescript building with a sign bearing a skull at the top and a sword and rose crossing beneath. They may be able to help you."

Grabbing both of Nefeli's arms, Deylan thanked her. He stared into her doe eyes once more before releasing her and heading in the direction that the Nem Pahlan man had gone. He needed to act fast.

VI

IT DIDN'T TAKE DEYLAN LONG to spot him. The easy swagger from earlier was gone. Now the man moved with stiff, jerky steps, his eyes darting to every shadow. His hand kept drifting to the pendant at his neck, his fingers clenching it like a charm of protection. Deylan kept his distance, ensuring there was enough space between them that it wouldn't be obvious at first glance that he stalked the man. However, he made sure that he never lost sight of his prey.

His efforts were quickly rewarded as the man led him to an old, worn-down building. The sign above the door had no letters, but it did bear the skull and sword and rose that Nefeli had talked about. Deylan was about to enter a legendary pirate's den – the favorite tavern of the Scourge.

Keep your head and you'll be fine. Focus on finding Dhruvasht. Don't draw attention to yourself.

The man disappeared into the tavern, leaving Deylan outside in the mid-day sun. The effects of the featherfew began wearing off, and the pain from his injury returned.

How long will I have to deal with this? Deylan wondered. He didn't know many who survived being knocked unconscious by a falling piece of a mast. He probably shouldn't have. *I need to find more featherfew.*

Deylan lingered outside, his breath shallow and his heart thudding in his chest. His palms slick, he wiped them on his trousers before exhaling and stepping inside. The tavern swallowed him. Darkness clung to every corner. Behind him, the door shut with a dull thud. The windows were boarded, creating a tomb-like atmosphere to the already all-engulfing darkness. Deylan took a cautious step forward. Then another. Every head turned. Eyes locked onto him, silent and unblinking. Even the ones at the back. A knot twisted in his gut – a familiar feeling he'd had five years earlier after he'd killed his siblings' father. He didn't belong.

Know your purpose, he told himself. *You belong here.*

Taking a moment to scan the room, Deylan pushed the pirates to the back of his mind. To him, they were no more than the strays outside. As long as he respected them and left them to their business, they had no reason to bother him. It took a while for his eyes to adjust, but once they did, he noticed the coward he had been following earlier talking to a heavily bandaged man. The shadows obscured most of the man's features, but Deylan decided to approach the duo.

No sooner had the young man start towards the back table did the patrons in the tavern turn away. He couldn't tell if they were disinterested, or quietly observing him. Deylan didn't look like a pirate. He never tried to. He found that if too many people knew just how knowledgeable he was then he would have a harder time finding ships to sail with.

The tables were crammed close together, as many as six or seven chairs to the small wooden tables. Even the bar stools were filled. Drink flowed freely and the general raucous chatter that Deylan was familiar with whenever he visited such establishments sounded louder due to the sheer number of people in the room. Very few appeared to be eating, but every soul in this tavern had a tankard in front of them.

Low candlelight from the candles on the tables allowed Deylan to navigate his way to the back. By the time he was almost upon them, the two at the table noticed him and stopped talking. Their bodies shifted as they turned to face him. In the light, Deylan managed to make out the greasy hair and thin scar that ran from the captain's forehead to his cheek, hitting the pirate's left eye in the process. Dhruvasht's tunic was loose and open, exposing the cloths that were wrapped around his ribs. Like Deylan, he had a thin strip of cloth wrapped around his head. The other man appeared relatively unscathed, the bastard.

Deylan went to remove his hat, but found his head bare. He would need to find another one soon. He felt naked without it.

Choosing to instead dip into a small bow, Deylan slipped into an empty chair across from the captain.

"It's good to see you, Captain," Deylan said.

The man next to Dhruvasht looked away, uncomfortable.

"I was afraid you had perished with the others. When I heard you'd survived, I knew I must find you." Lacing his fingers together, Deylan spared another glance to the man next to Dhruvasht, Bharam.

"I'm pleased to see that you are well." Dhruvasht's deep bass somehow carried over the low rumble of the tavern just as it had over the raging storm. "I too thought you dead. Graak has done well to keep us both safe."

At this, Dhruvasht turned to the man next to him and fixed him with a stern glare. The man's body withered and his eyes dropped.

"And I see that you have also been most fortunate."

Deylan loved the effect his words had on the man. Without looking up, the man mumbled a lackluster "Praise Graak." Dhruvasht cleared his throat, breaking the tension that had been building. Deylan's attention snapped back to the captain. He would have more fun with the other man later.

"Bharam was telling me of the baron's decree," Dhruvasht said. "He said that when Saijii heard the news he fled. It's a shame. He was a good sailor."

Deylan thought he heard a hint of regret in the man's tone. He never expected such an emotion from the stoic pirate.

"If you see him, bring him to me," Dhruvasht instructed. "He'll be killed for desertion."

A lump formed in Deylan's throat. He struggled to swallow it down as the words sunk in. The man no doubt had a price on his head at this point. He wondered if that was why Dhruvasht was in this tavern and not one of the others.

"So, tell me. When are you ready to sail?"

The question caught Deylan off guard.

"I'm sorry?" Deylan could only stammer out his question. His mind raced as he weighed the potential implications of his decision. "I heard the *Rose* was destroyed. With this ban, how will you get another ship so quickly? And a crew?"

It seemed ludacris that the injured captain would try to set sail with an injured sailor and a pirate who appeared to be questioning his choices.

What's his plan?

Dhruvasht glanced over at the bar, signaling Deylan and Bharam to follow his lead. Sitting on one of the stools was a red-headed woman drinking what appeared to be her third tankard. Deylan marveled at how such a small woman could put away so much alcohol. She had to be drunk. Next to her, a slim woman with dark skin sat and watched her. A glass of partially consumed wine waited for her to finish it. On the other side of the red-head was a man with deep bronze skin. A battle axe rested against his stool and a scimitar hung from his hip.

The man had a muscular frame, no doubt from years of fighting. He watched the red-head as she babbled about something, his expression never changing. He stuck out to Deylan. Like Deylan, there was something about the man, that no matter how hard he tried, he would not truly be one of them. That despite not looking like most pirates Deylan had seen, there was an air about the man the exuded power and confidence.

This must be the right-hand man of the Scourge, Deylan thought. *The warrior of Xan. The stories don't do him justice.* He watched as a small smile played on the man's lips after something the red-head must have said. *I beg the gods that he's not the one in charge of keeping the ports closed.*

"I've already spoken with the captain," Dhruvasht explained. "She has allowed us passage aboard her ship until we reach the Eastern Isles. There we will find our own ship and continue our sails."

"She?" Bharam gasped.

Deylan was happy he wasn't the one to ask. The news surprised him as well.

"Yes." Dhruvasht sounded annoyed. "I spoke to Kayna and she has been most generous. We need to find another man. I promised Kayna we'd have three men to help with ship duties. It was a damn shame the seas claimed Manesh. He will be hard to replace."

Of course, Deylan mused. *He can't be bothered to do any heavy lifting. Lazy bastard.*

Turning to his drink, Dhruvasht picked up his tankard and downed half of it in one gulp. Amber liquid dribbled down his chin. Taking Bharam's sleeve, the captain wiped his face. Bharam stared almost indignantly at his captain as he pulled his arm closer to his body, but Dhruvasht did not appear to notice.

"We leave in three days," Dhruvasht explained. "Kayna and her crew on *Graak's Fury* will be setting out tomorrow. Be quick."

And with that, the meeting was over. There was no room to discuss anything else now that the captain had given his order. Wishing he had ordered his own drink, Deylan dipped his head and stood up. Behind him, he heard Bharam speaking feverishly to Dhruvasht.

I wonder if he's trying to find a way to stay here without angering Dhruvasht? Probably wishing he ran when Saijii did. Damn coward through and through. I need to deal with him later. He's too much of a liability.

Wending his way through the overcrowded room, Deylan found himself back at the door and the center of attention. This time the chatter did not stop. Heads did not turn. Eyes did not follow him – not that he could see. Everyone appeared to be engaged in their own conversation, but the uncomfortable feeling of being watched brought back the lump in Deylan's throat. He wondered how many of these men would be on his new ship.

Oh gods, Deylan thought as he shut the door behind him. *I'm going to be killed. These people are merciless. I need a distraction.*

Pressing his palm to his forehead, Deylan fought back the pain of his aching head. *But where am I going to find someone who wants to go to sea with everything that's going on?*

After a particularly painful throb, Deylan decided that his first stop would be at the apothecary's. He needed to find some featherfew before he set sail. Some fresh cloths, a healing salve, and a hat were also in order. He couldn't sail without any of that.

"I wonder if Nefeli could tell me where the best shop is," Deylan muttered as he took another turn down the street.

As he searched for the apothecary and hat shop, Deylan reconsidered his options. It would be foolhardy to anger Dhruvasht when he still had so much he needed to do, but at the same time, it would be relatively easy for him to slip out of Kalimba and disappear into the north. Everyone believed he was from Ro'thre, no reason to not take advantage of an easy way to disappear. He knew the language well enough it wouldn't be too much trouble.

Have I gotten in too far? Should I just give up?

The further he got into the city proper, the more people Deylan saw. Normal people dressed in simple fashion. The people of the Bone Coast were not like the people of Zanir or Alocar, the two wealthiest nations in Corinth. Here, women wore basic dresses and men wore breeches and a tunic with loose sleeves. And Deylan, with his wide brim hat had fit right in.

It didn't take long before he found what he was looking for. At the end of the road, a little apothecary finally came into view. It looked relatively clean for a port town. Feeling his luck must be changing, Deylan entered the shop.

VII

THE SMELL of chamomile, lavender, peppermint, and other herbs hit Deylan as he stepped into the apothecary. Sunlight streamed into the shop, illuminating every crevice of the small store. Barrels filled to the brim with opium, poppy, and other remedies lined the walls. Along the back wall, a small cabinet filled with vials and flasks were locked behind glass doors. Deylan's boots echoed on the smooth wooden floor in the nearly empty room. Only a wispy man with well-oiled white hair moved around as if in a world of his own.

Deylan took the opportunity to check the barrels for featherfew and a few other herbs. It wouldn't hurt to get a little stock before he left. His hand ran along the thick oaken counter that stood between him and the locked salve cabinet. The grain had been worn down over time and the effects of countless hand oils left it feeling smoother than a baby. His attention turned to the cabinet. All of the salves looked practically identical, and none of them were labeled. Deylan gnashed his teeth as he struggled to remember the specific ointment he needed.

"Can I help you with anything?"

Deylan jumped as the shopkeep suddenly appeared behind him. His large, round eyes gave him an almost deranged appearance. A single eyepiece was wedged over his left eye, magnifying his already prominent eye. Deylan took a moment to compose himself as he took in the strange looking man.

"Yes," Deylan said after a moment. "I need some featherfew, a salve to protect me from the sun, and a healing salve to help treat cuts. I could also use a little poppy too."

"Ah, yes," the man said, fluttering off to one of the barrels in his shop. "I have just what you need." He began filling two small leather pouches with featherfew and poppy from the barrels, cinching each bag tightly with a flourish. "My salves are famous. We even supply the merchants who sell deeper in Corinth. You won't find anything better."

Deylan rolled his eyes. Better usually meant more expensive.

"Here," the shopkeep said, shoving the bags into Deylan's hand. "Take a sniff. There's nothing fresher."

Unsure if the man was just exaggerating, Deylan took the two pouches into his hand and opened them up. The poppy was strong and the featherfew light and sweet. They did smell better than the herbs Deylan usually purchased. Maybe the man wasn't exaggerating.

The jingling of keys caught Deylan's attention. The cabinet doors opened with a groan. The shopkeep began muttering to himself as his fingers danced in front of the glass bottles. Deylan couldn't make out what the man said, and nearly jumped when the man let out a sudden exclamation.

"I know you asked for just the protection and healing salves," the shopkeep said, "but I think I have one more for you."

Deylan fought back a growl. The man wasn't going to be making this cheap.

"What are you thinking?" he asked, pinching the bridge of his nose.

"I have been selling to your type for over fifty years," the shopkeep explained. "Those who know what they need." The man spun and placed his finger on his nose with a knowing wink.

"What do you mean, my type?"

With an exaggerated movement, he returned to the cabinet and pulled four bottles from the shelves. "I did a bit of traveling myself," the shopkeep said, ignoring Deylan's question. "I explored the lands across the Eastern Seas and found herbs and plants that we could never dream of in Corinth. I brought them back and began growing them myself. This," he held up a bottle filled with a pale purple cream, "is made from the purple flower of Tan'quao by the Pearl River. It only grows there. Her medicinal properties are astounding. They can heal almost any wound. Even burns."

"This," he placed the purple bottle down and held up a more liquidy vial Deylan hadn't seen. "Is an oil made with the sun flower of Shri. It provides better protection against the sun." The bottle hit the oaken table with a clink. They also appeared to be oils. "And these two. These are useful to both fight infection and protect from poison."

"Poison? Where do you think I'm going, good sir?" Deylan fought to keep the incredulity out of his voice.

"Ah, we do not need to know that, now do we?" Again, the shopkeep winked at Deylan, his magnified left eye appearing even more deranged. "Men like us are not happy staying idle. I have a feeling that you will not be on the Bone Coast for much longer. So, what do you say?"

The shopkeep leaned on his oaken table, watching Deylan intently. Deylan studied the man through the bottles.

What does he know? He's more than an eccentric healer. Deylan's eyes darted from bottle to bottle. *He's worked with "our type" before. Could he be a pirate?*

He had to take a chance.

"My good sir," Deylan said, looking up from the bottles and meeting the man's stare. "You are right. I am to set sail in three days and am in dire need of supplies. My old crew was caught in the last storm and we lost everything. Would this be enough for a journey with Lady Kayna?"

Deylan was rewarded by the shopkeep's brows twitching up for the briefest of moments. His ability to maintain his wide-eyed expression was impressive.

"Lady Kayna?" the man asked. "You travel the seas with the daughter of the Scourge? My good man, I insist that you take these. Please. I'll even give you one of the infection bottles as a gift from me."

"What will this cost?"

"For you, good sir, only seven gold and two silver."

The price was steep. Deylan felt himself recoiling from the owner, but fought to remain in place. He hoped the man didn't see the reaction.

"This is a bit more than I planned on spending," Deylan admitted. "I still have other things I need to purchase."

A cloud must have passed over the sun, because the room dimmed momentarily. As if triggered by the sudden change, the shopkeep took off his eyepiece and laid it down on the table next to the leather pouches and salves. His unmagnified eye no longer held the deranged appearance. Instead, Deylan could see a thin white scar that ran from his brow to cheek. The reflection of the glass somehow hidden the mark when worn. Now, the man's features took on a solemn, even haunted appearance as the muscles on his face tightened.

"I am more than a simple apothecary." Even his tone changed, becoming deeper and no longer carrying the joviality it once had. "I told you, men like us are not happy staying idle.

I have not traveled with the Scourge, but I know what his people get up to. If you are voyaging the waters with Lady Kayna, you are in for a shock. Her crew searches for treasures that one can't possibly even dream of."

The words hung in the air, collecting tension until Deylan found it difficult to breathe. This new demeanor unnerved him. How much of the shopkeep's previous conversation had been a façade? What was the man hiding?

"I see your hesitation. My name is Peniforth, but during my seafaring days I went by Pen. None of what I say will leave this shop, understood?"

For the first time, Deylan noticed a silver dagger hanging from Peniforth's hip. The sheath wasn't engraved like he usually saw on the more affluent merchants. This one was made of simple leather and looked to be well worn. Glancing at the man once more, Deylan noticed that his hands were calloused despite his working a job that didn't require manual labor. Deylan nodded, his throat tightening. He'd been in dangerous situations before, but this one felt different. He didn't think that he'd be able to talk his way out of it should he somehow anger the man.

"I have been to the isles past what Corinth calls the Eastern Isles. There is a world out there more magnificent than you could even imagine. Lady Kayna is quite familiar with these lands. As I said, I have been doing this a long time. I developed a pretty good eye for people who seek true adventure. I would not offer you something I didn't think you would need. And my goods are the best. You will find no better.

"You would be foolish to hit the seas so soon after being washed ashore in the condition you were in. The least you can do is be prepared."

Sunlight streamed through the windows as the cloud moved from the sun. The glass bottles sparkled in the light. Just as the cloud shifted, so did the mood in the apothecary once more. Peniforth put his eyepiece back on, assuming his wide-eyed expression. Now that he knew where to look, Deylan could barely make out the faint white scar on the shopkeep's face.

He found his hand rummaging through the coin pouch he kept hidden on the inside of his breeches. The one he used for show jingled on his hip as he searched for the total. Placing seven gold onto the table, Deylan held his breath. He hoped his gamble would pay off.

"Would you take seven?" Deylan asked. "I really do need to get a few more supplies."

Peniforth eyed the coins shining on his table. His gaze darted between Deylan and his table. The serious expression he'd revealed not a minute earlier returned. The eyepiece accentuated his brows as they knitted together. A darkness flashed across Peniforth's face as his hands encircled the coins.

Cold sweat broke out on Deylan's back. Without a word from the apothecary, Deylan stuck his hand into the pouch resting on his hip and fished out two silver coins. He did not want to press his luck after all. He placed the two silver coins on the table and waited with bated breath. Small streams of sweat dripped down his back, causing his tunic to stick to his flash.

The unease hung in the air, palpable. Deylan waited, not daring to break the silence first. The seconds dragged by.

"Thank you," Peniforth said at last. His wide-eyed expression returned and a smile graced his lips once more. "Since you are purchasing more than you intended to, I can do seven gold and one silver. As a gift, I would be honored if you still took the second infection bottle. Take it, and stay safe on your ventures. I hope to see you again."

Swiping all but one of the silver coins into his hand, Peniforth resumed his spot off to the side of his shop. A small stool sat hidden in a corner where the shopkeep perched himself once more. Deylan felt uncomfortable taking back his silver, but slipped it into his pouch. The herbs and salves were packed into a hip pouch next to a few small trinkets he kept stored.

He couldn't wait to leave the shop. As Deylan's hand wrapped around the knob and gave it a turn, he heard Peniforth's voice call out.

"Say hello to Kayna for me. You're in for a real treat. A voyage with her is worth its weight in gold. Take care, young sir. I'll be waiting for your return."

With a half-hearted wave, Deylan finished twisting the knob and pulled the door open.

VIII

T HE BONE COAST WAS COLDER than Heru imagined. Having grown up in Xan, a nation located in central Corinth, Heru preferred the more sultry climate. He rubbed his arms as a breeze struck him, sending goose flesh running through his body. The cries of the gulls overhead were loud and angry, nothing like the gentle symphony from the songbirds he knew back home. Even the smell of the Bone Coast was wrong. Instead of smelling like spiced meats and anise, there was a salty tang that filled the air.

"Why Father left for this godsforsaken place is beyond me," Heru muttered.

Reaching into his pouch for a bit of dried meat, Heru found his food stores gone. Muttering a curse, the young man searched for his coin pouch. There wasn't much left after his two-week journey, and he didn't want to spend it all on a hot meal and a room. Winding through the twisty streets, Heru searched for a tavern or inn where he could take a break. In his short-sleeved tunic and dark brown breeches, Heru stood out. He would've stood out regardless thanks to his two scimitars hanging from his hip.

He wondered if he would find the Flame, a god-blessed magi gifted in the art of fyre, who volunteered to move down to the Bone Coast nineteen years ago when Heru's father made the decision to give up his title of the Great Heart of Xan to live amongst the seafaring people. Knowing his father's pride, Heru doubted the Flame would be around. Still, a small part of him hoped that by finding the Flame, he would find his father.

People gave Heru a wide berth as he searched for a place to rest. His scowl matched his dark mood. Though he'd never been in a fight before, Heru was hoping that someone would give him a reason to unleash his aggression. There was just too much bottled up for the young man to handle. A man with silver hair and a wide brimmed hat exited a store right in front of Heru, nearly colliding with the young Xanan man.

"Watch your step!" Heru barked as he stopped abruptly. "Gods be damned."

A pair of amber eyes met Heru's. In an instant, the steely glint from when the man first turned to face him vanished, replaced by a more surprised expression. A feigned look of regret quickly followed. Whipping the hat off of his head, the young man twirled it as he brought it to his chest, the white feather swishing about with each movement of the hat.

"My apologies, good sir. I must admit that I've been preoccupied lately and must not have seen you."

Heru grumbled a curse under his breath in his native tongue. The man's brow twitched up, but he didn't care. Preparing to push past the silver-haired man, Heru noticed that the man remained where he stood, staring at Heru intently.

"If you value your life, move." Heru spat out his words with all the venom he could muster.

Weeks of frustration bubbled over. Mixed with his sore body and hunger, Heru's rage became unbearable. He gnashed his teeth as his hand hovered over the handle of his scimitar. He would not be the one to make the first move. To his dismay, the silver-haired man met his gaze. The corners of his mouth turned up in a grin that left the young Xanan man unsettled.

"What's so funny?" Heru asked, his hand now resting on the hilt.

The silver-haired man placed his hat on the ground under an awning and pulled out a dagger that had been strapped to his leg. Without changing his bemused expression, the silver-haired man flipped it casually in his hand. The sheath reflected the sunlight, accentuating the engravings that could barely be made out on it. A flash passed through the man's amber eye.

"Fate works in mysterious ways," the man said. "Today has been nothing but a series of unusual occurrences, and you, my good sir, are the final jewel to the crown." The glint returned to his eye as his smile finally vanished. "I normally avoid violence

– messy business, but if you so insist on engaging in these brutish actions, I will accept your challenge."

After a short pause, Heru removed his hand from his hilt. Emotion still roiled within him like a maelstrom and his muscles twitched as he sought to keep control of himself. Taking in his surroundings, Heru noted that the street had cleared. No barrels lined the road and there was nothing else to obstruct movement. Or to be used as a weapon. As Heru glanced about, the silver-haired man returned his dagger to its strap on his leg.

"Have a good day," the silver-haired man said.

Bending over to pick up his hat, Heru seized the opportunity and darted forward. The man flinched at the unexpected action, giving Heru a chance to kick him in the side. A grunt escaped the man. His arm went to his side as he clenched his teeth.

"You made a poor decision." The silver-haired man's words came out cool and even.

Before Heru could react, the young man lunged at him, wrapping his arms around Heru's body. Heru quickly found himself falling as the man's leg slipped behind his own, knocking Heru off-balance. The two landed on the ground with a heavy thump. Heru's breath was knocked out of him, leaving him struggling for air. The silver-haired man scrambled on top of him, wedging his knees under Heru's armpits and sitting up so Heru couldn't get a good hit in.

One. Two. Three.

The silver-haired man moved fast, his fists a blur and each punch landing with a sharp, punishing force. Heru reeled, his vision swimming as the sting of knuckles spread across his ribs and jaw. He raised his arms just in time, his forearms catching the next flurry of bone jarring strikes. When the silver-haired man paused to find a new opening, Heru thrust his hips up. The young man lost his balance and threw out his arms to brace himself as he toppled forward.

Slipping his hips out from under the silver-haired man, Heru broke free and went to take his opponent's back. Stars popped in his eyes and his mouth throbbed as the silver-haired man's boot recoiled. Blood quickly filled Heru's mouth. Rage blossomed in Heru's chest. He spat out a mouthful of blood as he moved to a crouched position. His hand moved to his scimitar's hilt. Before he could pull the blade completely free from its sheath, the silver-haired man's dagger pointed at Heru's throat. A growl escaped Heru, but he sheathed his weapon.

The silver-haired man's gaze bore down on Heru. As the seconds passed, the glint of aggression disappeared from his amber eyes. Slowly, he resheathed his dagger and stood up. Heru did the same. He found that he was breathing heavily after the fight. The metallic tang of blood still filled his mouth. Spitting out another mouthful, Heru wiped the blood from his face.

Stooping to pick up his hat, the silver-haired man kept his eyes on Heru. Heru's rage simmered, gradually cooling down as he caught his breath. He couldn't believe that he was beaten so soundly despite training for combat ever since he was five.

Had his masters gone easy on him because of who he was? Or was it because he let his emotions get the better of him.

I can't believe I lost my composure like that. If Freyna has truly blessed me on my journey, I can't let myself become undisciplined again. I cannot fail.

"Feeling better?"

The question caught Heru off-guard.

"Sorry?"

"Are you feeling better now that you got that out of you?"

The silver-haired man finally turned his attention back to himself. Heru noticed that under the man's, strips of cloth wrapped around his torso. He wondered what kinds of wounds the silver-haired man sustained.

"I... owe you an apology," Heru stammered. "I should not have let my frustrations get the better of me. Clearly, I was not in my right mind." Noting the man's injuries once more – a thin strip of cloth circling his head and the wraps on his bicep, Heru's shame deepened. "Please, let me buy you a hot meal. Or a drink."

"It's not necessary."

"I insist," Heru pressed. "My honor will not let me move on until I make this up to you."

The man stared at Heru. His amber eyes seemed to go straight to Heru's soul. The man had a way of looking at him that left Heru feeling exposed and vulnerable.

"All right," the man said slowly. "I know a place."

Dusting off his backside, Heru nodded. The two fell in step as they walked down the road. After a few turns, the streets became busy again. Heru wondered if they disappeared at the sign of conflict.

Not very brave for a town of pirates, he mused.

"I'm new to town," Heru said, breaking the silence. "If you could help me out, I would greatly appreciate it. I'm looking for someone."

"I don't know many, but I usually can find the right place to start looking."

The pair weaved around a family walking through the middle of the street. Children skipped around, oblivious to the two young men. The silver-haired man turned and touched the brim of his hat with a roguish grin and the wink of his eye. Heru caught the young mother's face flushing as she quickly turned away from him. The husband seemed oblivious to the interaction.

Heru found his lips turning upward slightly. *There's more to him for sure.*

"May I ask the name of my new companion?" Heru asked.

The silver-haired man turned to Heru. A sparkle appeared in his eye as he gauged how much to say.

Smart. I wouldn't be too trusting in this situation either. Heru didn't acknowledge how his actions impacted their relationship. It was in the past. Now was the time to move forward.

"Deylan."

Deylan maintained his stare with Heru.

Taking his cue, Heru replied, "Heru."

"And what are you looking for?"

"The former Great Heart of Xan. My father."

Narrowing his eyes, Deylan studied the young man. *Could he be related to the Xanan with Kayna's crew? He might be helpful to have on her ship regardless. He doesn't hate me; maybe he could be an ally.*

The buildings around Heru and Deylan became a little more spaced out. Their exteriors, though obviously old, were well-kept. The paint looked pristine despite not being fresh. No dirt or grime besmirched them. A large building bearing sign reading "Lost Siren" in delicate script loomed ahead. A beautiful depiction of a woman with the tail of a fish wrapped around the name. Though they were far away, Heru could tell that her features were both delicate and wild. A representation of the shop's patrons perhaps.

"The Lost Siren. Last time I was here, I enjoyed my meal. You have coin, yes?"

"Of course," Heru replied.

"Good. I may not be welcome here, so we should be careful."

Heru bit back an exclamation at the news. "What? Why are we going here if you are not welcome?"

"Because the food is good and I have someone I want to speak to. Besides, that was only this morning. Things may have calmed down a bit since then."

Pushing open the door, Deylan disappeared into the tavern.

"Freyna's mercy," Heru swore under his breath. "This better not be a waste of time."

Catching the door as it shut, Heru pushed it open and walked into the Lost Siren.

IX

THE ROOM WAS BUSTLING. Tables were filled and busty barmaids hustled about, weaving between the tables. The scent of lamb and ale filled the air, making Heru's mouth water. He scanned the floor and quickly located Deylan sitting at a table far away from the bar. He watched as the barkeep kept a steady stream of ale and mead flowing to the patrons in large glass tankards.

"This must be who he's hiding from," Heru muttered as he made his way to Deylan.

Chairs scraped against the floor as patrons shifted in their seats. More than one table held a group of men sharing a drunken conversation. One of the drunkards nearly ran into Heru as he tried to avoid a collision with someone at another table.

"Watch where yer goin'," the man slurred. "Nearly hit me, ye did."

His friends reached out to pull the man back into his chair. He fell into his seat and almost toppled over the other side onto his back. His companions broke into raucous laughter as the man's arms flailed. Heru ignored the group, determined to make his way to Deylan without getting into another fight that day. By the time he made it to the table, a young woman with wavy dark hair stood next to Deylan. The two chatted amicably, a boyish grin on Deylan's face and a soft smile on hers. Pulling out a chair, Heru slipped into his seat. He waited for the barmaid to turn her attention to him.

"Let me know if you hear anything," Deylan finished. "I leave in three days."

The young barmaid hummed in agreement before finally addressing Heru.

"What can I get you, love?" Her voice switched from the soft tone she had with Deylan to a more sultry one. "Our mead is the best on the Bone Coast."

"What did he get?" Heru asked.

"Lamb and a blackberry mead."

Her eyes sparkled as she glanced over at Deylan. Heru didn't miss the look.

"I'll have the same."

With a swish of her slim hips, the barmaid turned and went to place the order. Heru couldn't help but watch her as she sauntered off. Her body moved deftly between the tables, avoiding pinches and groping hands with the grace of a dancer. Noticing that Deylan's gaze never left the retreating woman, Heru raised a brow.

"Can't take your eyes off of her, can you?"

"She's a sweet girl, but I can't let her get involved with me. I won't be able to protect her. Anything we tried to build together would be taken away and it would leave her in ruin. She doesn't deserve to suffer for my sins."

A wistful smile played on Deylan's face that Heru couldn't ignore. The look was fleeting. Deylan's nonchalant demeanor quickly returned as he got down to business.

"We don't usually see people from Xan here, let alone someone so important."

Heru took a moment to gather his thoughts. Though his reason for coming to the Bone Coast was simple, there was more underneath that he still struggled with.

"I assume you've heard of the Gods Battle that happened twenty years ago?"

Deylan nodded.

"Well, after everything settled, my father left Xan for the Bone Coast. He gave up everything. His title. His influence. His family." Heru's voice trailed away as he finished. Though he felt the familiar pangs of loneliness that plagued his childhood, he maintained a steady gaze, not letting his emotions control him anymore. It was a practiced look, one he'd honed over the last twenty years.

Deylan rubbed his chin, his elbows leaning on the table. "Your father was god-blessed, right?"

"No," Heru replied. "Just favored by Freyna. His skill was all his own."

Humming in thought, Deylan clasped his hands. "The Gods Battle happened when I was very young. I never thought I would meet someone so close to it. Why did your father leave?"

"I don't know," Heru said with a shake of his head. "Mother said that the call of the sea was too great. Our current Great Heart said that Father was a man who craved power. He didn't say much, but he said that there was something out here that Father wanted to chase."

"The sea does carry an...allure," Deylan admitted. "She has a way of keeping us longer than we anticipate."

A shadow of emotion crossed Deylan's visage. Heru couldn't figure out what it was – it was a mixture of several. Deylan did not attempt to hide his reaction or mask it like he did when speaking of the young bar maiden. He let the sentiment linger.

"You've struggled to fight her hold," Heru noted.

"Sometimes we get pulled into the trap of thinking that there's just one more trip and then we can go home. But you never fulfill your desire. It's been five years. I wish I could go home. But I can't."

The honesty Deylan revealed surprised Heru. Here he thought the silver-haired man was just a foolish imposter. Someone masquerading as a no-name lordling in hopes of separating the rich from their money. Even after their fight, he didn't think there was much more to Deylan.

Two hot plates slid onto the table. Nefeli dropped them off quietly, promising to return momentarily with their drinks. The clink of silverware on the worn wood sounded unusually loud despite the general din of the rowdy and drunken patrons. The aroma of rosemary and butter hit Heru's nose, causing his mouth to water. The lamb looked delicious with just the right amount of fat marbling the pink meat. Deylan did not seem to notice the meal.

"I owe you an apology," Heru muttered as two tankards of blackberry mead were dropped off. "I seem to have caused you more grief than appropriate this day."

"No," Deylan said with a weak wave of his hand. He picked up his utensils and began cutting the meat. "I should have maintained my composure earlier. I try to avoid violence."

The two turned their attention to their food. As soon as his tongue touched the lamb, Heru found himself unable to control his hunger. He ate ravenously, as a man who hadn't had a true meal in several days is wont to do. The carrots and potatoes that accompanied the lamb were just as delicious. Soaking meat and vegetables in butter was a wonderful idea, one he wanted to bring back home to his mother and sisters.

The blackberry mead surprised the young Xanan as well. The light, fruity flavor brought a sweetness that cut the savoriness of the lamb. He soon found his tankard almost empty. He stared at his clean plate and the remaining mead in disappointment. Though his coin was almost gone, he found himself wanting another tankard of mead.

"You know," Deylan said, breaking the silence. His plate was empty as well. "I think I'd like another glass. Would you care to join me? I'll buy this round."

Excitement must have flashed across Heru's face because a bemused expression crossed Deylan's. Catching Nefeli's attention, he ordered two more tankards of blackberry mead, dropping a silver coin on the table. The dark-haired barmaid rested her hand on his shoulder a moment longer than she needed to before clearing the table and informing them that they would receive their drinks soon.

"I must say," Deylan added. There was a twinkle in his eye that, coupled with his boyish grin, made him look rather mischievous. "I never thought I would see two Xanans in one day."

Heru's jaw nearly dropped at the news. All anticipation that he'd had while he waited for his mead disappeared, instead replaced with a myriad of emotions that fought for acknowledgement. Two tankards appeared in front of the pair. Deylan looked at Heru over the rim of his glass. The sparkle in his eye still shining.

"Why didn't you say anything?" Heru's voice shook as he struggled to maintain his composure.

The spark disappeared from Deylan's amber eyes, but he did not stop himself from taking a drink. Heru waited for Deylan to finish up, his leg beginning to bounce with each passing second.

Patience, he chided himself. *The son of the Great Heart cannot be this impulsive. I can't let him get a reaction by playing with me.*

After several long seconds, Deylan put down his tankard. The noise level returned to what it was before Heru's exclamation and people turned away from the pair, resuming their conversation.

"I'm not sure, but I believe he was a son of Xan," Deylan said slowly. "As I said, I don't know many, but I usually can find my way to the right sources. I saw this man fleetingly this morning. I've had a long day, and I did not recall right away. Fate works in mysterious ways. Or maybe the gods?"

"What are you getting at?"

"You seek your father, journeying to find one so favored by the gods. I would presume that your quest is also blessed by the gods. I am in need of the gods' blessing to complete my goals. Perhaps we were destined to cross paths."

"For gods' sake," Heru grumbled. "Where did you see him?"

Circling the rim of his tankard with his finger, Deylan leaned back in his chair, taking Heru in. His aloof demeanor returned. He was in his comfort zone. The young Xanan studied his partner.

What is his end game? What does he want?

"What will this information cost?" Heru asked slowly.

"I have one more trip across the seas. I leave in three days." Leaning in, Deylan dropped his voice to a whisper so soft that Heru had to do the same. "My captain has a map, a map to an island past the Eastern Isles. There is a treasure said to be greater than all the riches of Enlil on that island. I can't go back home without them."

Pushing away from Deylan, Heru crossed his arms as he glared at the man. Growing up, he hated playing politics. He had no patience for them.

Maybe I should've let Bermet accompany me after all.

The thought of his older sister traveling across Corinth to the pirate coast did not sit well with Heru. His reasons were his own. If he wanted to find his father, he would need to master his emotions.

"I need a partner," Deylan continued. "Someone to cause a distraction. Someone to help me return. I've stolen from several pirates before." Lifting up his tunic, Deylan exposed the tip of a scar underneath the cloths wrapped around his ribs. "I'm no stranger to tricky situations. But since I will be going on a ship I don't know with a crew I've never met, it would be wise to have a partner. I'll take all blame."

"And if I go with you, how will you find my father? Who knows how long this trip will take."

"Rumor has it that Kayna has a strong warrior as part of her crew. Our type isn't exactly known as warriors," Deylan added with a chuckle. "I think they might be speaking about your father. If we go together, you'll have time to talk to him."

Three days. In three days he could be on the sea with his father. Three days was much too long.

"Why can't you take me to him now?" Heru asked.

"I can," Deylan replied. "I was hoping you would agree to help. The son of a god-favored warrior would be a great boon on my search."

It was now Heru's turn to take a long draught from his tankard. The sweet mead refreshed him, soothing his adrenaline. Or perhaps it was the alcohol in the drink. Either way, Heru found the swirling sensation in his stomach subsiding.

The bones are in my favor once more, Heru thought. *It's been a long time. The Great Heart said that fortune favored Father. Fortune, and Freyna. If I want them to bless me, I need to show them that I'm worthy. To give them a reason to watch over me like they did Father.*

He didn't rush at responding to Deylan. Putting his tankard down, Heru crossed his fingers and rested his chin on top of them. To his credit, the silver-haired man did not lose his composure.

"I don't want to put my life in any unnecessary danger," Heru said. Though his expression didn't change, Heru could see Deylan's shoulders droop a little. "But my honor will not let me deny you this. I have not acted as I should and put you in an unfavorable position. You have my swords for your quest. May Freyna smile down on both of us."

Relief washed over Deylan's face. Heru could see that he tried to suppress his feelings, but he couldn't stop the mask from slipping. He picked up his flagon once more and took a long drink. The noise in the tavern dropped by half as the two tables of drunks walked out. With the new quiet came a sense of being watched. Heru leaned back in his chair, keeping his posture nonchalant as he tried to find the source of his discomfort. He noted that Deylan's eyes darted over his shoulder towards the back of the tavern. The silver-haired man took another drink, finishing his mead as he stared at the bar.

Heru twisted in his chair, craning his neck to look at whatever held Deylan's attention. A large man stood behind the bar, wiping down the glasses. A layer of muscle, no longer defined but still visible, combined with his dark hair and beard, gave him the appearance of a bear. His massive hands delicately held the cup as his rag cleaned the same spot over and over. Standing out from the man's size were his eyes. The man's unwavering glare at their table. Finishing his stretch, Heru watched Deylan. The silver-haired man picked up his hat, his characteristic smile plastered onto his face and exuding confidence despite the tension in his body.

"I think it's time to go," Deylan said. "I don't know if it's a good idea that either of us come back here for a while. Shame. I rather liked the mead."

"I agree."

Placing a small handful of coins onto the table to pay for their meal, Heru stood. The pair made their way to the door. As they wove through the tables, the barkeep's eyes stayed trained on the them. Heru glanced at the man and noticed that he'd given up all pretense of cleaning his glass and just watched the two as they left. The young barmaid who served them earlier peeked out from behind the kitchen doors, but didn't dare come into the main room of the tavern.

They couldn't reach the door fast enough. As Heru gripped the knob, he noticed the bear of a barkeep step out from behind the bar. He didn't want to wait to find out if the barkeep was following them. Pushing the door open, Heru and Deylan stepped onto the street in front of the Lost Siren.

X

THE YOUNG XANAN STALKED OFF, leaving Deylan to catch up. His heavy step reminded Deylan of when they first met, angry and full of turmoil. The young Xanan clearly had a lot that he needed to work through. Being abandoned by your father, a great war hero at that, must have left deep scars and insecurities for the young man. As a member of the warlord nation, Deylan expected more aggression from Heru.

Falling into step with Heru, Deylan let him walk in silence. Deylan's own mind wandered. There must be a reason why the barkeep, Ketes, held a grudge towards him. He racked his mind trying to figure out where he knew the barkeep. All the while, he directed Heru to the Scourge's personal tavern. Halfway to the tavern, Deylan gave up on trying to remember Ketes.

He probably blames the attack on the Rose *for the coast closing. Everyone needs someone to blame.* Turning one final time to see if they were being followed, Deylan allowed himself to relax a bit when he saw that there wasn't another soul on the road besides Heru. *I'll have to find another way to contact Nefeli. I doubt Ketes will let her out of his sight for a while. I wonder if this Kayna knows anything about him.*

As the buildings became a little more ramshackle, Deylan found himself struggling to remember where to go. The only time he'd been in that part of town was when he was following Bharam. Cursing himself for not paying attention to his surroundings, Deylan questioned his ability to find the tavern.

"You're not going to betray me?" Heru asked. His hand moved to his scimitar on his hip. "I thought we made a deal."

"No," Deylan said quickly. "To be honest, I don't remember exactly where I'm going."

Spinning to face his companion, Heru fixed him with a disbelieving stare.

"I've only been there once. This morning in fact. I'd just woken up after being unconscious for three days. I think that earns me a little grace."

Heru gnashed his teeth, grumbling a curse in Xanan. Deylan was beginning to like the young man more and more.

"Remember, I have an uncanny ability to find my way," Deylan added with a wink. "We won't be lost for long."

A steady stream of curses continued from Heru, albeit softer and less aggressively. He didn't argue with Deylan further, and allowed the silver-haired man to lead him. With a deep breath, Deylan stopped and looked around. Nothing stood out to him, yet there was an air of familiarity to it. Following his instinct, Deylan took them down a narrow side road. The two squeezed through the tiny street, taking several turns. Worry crept in as they appeared no closer to the tavern when suddenly Deylan saw the worn sign with a sword and rose under a skull.

"See?" he pointed to the young Xanan. "I told you I'd get you to where you need to go. It's not much further."

The two followed the path as it sloped downward towards the coast. The road widened enough for the two of them to walk side-by-side once more. As they neared the tavern, Deylan found a heaviness settle over him. It sent his heart racing and made his legs feel heavy. A cold sweat broke down, dampening his back and making his hands clammy. He glanced around, trying to find the source of his discomfort. However, apart from him and Heru there was no one on the streets. The buildings appeared empty. No sounds came from them, and no shadows went by the windows. The entire area seemed empty.

Taking a steadying breath, Deylan worked to calm the adrenaline that surged within him. The closer he got to the tavern, the more he began to wonder if it was the prospect of seeing such daunting pirates again. It made no sense to him. Deylan had spent almost five years with seafaring men of varying levels of repute and never felt this level of trepidation with any of them. His silver tongue always managed to smooth over any temper. Then why did he feel this way? This was nothing he shouldn't be able to do.

Am I pushing my luck? he wondered. *Is it worth it?*

The thought of potential retribution from Kayna and her crew sent shivers down his spine. Dhruvasht he could handle. Bharam did not scare him. But the three sitting at the bar and the power they exuded unsettled him. He didn't even need to see them in action. Just the presence they commanded was enough for Deylan to know that he was entering into some very dangerous waters.

Can I even go back now?

The notion of giving up pained him. Deylan knew he'd done enough to hopefully pay off his Redemption, but he couldn't be sure. A life was not a cheap thing to repay. His heart ached at the thought of not going back. He missed his family, but it was not worth the risk to his mother and sisters.

And then there was Heru. Deylan worried that bringing a Xanan into this world would end in disaster. The boy had some skill in combat, but his impulsiveness could be their downfall. He wasn't sure if Heru was up to the task Deylan had in mind. There was also a distinct possibility that Heru would leave after finding his father, assuming it was the man Deylan had in mind.

Why did I have to make things so complicated?

It wasn't long before the worn-down sign of a sword and rose under a skull hovered above the two. The pair looked up at it as it rocked slightly in the breeze. Inside Deylan could hear muffled chatter. It seemed as though the Scourge's tavern was always busy.

"I wonder what the name of this tavern is?" Heru remarked. "Strange seeing one without a proper sign."

The comment brought a smile to Deylan's lips. There was a time when he was naïve too. The sea quickly disabused him of his innocence, and he'd had to adapt quickly if he wanted to survive. Hopefully Heru could do the same.

"If you're around long enough, you'll find someone who knows. I haven't broken into the inner circles of this level of brigand. This will be an adventure for the both of us."

Out of the corner of his eye, Deylan caught Heru smirking at him. The young Xanan appeared to be taking everything with good humor. Opening the door, the pair entered the Scourge's tavern. As the bright afternoon sun burst into the room, the muted conversations stopped. Heads swiveled towards Heru and Deylan, just like they did that morning when Deylan first entered the tavern.

Once their eyes adjusted to the darkened room, Deylan noted that the crew watched the two intently. Grizzled faces, the flesh tanned and resembling leather from the constant sun exposure, and a number bearing scars, glowered at the young men. The feeling of heaviness and anxiety that Deylan felt earlier threatened to return. He felt his breathing want to become more ragged and his hands became clammy. He took a deep breath. Now was not the time to show weakness.

Deylan scanned the room, looking for an empty table or familiar face. For once, he hoped to see Dhruvasht or his coward of a crewman. He found neither. He did spy an open table. Without a word, Deylan made his way to the empty table on the side of the room. Heru followed, seemingly oblivious to his situation. Once they were sat at the table, Deylan pressed his palms into his face and heaved a sigh.

"I'll get some drinks."

The young Xanan's casual tone snapped Deylan's head up from his hands. Without so much as a second thought, Heru wend his way through the tables, ignoring the hostile stares that greeted him, until he reached the bar.

"Oh gods," Deylan muttered. "At least he's confident."

Heru spoke to a man behind the bar who was so massive that he made Ketes look like a small man. Scars marred his arms and face, several crossing into Xs along his arms. The two spoke quietly for a bit. The air in the tavern lay heavy as all eyes were now on the young Xanan and the barkeep. After several tense minutes, the barkeep let out a bellow of laughter and slapped the bar before turning to grab the drinks. He filled two huge flagons with ale until they overflowed. Heru dropped a singular coin on the counter and grabbed the drinks, foam and ale sloshing onto the well-stained floor.

Conversation resumed almost instantly. If anyone watched Deylan or Heru, it was not as obvious. Instead, they focused on those around them once more. A peal of laughter could be heard, cutting through the tension that had built up in those few minutes. More ale spilled on the table as Heru passed Deylan his flagon, the golden liquid seeping into the stained table. Deylan took a sip, taking one last scan of the tavern before turning to Heru. The drink was unusually light and sweet. Not what he expected from a group like this. The drink helped ease the tightness Deylan felt. He wouldn't fully let his guard down, but allowed himself a moment to relax.

"You seem to have impressed that beast of a barkeep," Deylan said. His relaxed demeanor contrasted with the adrenaline that still coursed through him. Hoping to keep the attention off the two of them, he forced himself to keep the tone light. "How did you manage that?"

Heru slowly sipped his own drink. His brow quirked up as if to express his own shock at the ale's flavor. "I didn't expect that," he muttered. "It wasn't as hard as you'd think."

Deylan waited for a follow up to the response, but the young Xanan did not oblige. Deylan snorted. "A true man of many words," he said before taking another sip. "I'm glad your gilded tongue saved us."

It was Heru's turn to smirk. "Not everyone is as gifted as you. I told him that I recently joined your crew and am about to take my first trip. I asked for the best drink to help prepare me. Apparently, I'm in for an adventure."

"I believe I told you that," Deylan replied. "Glad I wasn't wrong."

"You two are cut from the same cloth. Are all you seafarers the same?"

With a shake of the head, Deylan replied, "Not all. Some are great conversationalists like you. Others talk more with their sword and fists. You'll figure them out pretty quickly."

Staggering into their table, a lanky man fell into Heru's chair. Spinning around, the young Xanan shot a withering glare at the drunkard. As if oblivious to their presence, the lanky man mumbled something, not apologizing for hitting them. Deylan opened his mouth to say something when he noticed a darkness crossing the young Xanan's visage. The look couldn't be more different than the one he'd seen when they first met. It was calculating and deadly.

"Watch where you're going," Deylan said, adopting a light-hearted tone. "You nearly spilled our drink."

Heru sneered at Deylan, his eyes narrowing. The intoxicated man stammered out an incoherent response, possibly an apology, but Deylan couldn't be sure. The nearby tables turned to observe the exchange, expressions hungry. It was almost as though they were waiting for a punch to be thrown.

Acting fast, Deylan added, "I know we're outsiders here, but surely we can clear this up to everyone's satisfaction."

Crossing his arms, Heru leaned back in his chair. He focused on the lanky man once more, waiting. The man looked down at the two before walking off. The sound of chair legs scraping against the floor seemed unnaturally loud in Deylan's ears. It was as though the chair protested the drunk man's actions before the young Xanan did. Heru shot up out of his seat, his hand coming precariously close to pulling his blade free. Deylan followed suit, not wanting the situation to escalate.

"Do you wish to die?" Heru asked.

The man babbled out a response, not bothering to stop. His unsteady gait and the crowded tavern prevented him from moving far. Heru grabbed the man by the shoulder and spun him around until the two faced each other.

"I will not endure your disrespect." Heru's voice came out strong, silencing the room and drawing all eyes to them.

Deylan made to get between the two, but was stopped by a man at another table. The man rested a meaty hand on Deylan's shoulder, preventing him from moving forward. Deylan turned to face the man. He did not appear to be acting in aggression. The man watched the dispute between Heru and the drunk intently, waiting to see what would happen.

"This isn't yer battle, lad," the man warned. "Let them handle it like men."

Deylan wanted to protest, but he knew that doing so would instantly ruin any relationship he could hope to build with them. It would be foolish to make so many enemies with one move. Letting himself relax, Deylan placed his wide-brimmed hat onto the table, being careful to keep it from soaking up the spilled ale that still dampened its surface.

"This is your last chance," Heru warned.

"C'mon Michail," another man called out. "Apologize to the boy. Yer three sheets to the wind and about to be ploughed."

Michail wobbled where he stood as he attempted to look at his companions. The motion almost seemed to be too much for the intoxicated man and he nearly fell over. Heru stood in front of the man patiently. Deylan noted that the patience would not last much longer. Finally, the drunkard mumbled out a proper apology before staggering off once more. Heru muttered a curse before pushing his chair back into place. The two men who intervened moved to follow their friend. As the man behind Deylan released his hold on Deylan's shoulder, the silver-haired man felt emboldened.

"Could you help me find someone?"

The man grunted, pausing for a moment.

Taking this as a sign to continue, Deylan asked, "Do you happen to know a man from Xan?"

The question caught Heru's attention. He followed up asking, "He would be nearly fifty summers. Master of the battleaxe and scimitar."

Recognition crossed the man's face. A few others made comments while they were seated at their table. Deylan felt confident that he found the right place. Glancing over at Heru, he saw what appeared to be hope on the young man's face.

"Are ye lookin' for Len?" the man asked.

"Yes," Heru blurted out. "Have you seen him? I've heard that he frequents the Bone Coast. He might consort with a Flame."

"A Flame?" the man asked. "We haven' seen any god-blessed in a few years. They were run out when the new baron moved in. But Len, I know him. Been sailin' with him for over ten years."

"Where is he? I'd like to speak with him."

Deylan could almost feel the excitement radiating off of Heru. There was an energy exuding from him. He almost seemed to be trembling in anticipation. A sense of peace filled Deylan. It was the first true moment where he felt at ease in the Scourge's tavern. Len's presence did not seem to be a sore subject for these men. Perhaps the former Great Heart would afford them both a measure of protection.

"Sorry, lad," the man said.

Deylan's rising feeling suddenly dropped. The tavern sudden became stifling despite the conversation having returned to its normal level once the confrontation between Heru and the drunkard passed. He glanced over at Heru and saw the dismay on the young man's face. The Xanan fought well to mask his disappointment, but it still slipped through.

"Len left earlier this mornin' with Maya and a small crew. *Graak's Fury* is set to meet up with them later, but we don' know when. When Maya takes a crew, it's usual for big trips. Usual high risk."

The man walked away, ending the conversation. His comrades followed. Deylan couldn't help but feel deflated. After all their efforts, it felt as though he fell short of his goal even though he found the former Great Heart's crew. Out of the corner of his eye, he noticed Heru sliding into his chair. The young man made no effort to hide his disappointment, his eyes downcast, staring at his knees. Deylan believed he saw the young Xanan's eyes glisten in the darkened room.

"It's not an impossible task," Deylan said softly as he returned to his seat. "The ships are set to meet up. Your father will only be a few days ahead of us. There's a good chance we run into him at the Eastern Isles when we restock supplies."

"Every time I get close, he manages to slip away," Heru mumbled. "Why does Freyna keep him away from me?"

The two sipped their remaining ale in awkward silence. No one bothered them in the tavern. In fact, no one seemed to leave. Deylan got the feeling that the tavern was actually a cover for the Scourge's crew and they shared bunks somewhere in the back. He tapped his fingers on the side of his flagon, not wanting to disturb Heru's thoughts. Where did these people go for a bite? He hadn't seen anyone bring out food since they'd arrived.

The door opened and a familiar face entered the darkened tavern. The light pained Deylan's eyes. He wondered if that's why everyone seemed annoyed when he walked in. Checking the tavern floor once more, Deylan felt a spike of adrenaline as he watched Bharam take a seat at an empty table on the opposite side of the tavern. Dhruvasht was nowhere in sight. The Nem Pahlan man furtively checked the room, rubbing his hands together as he searched for whatever he was looking for. Deylan couldn't believe his luck.

Perhaps the gods are blessing me after all, Deylan mused. *I think it's time to pay this coward a visit.*

Turning to his companion, Deylan saw Heru hadn't moved much from his original position. When he wasn't drinking his ale, Heru stared at a spot on the wall in a dark corner. His eyes were no longer rimmed with moisture, but he still clearly fought with emotions from within.

"I'll be right back," Deylan told Heru. "I have some business that I need to attend to. If you can wait, we can grab a pint together. I know a good place where we won't be chased out like at the Lost Siren." Deylan hoped his attempt at levity would be well received. It was not. "We can discuss our next steps and gather supplies. Once we reach the Eastern Isles, we can jump ship and join your father on *Graak's Fury*. I can complete my business by then."

An empty stare met Deylan. Somewhere behind those hollow eyes, Deylan thought he saw a spark of hope. Tipping his hat to Heru, Deylan got up and walked to the opposite side of the bar.

He'll be all right, he tried to tell himself. *Someone like him, he'll be back to his brooding self by the time I return.*

Bharam didn't notice Deylan until he pulled out the chair opposite him and sat down. He was rewarded with the Nem Pahlan man jumping in his seat. It seemed that the only surviving member of Dhruvasht's crew was not anticipating a visit from Deylan.

With a trembling hand, Bharam reached up and touched the religious pendant he wore around his neck. The action was brief, but it told Deylan a lot. The man was a coward – always had been. He was not fit to traverse the seas or face the consequences for his inaction. Deylan almost felt sorry for him. Perhaps after their conversation he would actually feel remorseful. At this time, he wanted to sow a few seeds of discord.

Plastering on a disarming grin, Deylan placed his hands on the table, palms down. He hoped the Nem Pahlan would take the bait and see him as open and honest. Then he would be putty in Deylan's hands. He noticed that Bharam took note of his posture, the recreant's body relaxing visibly as Bharam placed his own hands on the table, albeit closed.

"How goes your health?" Deylan asked. "Last I saw, it appeared that you were lucky and avoided any real injury when the *Rose* was destroyed."

Deylan didn't want to give the impression that he was vulnerable, but his injuries weren't exactly something he could conceal. Bharam would no doubt have already seen the bandages around his head. He might even have seen the ones around his chest through his shirt, or the one on his arm. There was no use pretending he hadn't been injured.

"Maa'zhun has blessed me with her protection." Pointing to Deylan to accentuate his statement, Bharam added, "This is what comes from praying to heathen gods. Turning from the path of true divinity places you in line for her displeasure."

It took a lot of effort for Deylan to not roll his eyes at the man. Though he often found himself following seafaring tradition and paying his respects the gods of Ayr, Deylan no longer believed in the gods of old. They'd betrayed him one time too many, and he couldn't understand how those who were supposed to protect him could abandon him. People like Bharam, people who put so much faith into such deities confused him. And in Bharam's case, he just annoyed Deylan. The overly pious attitude did not help ingratiate him to Deylan.

Keeping his tongue in check, Deylan forced a pleasant expression and placed his hat onto the table. "Perhaps you're right. You'll have to teach me about Maa'zhun once we're aboard the ship. I have a feeling that these guys know how to keep their journeys smooth." Deylan motioned in the general direction of the tavern's patrons for effect. "Now then, what do you say to a drink?"

Suspicion flashed across Bharam's face, but he didn't decline the offer. Deylan found the look strange. The two barely interacted during their time on *Death's Rose*. There should be no reason for the man to distrust him. Unless it was because of a guilty conscience.

"Maa'zhun does not approve of frivolous things like drinking," Bharam said. The Nem Pahlan's voice betrayed the shame buried under the feeble attempt at indignation.

Deylan had seen Bharam drinking with the rest of the *Rose's* crew many times during their voyage. The man was trying to paint a different picture of himself. A self-righteous one.

Deylan wouldn't call him out on his deception just yet. Now was not the time. But he could push a little.

"Oh, come now. Surely, she would forgive a little indiscretion. After all, wine and ale are practically our blood. We drink it more than water when we're at sea. A little can't hurt. Look, I insist. As a gift before our next trip."

The man stammered for a bit, attempting to articulate a reason why he couldn't join Deylan for a drink. Deylan just held eye contact and waited for Bharam to finally say something. After several seconds when he couldn't come up with a good excuse, Bharam conceded. Slapping the table in pleasure, Deylan popped up and made his way to the bar. He turned around constantly, making sure that Bharam didn't run off while he was gone. To his relief, Bharam remained seated, an almost defeated expression on his face.

"I wonder if he found someone for Dhruvasht like I did?" Deylan mused. "It would be nice to have an extra set of hands onboard."

There wasn't much time for idle thought. The large bar was maybe fifteen steps away from their table to begin with. Behind it, as massive as always, stood the barkeep that Heru managed to charm. The beast of a man loomed over Deylan a good foot, and his body was so broad that Deylan could almost imagine that another half of him could combine with himself before he was the same width as that man. The scars were more jarring up close. Deylan could see that they weren't delicate lines like he usually saw. They were the deep gashes that only come from intense combat. Combat, or punishment. Deylan's hand twitched, wanting to go to his chest at the sight of the scars on the barkeep's arms. Phantom pains from his past blossomed in his chest. He'd tried hard to forget that day.

The barkeep lumbered behind the slab of wood that served as the bar counter. He didn't stop and ask Deylan what he wanted like a normal barkeep. Instead, he worked while he waited. Deylan found that his mouth was dry, like if he had put a bit of salt in his mouth. His eyes darted back to Bharam. The man watched him intently. Deylan knew he couldn't let his nerves get the best of him.

"My good sir," Deylan began. He hoped his words did not offend the man. Part of him wondered if the barkeep would take kindly to such flowery language. "May I bother you for a couple of drinks? My tablemate and I are joining Lady Kayna on her next voyage in three days and we would love something strong before setting out."

The barkeep raised a brow, finally stopping and facing Deylan. The silver-haired man balked at the large man's change. He didn't expect the man to stop like that. Wondering if he made a mistake, Deylan found himself pushing forward. Changing his demeanor would be a dangerous idea, so he continued on with his usual routine.

"Both of us need this little bit of help after our last ship was destroyed by an unexpected storm not three days ago. I'm sure you heard of it?" The man's arms crossed across his chest, but he said nothing. "I don't know about my tablemate, but I am not wanting to earn Graak's ire once more. A drink would be most helpful in calming the nerves."

"I don't like your kind," the man growled. His deep bass shook Deylan to the core. "Too much fancy talk for my tastes."

"I'm sorry," Deylan faltered. "I would like two ales, please."

The beast of a barkeep turned and prepared two flagons of the sweet, golden ale. The drink went up to the brim, threatening to slosh over the sides and stain the bar counter. Deylan offered the man a coin, hoping to smooth over the apparent misunderstanding. However, the barkeep pushed it back to Deylan.

"You should try to be more like your friend over there," the barkeep said, jutting his chin out towards Heru. "You talk too much. He's ready for the sea."

Stammering out an apology, Deylan took the drinks. Bharam continued to watch their interaction with a critical eye. Deylan hoped he didn't hear the conversation. It was loud enough that the bustling tavern covered their exchange.

"Boy," the barkeep said as Deylan took his first step.

Spinning around with the grace of a dancer, Deylan faced the barkeep without spilling a drop. Deylan felt his soul bare open as the barkeep's one good eye bore into him.

"You're traveling with Kayna?"

Deylan nodded.

"Keep your wits about you. The Scourge's daughter attracts some dangerous folks. If anyone gives you trouble, tell 'em you and your friend are protected by Sam." With a slight nod, the barkeep stared expectantly at Deylan.

"Thank you... Sam," Deylan said, fishing a couple gold coins out from the pouch on his hip, somehow still managing to not lose anything from his flagons.

The monstrous barkeep pocketed the coins faster than Deylan could blink. Ignoring the question that hung at the end of the sentence, he gave Deylan a dismissive nod. Nonplussed but relatively pleased with the exchange, Deylan turned once more and returned to the table with his two ales. Bharam waited for Deylan's approach with wide eyes. He looked as though he wanted to burst. The uncharacteristic expression confused Deylan.

"What did he say?" Bharam leaned in and asked in a sort of whisper. It wasn't too quiet that he needed to truly whisper, but the general ambiance was soft enough that if they wanted to have a private conversation, they needed to lower their voice. "Why did he call you back?"

"He wanted to give me a bit of warning about the seas," Deylan said. He chose his words carefully, not wanting to repeat Sam's words. "Didn't think I was the seafaring type."

The answer didn't seem to satisfy the Nem Pahlan man. He was thirsty for information. His eyes gave it away. There was no effort made to conceal his desires. This was a completely different man from the pious coward Deylan knew.

"Come now," Bharam pressed. "He returned your coin. What is your relationship to him? Does Dhruvasht know?"

The pressing interest in Sam the barkeep's warning left Deylan growing uneasy. Did Dhruvasht have a quarrel with

Sam? Would this change the dynamic on the ship when they left in three days? Deylan sipped on his ale, buying time while he tried to formulate an answer.

"I don't know the man," Deylan said honestly. Leaning back in his chair with an amused grin, he placed his hands behind his head, interlacing his fingers together. "He just said that I don't seem like the seafaring type. Shame he's never traveled with me. We'd have a great time."

Disappointment filled Bharam's face. He picked up his flagon and took a deep drink. Deylan studied him, enjoying a stretch before resting his arms on the table. It felt sticky. The furniture here probably saw a lot of spilled ale over time. Deylan wondered if he sniffed them if they would smell like the sweet ale or something else.

"I would have agreed when we first met," the Nem Pahlan grumbled. "You're too happy even when food stores are low. You'd almost think you're Fukur'okuju reincarnated."

"Fukur'okuju?"

"Our god of joy. Maa'zhun, as you know, is our goddess of the sea. If we continue together, you will become well versed with the true gods."

Deylan made a non-committal grunt behind his drink. The man seemed to be warming up to him. Perhaps he was hoping for some information. Deylan didn't believe that he gave up on the curiosities of his earlier line of questions.

"Have you found someone to join us in three days?"

The Nem Pahlan man seemed to be coming up with any small talk he could to keep the conversation from turning to awkward silence. Deylan almost enjoyed the man's discomfort. He wanted to continue playing with Bharam, but he was beginning to get tired and the next few days were going to be busy.

"I have a promising lead, but I want to continue searching. Dhruvasht wants us to come back here to board the *Fury*, right?"

His companion nodded. "He didn't say much, but the captain is resting in a room at one of the nearby inns. I don't expect him to show himself until we leave."

"That sounds like a good idea," Deylan mused. "I could use a good nap." To accentuate his point, Deylan let out a big yawn. His arms stretched wide to the side, his hand bumping into Bharam's side without apology. "Where are your lodgings?"

"I – uh am staying at the one down the road. The Feathered Plume, I think. There are some merchants staying there while they try and figure out the whole ban on travel."

Bharam busied himself with his drink. If he had been paying attention, he would have noticed the glint in Deylan's eye and how he perked up at the news. A merchant inn was exactly what the silver-haired man needed.

XI

"**D**ID YOU MANAGE to get any information from your little friend?" Heru asked.

The young Xanan leaned back in his chair taking in the tavern as he sipped the last dregs of his drink. Deylan dropped into his seat, his tankard hitting the table with a louder thump than he intended. He watched his ale swish to the rim of the mug, nearly splashing over the side. To his relief, none of the sweet liquid was lost. It would have been a shame to have spilled such a delicious drink.

"Not much," he said with a smile. "Just the name of a place for us to stay while we wait to leave. It should be a good spot to rest and stock up on supplies."

Heru shot Deylan a questioning look, his brows knitting. "Why are you smiling if you haven't gotten any good news?"

"On the contrary," Deylan said, his tone reflecting the grin that spread from ear to ear. "This is wonderful news."

A flash of gold sparkled briefly in the darkened room. Deylan watched, amused, as Heru's eyes followed the movement of his fingers as he twirled the gold coin across the back of his hand. He waited for anything other than a quizzical look to cross the man's face. When none came, Deylan let himself relax as he continued flipping the coin.

"In fact," he continued, "My dear friend has graciously offered to pay for our first night there."

For the first time since he met the young Xanan, a smile broke out on Heru's face. Deylan let the coin drop to the table with a small tinkle before pocketing it. Raising his glass with a wink, the two shared a drink to their newfound fortune.

~~~

It wasn't long before the two stood outside the Feathered Plume. The large inn was a pristine white with pale blue trim. Delicate carvings around the elaborate wooden sign looked like seashells. Underneath the inn's name, an elegant feather accentuated the establishment's name. The building bespoke wealth. Only those who could afford her beauty were allowed to stay – the complete opposite of those who frequented Kayna's tavern.

Sifting the coins in his pouch through his fingers, Deylan enjoyed the feel of their coolness against his flesh. This definitely would be a step up for him during his stay at the Bone
~~~

Coast. A welcome one at that. Tugging on the brim of his hat, Deylan took a deep breath and prepared to enter.

Next to him, Heru stood stiffly. The young Xanan's attention darted around, taking in his surroundings and studying everything intently.

Gods, he's going to give us away if he can't relax, Deylan sighed.

"Calm yourself," Deylan whispered. "You'll get us banned from the establishment before we even set foot in it."

He was rewarded with a grunt from his companion.

I'll need to train him up a bit if we're going to have any measure of success.

Smoothing down the front of his tunic, Deylan gave his body a little shake to alleviate the stress. It was showtime.

"Let me do the talking," he instructed.

Before Heru could respond, Deylan pushed open the door and stepped into the sprawling building. The inside of the Feathered Plume was immaculate. Plush furniture dyed in rich, vibrant colors dotted the room. Deep purple cushions, the likes of which even kings probably had never seen, were framed against dark woods. The luxurious cushions begged to be sat in. Small tables with graceful legs rested next to the chairs, an occasional drink from the adjoining tavern resting on their polished surface.

Etchings of no doubt important people hung on the walls. Though he couldn't see the images clearly, he could tell that they would be detailed based on the varying greys he could see from the inn's entrance. Deylan fought to keep his jaw from dropping at the pictures. He'd never seen the likes of such wealth before. Running his hand absentmindedly over the moldings on the column next to the front door, Deylan noticed that his finger came back clean. There didn't appear to be a speck of dust to be found.

Throughout it all, women in beautiful gowns and men dressed in crisp, clean outfits milled about. Their brightly colored clothes implied a scale of wealth that Deylan could only dream of. Beside him, Heru let out a soft exclamation of amazement mirroring his own. He hoped Heru's dirty clothes and his still noticeable injuries wouldn't keep them from obtaining lodgings. These places tended to be exclusive.

Heads turned as the two made their way to who Deylan presumed to be the innkeeper near the bar on the right side of the room. Women scrunched their noses, fanning themselves with their hand fans as they passed. Taking a sniff, Deylan couldn't figure out why they were acting like the two of them smelled. It was almost an insult.

His fingers itched as he took in the opulence. All in good time.

Poorly veiled conversations behind fans followed the pair. Taking it in stride, Deylan kept his face relaxed. Occasionally, he flashed a charming smile at some of the women. He was rewarded with a slight flush tinging their cheeks as they faltered in their gossip. A few even returned the gesture, an alluring grin unconsciously appearing.

The men in the room appeared to be less bothered. Some shot the two a glance, no doubt taking in the surly young Xanan or his fine wide-brimmed hat. As long as Deylan carried himself like one of them, the men wouldn't give him any problems. He was unconcerned.

The bar was made of a fine dark wood polished to absolute perfection. The grains moved in harmony, creating a delicate flow on the surface. The very wood itself was smooth as the flesh of the most beautiful woman – soft and without blemish. Intricate designs were carved into the front of the bar. Dainty swirls framed the edges while the exquisite dark wood stood out as the centerpiece.

An older man with a finely oiled mustache stood behind the bar. He didn't tend to his crystal-ware like most of his ilk. Instead, he stood casually, finishing up a conversation with a patron. Deylan waited patiently for the two to finish, the pair glancing in his direction in acknowledgment. However, they did not rush their discussion. Deylan could feel Heru growing impatient next to him. Before he could say anything, Heru walked off, sinking into a chair by a large oriel window.

Thank the gods he went over there, Deylan sighed. *His damn attitude would have made this more difficult.*

A few more moments passed before the man turned from the mustached man. Deylan gave him a few seconds before approaching. He assumed the man was the owner, but Deylan wanted to gauge the barkeep to confirm. It wasn't common, but sometimes the barkeep was just a front for the establishment.

"Good afternoon, sir," Deylan said. He let sunshine ring from every word as he let his hands rest on the finely crafted bar. "I'm hoping you have a room for rent. My friend and I have just arrived after a long journey and are in need of a good night's rest."

The man's eyes narrowed as he looked over at Heru. The Xanan lounged in the luxurious aubergine cushions, letting his body melt into the plush pillows. Deylan was surprised to see the corners of Heru's mouth turn up in a rare look of contentment.

"I do have a few rooms available." The man's voice was as oily as his mustache. "How long are you planning to stay?"

"Two nights. We will leave on the third day," Deylan replied. "It's been so long since we've had a proper bed, and I'm sure my friend is ravenous. There weren't many inns with good food either and he eats quite a lot."

As if on cue, Heru got up and chased down a young woman carrying a tray. The two shared a quick word before parting and Heru returned to his chair.

The owner raised a brow, but didn't say anything. He ran his fingers over his mustache, deep in thought. Deylan noted how the man's gaze kept darting towards Heru. The young Xanan sat peacefully in the chair, taking a bit of bread from the barmaid he'd spoken to earlier with a nod of the head. The owner's nose crinkled as he saw the barmaid attempt to make small talk with the Xanan. It looked like disgust.

"Is there a problem?" Deylan asked.

The man jumped, not expecting the question. "I beg your pardon?"

"Our room," Deylan prompted. "You were telling us about the ones you have available."

Pulling out a gold coin, Deylan casually placed it on the bar. The obvious display of wealth caught the man's attention. Deylan noted how the owner stared at the coin, but his body didn't so much as twitch in anticipation at the payment.

"Oh yes, of course. I assume you are fine with sharing a bed? Our bigger rooms are considerably more."

The mustached-man studied Deylan like a hawk, the sparkle of the gold reflecting in his eyes. He was a simple man, Deylan noted. That would make their stay more difficult, but it would at least keep them from being thrown out – for now. He could only hope that the man's dislike of the young Xanan wouldn't cost them too much.

"A single bed will be fine. I daresay, we're so exhausted that one of us could even sleep on the floor. That won't be a problem, I hope?"

Taking the opportunity to lock eyes with the innkeeper, Deylan made sure to hold it without breaking his confident demeanor. The man met his gaze, his own self-assuredness wavering after several long moments. The man's attentions darted to Heru relaxing in the chair and back. Every time he glanced at the Xanan, the innkeeper's eye would twitch.

Almost there, Deylan noted.

With a heavy blink, the innkeeper turned away, pulling out a ledger. A pot of ink and quill followed shortly after. The small victory filled Deylan with pride. He usually never tested his luck against the upper classes. People were motivated by the same things after all. Gold would be his secret to success once more. The innkeeper rambled through his well-rehearsed spiel not looking up as he spoke. The rules of the inn were laid out as well as the amount owed for the stay. The price nearly broke Deylan's well-practiced façade.

"Twenty gold is quite a lot," he stammered. As soon as the words left Deylan's lips, he cursed himself. He should have maintained his composure better. "Two nights at ten gold is more than I've heard. Even nations in the heart of Corinth don't charge that much."

Finally, it was the innkeeper's turn to win their little exchange. Jutting his chin in Heru's direction, he fixed Deylan with a greedy stare.

"We add an additional fee when dealing with those who do not belong." Contempt dripped from every word. "You could have stayed for six gold a night. But when you bring brutes from the warlord nation, we must find an assurance that any damage he may cause will be covered. After all, their type aren't exactly known to be refined. My girls will have to work extra hard to clean the smell of sumac from our linens."

Anger burned Deylan's face. His cheeks threatened to betray the emotion simmering within and blaze red. He fought the urge to gnash his teeth – he would have to let his frustrations out in another manner. The ledger was slid over to him with a grin. The quill waited for him to grasp its delicate shaft. Deylan noted, through his disgust, that the feather was pristine. Pulling the ledger closer to him, Deylan saw that despite the room being full with patrons, there weren't many pages of the ledger completed.

This sent a wave of suspicion coursing through him. He scanned the page, but nothing seemed amiss. No hidden messages or underhanded text graced the page – just a handwritten price scrawled onto the page next to where their names were to be. He could deal with this later. Dipping the quill into the rich black ink, Deylan wrote his name into the book.

"Does your friend know how to write?" the innkeeper asked. A bemused expression filled his face as though he made a humorous joke. "You can fill in his name, if that would be easier."

"You're too kind," Deylan murmured. He managed to plaster on his charismatic air once more. "We've had such difficulties getting lodgings from fine inns like this. This will undoubtably be a trip to remember. Will you be escorting us to our room?"

The bronze key, polished and without a hint of grime, slid across the wooden bar.

"I'm afraid I have other matters to attend to. You'll be on the third floor. Room six." His fingers moved to his face, stroking his oiled mustache as if he were deep in thought. "Try not to start any problems with your friend over there. I am extending you a courtesy. We don't take kindly to his type."

With a dip of his wide-brimmed hat, Deylan scooped up the key and bid the man good day. He didn't waste any time and headed towards the Xanan. Heru dozed in the chair, his arms laying on the intricately carved armrests. His weapons rested against the side of the chair.

"How can he keep these out here so casually?" Deylan hummed. "The axe isn't even sheathed. At least he wipes the blade."

Poking the slumbering Xanan, Deylan bit back a laugh when the man didn't wake up. Not wanting to scare his companion, Deylan gave Heru one last poke before grabbing his shoulder and giving it a shake. The Xanan's eyes remained closed, but his hand swatted at the silver-haired man.

"If you value your life, don't bother me," Heru muttered.

"For gods' sake," Deylan hissed. "Get up. We got a room. Grab your shite and let's go. We can't leave weapons just lying about for any child to grab."

Cracking open an eye, Heru glared at Deylan.

"Up," Deylan said with more urgency. He nearly slapped the Xanan's arm, but stayed his hand.

His patience proved to be a good decision. Heru growled softly at Deylan before pushing himself up from the velvety chair. The deep purple fabric held the Xanan's imprint momentarily before returning to its regular shape. Deylan envied his companion for being able to enjoy such a magnificent chair. He would have to find a chance to enjoy it before they left.

Gathering his weapons, Heru followed Deylan towards the winding staircase leading to the upper levels. The banister was a beautiful pine. The wood was a pale brown, so pale it was almost white. Smooth and rounded, the banister fit the hand like a glove. The carpet on each step was soft, cushioning each step of Deylan's boot. The difference between the carpet and wooden steps was astounding. The Feathered Plume was luxury exemplified.

Each step left a muffled thump as the two made their way down the corridor to their room. Only ten rooms were on each floor. A single table made from the same rich, dark wood as the bar sat in the middle of the hall. A simple glass filled with fresh, white flowers lay on a delicate piece of lace. Spying the rare decoration impressed Deylan. It was so uncommon that he assumed only royalty had the accent fabric.

Room six lay at the end of the corridor next to a large oriel window. Like the rest of the inn, the panes were extraordinarily clean without a streak or any salt crystals from the tangy sea air. The key clicked into the hole and the door opened. Pushing his companion into the room, Deylan glanced around the corridor and shut the door behind him.

"Why did you bother –" Heru began, but Deylan shushed him with a motion of his hand.

"You, my dear friend, will need to keep your temper during our stay." Deylan said. "We're on a thin rope as it is. You will *not* give them any reason to kick us out. We've paid an exorbitant amount in advance and I can't afford to lose that much."

"You've already told me that they're high end."

"No," Deylan replied, urgency tinging his words. "You are the issue. The owner believes that the warlords are all savages, though he didn't outright say as much. He's looking for any excuse to deny us our stay and keep our coin."

Looking like a fish gasping for air, Heru's mouth opened and closed without any sound. For once, the Xanan was stunned. Multiple questions flashed across his face as he struggled to find his voice. A twinge of sadness pulled at Deylan. The young man was proud, but innocent enough. He'd probably never been outside of Xan prior to this. This was a tough way to find out how cruel the world could be.

Like a cloud passing, Heru managed to regain his composure and closed his mouth. The questions were still there, but not visible anymore. He confidently crossed the room and placed his weapons upright in the corner. The change was striking.

"So we are to bow down to these bastards and let them walk over us like beaten dogs?"

A darkness flashed in Heru's eyes that startled Deylan. He was glad the Xanan's weapons were resting against the wall.

"Not at all," Deylan replied. He found the corners of his mouth turning up as he spoke. "Just leave the rest to me. You be a good boy and play the perfect traveler. I'm not nearly as noticeable if I don't want to be. Come, let's get some dinner. I'm exhausted and need a good night's rest."

Glancing at his scimitar, Heru's hand twitched, the motion momentarily resembling him grasping its handle. With a bit of effort, he turned away from his familiar blade. Tossing his bag onto the ground, Heru nodded.

"I could use a bite myself. Just ale makes for a poor day's meal."

XII

SOFT MUSIC PLAYED by the staircase as a woman with a lute sang. Her voice lilted with a heartbreaking beauty as her fingers played deftly over the strings. Deylan caught a few lines about a young princess and her unrequited love, but paid the song no mind. He had more important matters to attend to. It was easy for the two to find a table. A barmaid quickly stopped by and took their order. Unlike the serving women of the less savory taverns, these women felt sacred. Their young faces shone with innocence and purity. Their dresses were simple yet elegant – a white chemise with a blue dress on top. The pale blue ribbons cinched the front together tightly without leaving them exposed. These weren't the type of women who could be persuaded with a few sweet words to spend extra time with a patron.

Deylan found himself frustrated knowing it would be more difficult to get information. Difficult, but not impossible.

The musician finished up her song by the time the food arrived. Her final note a breathy one filled with hope. A polite smattering of applause filled the room. It lacked the enthusiasm of the taverns Deylan had been to despite the young woman being one of the better singers he'd heard.

Salted cod lay on the plate with a little section of lemon on the side. The plate was clean, the fillet resting nicely in the center. Small carrots and some type of green vegetable that tasted bland and of water waited on the side. He glanced at his companion and noted the Xanan eyeing the fish. His fork hovered over the slab of cod, unsure.

"We should have asked for something more familiar," Heru mumbled. "We don't have fish at home."

"Just eat it. If you are to fit in with these popinjays you'll need to appear to enjoy it."

A thin stream of lemon flew in Deylan's direction as Heru struggled to squeeze the fruit over his meal. Deylan fought back a chuckle as the Xanan managed to redirect the juice onto his fish. Doing the same, Deylan then took a bite. He was pleasantly surprised at the firm, flaky texture. The taste was mild and slightly sweet. Having never tasted the finer meats, Deylan found himself digging into the meal with vigor. Peeking up from his plate, Deylan noticed that Heru also appeared to be enjoying his dinner.

A new entertainer took the stage. The musician appeared to be not much older than Deylan. He pulled out a lute and plucked a few notes. The strings sang in harmony. Clearing his throat, the young man began singing in a beautiful tenor. Deylan didn't pay much attention to the song. Instead, his attention was on the patrons of the inn. The tables were filled with finely dressed men and women all engrossed with the young singer on the bottom steps of the staircase. Wine and ale flowed freely from the kitchen. Barmaids wove between the tables grabbing empty glasses and replacing them with full ones as if in sync with the song.

Wondering if his luck had run out for the night, Deylan sipped on his wine ready to give up for the night. Heru leaned back in his chair, listening to the singer as his eyelids drooped. There wasn't much time left.

Then he spotted her.

Sitting in the far corner opposite his table, Deylan saw a woman watching the show with a less than amused expression. Her blonde hair was twisted into intricate curls atop her head, leaving her shoulders and back exposed thanks to the lowcut top of her dress. There was no one accompanying her for dinner. Excusing himself, Deylan told Heru that he would be back later. Whether the drowsing Xanan heard him, he would have to find out later. A round of polite applause rang out as the musician finished his song. Deylan moved between the tables, dodging the barmaids as they scurried about. A half-drank glass of dark wine sat on the table in front of the woman. Judging by the way she swayed with the music, Deylan guessed that she had at least a couple others before.

"Excuse me," Deylan said, startling the woman. "Might I join you?"

A faint flush tinged the woman's cheeks. Deylan wasn't sure if it was because she had a few too many drinks. A light layer of freckles dotted her skin, hidden under the pink that blossomed on her face.

She let out a breathy response, moving her chair despite Deylan being next to an empty one. Sliding into the chair across from her, Deylan leaned in. He was rewarded by her mimicking him.

"The music is lovely tonight," Deylan said softly. "However, it is paled by your splendor."

A brighter flush spread over the woman's face.

"Is your name just as exquisite?"

The woman giggled behind her hand. "You know how to charm a woman." Her husky voice in combination with the exotic dark paint she had around her eyes intrigued Deylan. He found his gaze lingering on her face. "What business does a young man like yourself have in a place like this? Are you just here to bed vulnerable women?"

Deylan brought his hand to his chest, his face taking on an expression of feigned disbelief. "My dear woman, I am hurt by your insinuation. I am here on business with my partner. We are meeting with the local apothecaries to find dealers for our tinctures."

"Oh, I'm sorry," she replied. "I just assumed that you approaching a lone woman came with ulterior motives."

Maintaining his hurt expression, Deylan waved his hand as though he were trying to alleviate her worry. "Understandable. It's not often that a man approaches a beautiful woman like yourself without wanting a little more. Please, tell me more about yourself...?"

He let the end of his sentence trail off like a question. He hoped she would take the hint and provide her name. He was pleased when she complied.

"Marie," she provided. "And you?"

Deylan replied in kind.

The two discussed their business on the Bone Coast. Deylan made sure to let Marie do most of the talking. She gradually finished off her glass of wine, offering him a glass of his own while they talked. In the background, the entertainers switched as the young man ended his set. By the time the wine was consumed, Marie was all smiles as they shared an intimate conversation. Her soft hand touched his several times and her eyes sparkled as she laughed.

"So," Marie said, pausing as she rubbed his hand once more. "How long will you be staying?"

"I leave in two days."

Her lips turned in a pout. "I would hate to not spend more time with you."

"I feel the same." Deylan picked up her hand and entwined his fingers with hers. "But I'm afraid I have meetings during the day. I don't have much time to myself."

"Then why don't we make the most of our time together?" Marie's lips turned up as she held his gaze. "I'm sure we wouldn't regret it."

Glancing back at where Heru sat, Deylan saw the Xanan leaning back in his chair with his arms crossed in front of him, asleep. Thanking the gods that he kept the key and handled the bill that night, Deylan turned his attention to Marie. Heru could fend for himself – hopefully in an appropriate manner for the likes of the Feathered Plume.

"That sounds lovely," Deylan replied.

〰

Marie's room turned out to be larger than Deylan's. The faint scent of rose filled the room. He wondered if she placed rose petals in her drawers to keep her clothes smelling fresh. He didn't spend much time taking in the room before Marie wrapped her arms around him. The two shared a deep kiss. Her plump lips cushioned his, her tongue shyly playing with his. His hands wandered down her back until he reached her back-side. Her body pressed against his.

Letting her take the lead, Deylan brought one hand to her breast. They were small, but firm. His other hand moved to the front of her skirts. She didn't stop as he bunched up her skirt, searching for her soft flesh. He found what he was searching for. His fingers rubbed against her, enjoying her body's reaction to his touch. Her body quivered as his fingers went deeper.

Pulling away from her lips, he found the bed. Guiding her to the bed, Deylan gently laid her down and climbed on top. Her body pressed against his, her hips moving up to meet his. His hands worked to undo his pants while hers pulled his tunic off. Once he'd removed his clothes, Deylan worked on Marie's. Soon her dress lay in a heap on top of his clothes. Her body was smooth and fit with his perfectly. His hands cupped one of her breasts, the other returning to between her legs. He let Marie determine the pace. Her breathing became heavier as his fingers moved deeper and faster within her.

As a moan escaped her lips, he knew it was time. Maneuvering his hips, Deylan felt himself slide inside. Her body shuddered around him as he thrust his hips. Her gasps became high-pitched moans. A moan broke free from Deylan, Marie's enthusiasm exciting him.

〃〃

Pale moonlight streamed through the sheer curtains. Deylan lay on his back, the cool pillow cradling his head gently. Marie's arm was draped over his chest. Her heavy, rhythmic breathing called to him. He longed to slumber. His fingers traced the small of her back. They'd spent the evening wrapped in each other's arms and remained that way late into the night. Her stamina was that of a warrior.

Deylan wondered if Heru found peace in their room without him. Despite being on the Bone Coast and surrounded with people of questionable character, Deylan realized that there were going to bigots everywhere, and with Heru not fitting into their perfect little mold of what a proper person should be, Deylan hoped his little rendezvous wouldn't cost them more before their stay ended. The innkeeper seemed more than willing to take their money. Their departure couldn't come fast enough. They could have gone to a more affordable place, but he wanted to keep an eye on Bharam. Deylan also wondered if Dhruvasht was staying at the Feathered Plume as well.

Marie let out a soft sigh and rolled over. Deylan wished he could spend a few more days with her. She proved to be more fun than he'd imagined. His eyes grew heavy. The moon hung high in the heavens. Tiny pinpricks sparkled in the sky like little diamonds. It had been a long day. Giving in to exhaustion, Deylan closed his eyes and let sleep take him.

～

Deylan slept fitfully despite his fatigue. Images of the sudden storm that sunk *Death's Rose*, her sails and ropes whipping wildly in the wind, flashed through his mind as vividly as the lightning that illuminated the darkness. He heard the sickening crunch of the man who fell climbing out of the bird's nest, his shrieks quickly disappearing with the heavy *thump* and the crack of wooden planks. Somewhere in the back of his dreams, as though watching him, was an even darker presence floating amongst the roiling waves.

The visions of his final moments on *Death's Rose* eventually subsided, like the raging winds, and were replaced with ones of Heru. Deylan replayed their battle and subsequent walk to the Feathered Plume. He felt his chest tighten as he listened to Heru talk about finding his father. Tears welled at the corners of Deylan's eyes. He remembered what it was like to be lost.

As his hand reached out to open the door of the Feathered Plume, Deylan saw it had shrunk. In the faint reflection of the glass window, Deylan saw himself. Lost. Scared. Fifteen once more.

His mother's voice spoke urgently to him, echoing in the recesses of his mind. She spoke words he'd both tried to forget, and fiercely held onto as though they were the last bit of driftwood keeping him afloat in the tumultuous seas.

"Go, be happy," she'd told him through tears. "Live your life."

"But what about you?" his younger self asked.

Deylan's jaw trembled and tears rolled down his cheeks. He had no money, and he didn't want to leave his family.

"We will meet again someday. I would rather lose you and have you live a good life than lose you forever. We will meet again. I promise."

She was gone, and Deylan was alone once more.

The morning light streamed into room six. Birdsong could be heard through the closed windows, their aria punctuated by the raucous cries of gulls. Somehow, the squawking didn't break the peaceful ambiance created by the birds' chorus. Deylan hummed a tune of his own as he walked into the room. Despite the early hour, he found Heru sitting shirtless on the bed. The young Xanan laced up his boots, his tunic thrown over the back of the lone chair.

"Late night, huh?"

Deylan stopped humming. Glancing in Heru's direction, he saw the twinkle in the young warrior's eye. A familiarity colored his words – as though the two had been friends for years and regularly partook in teasing each other.

"Aye. It was definitely one to remember."

"How was she?"

Leaning back on his hands, Heru gave Deylan his full attention.

"Insatiable."

Heru let out a bark of laughter. Throwing on his shirt, Heru clapped Deylan on the back.

"Glad you managed to satisfy her. Did she satisfy you?"

A sheepish grin spread over Deylan's face. Reaching into his pocket, he pulled out a thin gold chain with a blue stone in the center. Heru's eyes widened as Deylan dangled the bracelet in front of him.

"Quite nicely," Deylan replied.

"Are you mad? You're going to get us thrown in the gaol. And you told me to behave."

"I'll take care of it, I promise." Deylan pocketed the bracelet once more. "Will you need the key, or should I keep it with me?"

"I got one of the girls to let me in. Shall we meet at midday for lunch?"

"That should be plenty of time. I'll see you then. I want to hear about your evening."

Playfully nudging the Xanan, Deylan was rewarded with a slight grin. He was beginning to like Heru and had hope that the two would get along quite nicely once out at sea. Picking up his wide-brimmed hat, Deylan left Heru and the room.

XIII

SLIPPING INTO THE LOST SIREN, Deylan sat down at a table on the outer edge of the tavern floor. Keeping to the few shadows he could, he studied the women moving from table to table, serving the patrons. His eyes darted to the bar, hoping to not find Ketes cleaning glasses or pouring drinks while he searched for Nefeli. Deylan heaved a sigh of relief, his shoulders dropping as the tension left him. Ketes was nowhere to be seen. After several long minutes, he spied Nefeli's long, wavy brown hair a few tables away.

Whistling a short blast, the note coming out like birdsong, Deylan caught Nefeli's attention. The young bar maid's face lit up, her eyes twinkling as she noticed Deylan. With a grin and a nod of his head, he motioned her to come over. Now that she'd seen him, Nefeli was clearly distracted. She finished up her in-teraction with the men at her current table, her now curt discussion with them earning Deylan a glare from the men once they realized that she would not entertain their advances.

"I didn't think I'd see you so soon," Nefeli said, her face flushing as she met his gaze. "I thought Ketes scared you away."

Feigning indifference at the mention of the barkeep, Deylan waved his hand. "His threats of bodily harm would never dissuade me from seeing you."

Slipping his fingers around her dainty hand, Deylan held it for several heartbeats. A thrill coursed through him the moment he touched her soft skin. He could see her face flush deeper, her eyes hiding behind her thick lashes.

"Nothing could, Feli."

"You flatter me," she murmured. "Surely, you've found more desirable women during your travels."

"Nonsense," Deylan replied, still keeping hold of her hand. "None can hold a candle to you."

Their gazes lingered, just like their touch. The noise of the Lost Siren vanished into the distance as time seemed to stop for the two. A moment later, it was gone. Just like that, Nefeli pulled away, her flush fading and her usual sweet, yet alluring tone returning.

"And what can I get you?"

Her words poured from her mouth like a purr, and Deylan felt his cheeks betraying him and becoming warm.

She's good.

"I am in need of some coin," he replied. "I'm to set sail in a few days, and I need money to pay for my lodgings and food. I have a few trinkets I picked up that I would like to see if I can exchange. I know some businesses may hesitate if they think I'm one of the seafaring type. I'm hoping you can help me find someone who can meet my needs."

Nefeli's brow disappeared into her brown hair and her head cocked to the side, questioning, deciding. "Meet me out back," she said, her voice falling to hushed tones. "I'll be a moment."

With a swish of her hips, Nefeli made her way back into the sea of tables. Her body moved deftly, managing to avoid the rogue hands that reached out to pat or pinch her backside. A stone slid into Deylan's stomach. Nefeli was young. She shouldn't be so adept at navigating such treacherous waters.

Behind the Lost Siren, the streets were bustling. Bodies flowed like a river. No one paid attention to Deylan or his wide brimmed hat – the magnificent plume and his pristine clothes providing the perfect cover. No one suspected who he was. Nefeli found Deylan quickly, her wavy brown hair catching the light of the sun and shining like amber. Deylan found his heart beating a little faster as her hand lightly grabbed his.

"I know a place," she said.

The two set off down the street, Nefeli taking the lead. They moved easily together, their bodies occasionally touching and the conversation flowing freely. Whenever Nefeli laughed, Deylan felt something practically glow inside his body. He found himself getting lost in the memory of their one afternoon together when he first woke up, the sound of her voice muted in the background. He remembered the way her body moved against his, the breathy gasps that escaped her as their passion reached a fevered pitch, and the delicate smile she flashed him as he laid on top of her when it was all over.

The buildings passed in a blur. Deylan tried to memorize the route they took, but he got lost in his conversation with Nefeli. The scent of honeysuckles that lingered around her reminded him of the meadows he used to run through as a child.

"Here it is," Nefeli said pointing to a nondescript shop in front of them.

A faded sign with the image of an anchor hung in over the door. The buildings in this part of town were unremarkable, not derelict, not pristine and welcoming. They were shops that most would pass without a second thought.

"Perfect," Deylan said with a grin. He held out his elbow, waiting for Nefeli to grab it. "Shall we?"

⌁

As expected, the shop proved to be exactly what Deylan was looking for. The proprietor did not question Deylan too hard or seem particularly interested in his story. With a curt word, his voice gravely from too much tobacco, the man examined the gold and gems in the jewelry before fishing out a handful of coins and sliding them across the table to Deylan.

Like a true gentleman, Deylan escorted Nefeli back to the Lost Siren. Before she disappeared into the kitchen, he took her hand and lightly brushed his lips across the back of it, causing her face to flush.

"I'll see you again?"

Hiding a giggle behind her hand, Nefeli shot him a glance behind her thick lashes before slipping back into the Lost Siren. Tapping the coin pouch on his hip, Deylan spun on his heels and made his way back to the Feathered Plume. Each step bounced as though he were walking on clouds. He was ready to make some more money.

～～

Deylan and Heru's stay at the Feathered Plume turned out to be quite pleasant. Deylan's fears that the innkeeper would tax them and then throw them out proved to be unfounded. Heru maintained a level of sophistication that caught even the snootiest in the inn off-guard. Using the mystique of a traveler to his advantage, Heru managed to lure more than one of the barmaids to bed and leaving Deylan a little jealous. Deylan, however, found success as well. After his encounter with Marie, he both avoided running into her again while finding two more women to spend the night with. Each proved to be more lucrative than the last as he returned to his room with some trinket he managed to slip out with him in the morning.

By the second day, one of the male serving staff approached Deylan to inquire about the missing jewelry. In the background, Deylan observed the owner following him with a hawk-like gaze. But thanks to his meetings with Nefeli and her knowledge of the best places to sell gold quickly, Deylan was able to show the man that he had nothing of the sort in his room. After each meeting with the young barmaid, his stomach would knot. He found himself thinking of her during his free time. Each time they parted, Deylan found it harder and harder to say good-bye.

Despite the staff being on alert of the potential theft, Deylan had no difficulty meeting wealthy women during his short stay. By the time they checked out of the Feathered Plume, Deylan's coin pouch jingled as it weighed heavily on him. The jewelry he sold more than made up for the exorbitant boarding cost for the Feathered Plume.

Neither Deylan nor Heru ran into Bharam while staying at the inn. Their days were spent in the Scourge's tavern watching how the crew prepared for their journey. They noted how supplies never seemed to be mentioned. Instead, the men just sat around eating and drinking. The banter, Deylan found, painted a much more interesting picture of the social dynamics of the crew.

Though they all held an imposing and deadly air, the main group frequenting the tavern seemed to defer to Kayna without a second thought. The Scourge never set foot in the tavern and both Deylan and Heru were quite intrigued by this mystical man. A few members of the crew gave the two a little insight about the Pirate Lord over a few tankards of ale. From what they gathered, the Scourge was a man who ruled the seas with an iron fist. The other captains of the different crews held the man in great regard. No one disobeyed the Scourge.

Stocked up on what supplies they thought they might need, Heru and Deylan waited at the Scourge's tavern on the third day waiting for Dhruvasht and Kayna to provide them with orders before boarding. The air in the Scourge's tavern no longer unnerved Deylan. He still kept his guard up, but the longer he remained in their presence, the more he felt he could possibly become one of their own.

"Where is that captain of yours?" Heru asked Deylan.

"I don't know."

The conversation in the tavern felt different from the days before. Fewer men sat at the tables drinking. Laughter wasn't as pronounced as it had been three days prior. Even Sam, the barman, appeared more alert. Deylan noted how the man more obviously watched the door as he cleaned his glasses.

"We should see him soon. I can't imagine us waiting too long to depart with the sailing ban that's taken effect," Deylan added.

With a grunt, Heru headed off to the bar for a drink. Deylan moved to follow, but something caught his eye. Slipping into the tavern and scurrying towards a darkened corner, Bharam made his way to the farthest table in the room. Deylan watched as he pressed his back to the wall and began fumbling with something, probably his religious talisman, around his neck. Time had not dampened Deylan's disgust and distrust of the man. Anyone who could abandon their crew so easily could never be trusted.

"You found your friend, I see," with a smirk, Heru pressed a flagon of the sweet ale into Deylan's hand.

Without thinking, Deylan took a drink. The ale refreshed him. He realized he would miss it once they hit the sea. "He doesn't appear to want to be seen," Deylan replied. "I wonder what scared him."

"I can't imagine people like him getting along with men like these," Heru waved his hand in the general direction of the tavern. "Cowards can never be held accountable. I would wager that he's angered more than one man and is trying to remain inconspicuous."

Deylan grunted in agreement. The young Xanan had a habit of being very blunt.

The two searched for an empty table. Though the tavern wasn't nearly as crowded, there were still enough people inside that they had to settle for a pair of seats at an already occupied table. No one batted an eye at them as they slipped into their seats.

"No one is drunk," Deylan observed.

"This journey must be more important than you thought."

"The apothecary I was telling you about, Peni, said that Kayna's crew is the only one that brings back the rare plants for his oils and such. I can't imagine it's a leisurely trip."

Heru nodded and took a sip. He scanned the room, his eyes peering over the rim of his flagon. The men sitting across from the two didn't seem to pay them any mind, so Heru's scrutiny went unnoticed.

What has he noticed? Deylan wondered, narrowing his eyes as he took a quick look around the tavern himself. His back was to the main door, leaving him feeling a little exposed. *There is a heaviness.*

Though he couldn't figure out why, Deylan found himself shifting in his seat. His head swiveled a few times before scolding himself.

Calm yourself. Nothing good comes from panicking.

"Look," Heru muttered.

Trying not to draw attention to himself, Deylan cocked his head. Fighting back a gasp, Deylan watched as Dhruvasht's broad figure clomped through the tavern. He stopped in the middle of the room as if searching for someone. His body spun around several times before making his way to the darkest corner – where Bharam sat.

"I wonder what those two are talking about?" Heru mused. "I noticed that neither brought someone to man their ship like you did."

"Dhruvasht can't be bothered," Deylan murmured. "Too busy being important."

"Does he have the skill to be this arrogant?" Heru sat his flagon down on the table, his eyes glinting.

"I've never seen him, but his crew respected him. I wouldn't try my luck with him without some thorough planning first."

The Xanan's eyes narrowed, but he didn't say another word. They quietly observed the two as they sat huddled in the darkened corner. Through the shadows, Deylan saw that Bharam spoke quickly, Dhruvasht barely saying a word. Occasionally, the captain would nod or respond, but the discussion was short and one-sided.

"That's a slippery one," one of the men sitting at the table with Deylan and Heru noted. "Glad I'm not going to be on the *Fury* with them."

Deylan and Heru shared a glance while the man's companion agreed. The two pirates shared a hard look at the two in the corner before changing the conversation once more. Deylan opened his mouth to speak, but Heru gave the slightest shake of his head. Now was not the time to speak.

The two finished their ale in silence, watching the furtive duo. The discussion abruptly ended when Dhruvasht made a statement, his hand slamming onto the table to accentuate his point, before storming off. Bharam appeared shaken, but Deylan quickly had to look away as his former captain approached. Dhruvasht stalked past the table, suddenly noticing Deylan and his companion.

"Is this who you managed to find?" he asked curtly.

Deylan fumbled for an answer, acutely aware that more than a few pairs of eyes watched this exchange with interest.

Heru sat mutely, his empty flagon of ale pressed to his lips as though he were taking a long drink. A smirk played at the corners of his eyes as he let Deylan suffer.

Damn bastard, Deylan groused. *The one time he decides to stay silent.*

Dhruvasht's glare bore into Deylan the longer the silence stretched. Deylan almost thought he saw a vein on the man's temple begin to throb. What he would give to let this go on for a few more moments. The hush around him intensified as a few more heads turned his way. They didn't even attempt to be discrete about their curiosity. Satisfied that he'd thoroughly annoyed his former captain, Deylan cleared his throat.

"It is," Deylan said at last. "I have had the pleasure of talking to him the last few days, and he seems up to the task. What exactly are we doing?"

Deylan hoped Dhruvasht would answer the question. But with all the prying eyes, he doubted he'd get an honest answer. The former captain of *Death's Rose*'s lip curled in a snarl. Something was bothering him and Deylan was dying to find out what.

"We will talk on the ship."

Without further explanation, Dhruvasht took one last look at Heru and stomped out the tavern door. Despite the general din, the slamming door rang in Deylan's ears. Heru kept his gaze on his companion, his flagon now resting on the table once more. The surrounding tables stared at the two. Deylan was highly aware that he was being watched. He hoped that Bharam didn't notice the exchange. He wanted to speak with him before they left.

"What a cunt," the man sitting next to Deylan said with a laugh. He slapped Deylan on the shoulder as the others joined in his mirth. "Good luck surviving this trip with him."

Out of the corner of his eye, Deylan saw Bharam head out the front door. Without a word, Heru got up and followed the man. Taking the moment, Deylan remained seated. He would have to follow Heru later.

"I take it our dear captain Dhruvasht hasn't ingratiated himself with you," Deylan said with a bemused grin.

"That damned Dhruvasht has been parading about as a captain for over a decade now. He may know his way around a ship, but that doesn't mean he's earned the title."

"He's smart though," another man added. "He's stayed away from our crew long enough."

Another round of laughter broke out. Deylan joined in, but he didn't share in their amusement. His mind raced as he pieced everything together.

"I take it he's been on a thin rope for a while now?" Deylan asked.

"Those who don't heed the Scourge's laws face our wrath. Kayna metes out justice, and sometimes we act as her sword."

There was a glint in their eye that left Deylan feeling unnerved once more. He'd grown familiar with the men and started to think that they wouldn't hurt him, but now he questioned is judgment.

"Are the Xanan and I safe amongst you?"

The words struggled to come out, his mouth suddenly was so dry. The laughter stopped. More heads turned his direction.

"Leave 'em alone."

Sam's gruff voice carried over the last remnants of conversation. No sooner did he speak, then a hush fell over the rest of the tavern. The few who were talking now faced Deylan and his table.

"No one will harm you," Sam added. "They're just having a laugh. You'd have to fuck up good to earn our ire."

"Do we need to know somethin'?" the man asked. When Deylan blanched, he burst out into laughter. "I'm kiddin'!" The man slapped Deylan on the shoulder, nearly knocking him out of the chair. "If Ol' Black Sam trusts you and Kayna's not worried, I'm not bothered."

Readjusting his hat, Deylan pushed his agitation away. He emptied the flagon, exhaled, and let it drop to the table with a muted *thunk*, the kind that said satisfied without needing a word. He fixed his neighbor with an amused grin before joining the others in a round of laughter. Heads turned away and Black Sam resumed his duties. The man next to Deylan turned to his friend as they finished their laugh, leaving Deylan alone at the table.

A sudden outburst outside startled Deylan. The two men closest to him craned their necks towards the door, but didn't seem all that concerned. Not seeing Heru return, curiosity got the better of Deylan and he got up from the table and headed outside.

Heru stood in the middle of the street. Not more than a foot away, Bharam was rooted in place. The Nem Pahlan clutched the token on his necklace, his other hand clenched at his side. Both glared daggers at each other. Bharam appeared to be trembling. Whether it was rage or fear, it was hard to tell. Deylan glanced around and saw that Dhruvasht was nowhere in sight.

"Apologize," Heru commanded.

Ever the man of few words, he didn't elaborate. He didn't even notice Deylan standing in the doorway. Bharam's jaw clenched, but he didn't say a word.

"What's going on?" Deylan asked.

Bharam spoke quickly, as though he were afraid to let the Xanan get in the first word.

"This ungodly man dared to impugn me. He's accused me of cowardice and of not fulfilling my duties."

"Because you betrayed your brothers," Heru replied.

"You know not of which you speak!" Bharam's voice trembled and his eyes blazed. At his side, his fist shook as though it took every ounce of strength he possessed to not strike the Xanan. "You cannot disobey the gods."

Heru's body relaxed. A stream of curses spilled out of his mouth. Crossing his arms, Heru fixed his opponent with a withering stare. Anger no longer filled his face.

"Go down to the docks," Deylan interjected. "Let's get ready to set sail. If we're to be on the *Fury* together we should at least get along. Otherwise it will be a long trip for all of us."

Bharam took a step back, his body tense but no longer trembling. Finally breaking his attention away from Heru, the Nem Pahlan focused on Deylan. Disdain rimmed his eyes. He obviously didn't care for either of them. He backed away slowly, not exposing his back to the two. No one else waited in the street. Just the three stood together, tense.

Heru didn't move a muscle. He watched the Nem Pahlan slink away, still trying to maintain a bit of dignity. Once he'd created a bit of space between the two, Bharam turned and began walking away.

"He looks as dumb as he does strong," Bharam muttered.

He must have thought he said it softly, but he was wrong. In a heartbeat, Heru crossed the distance between them and slammed his fist against the side of Bharam's head. Bharam stumbled forward from the force of the blow. His knees buckled and he toppled to the ground, barely managing to keep himself from landing flat on his face by throwing his hands out in front of him.

Deylan tried to wrap his arms around Heru's body, but he missed as the Xanan continued forward. He watched as Bharam landed roughly on the ground, his body jarring as his hands and elbows hit the cobblestones. A grunt escaped Bharam as he hit the street. His legs scrambled to get beneath him as he gasped for breath. Before Deylan could react, Heru threw himself on top of the Nem Pahlan.

XIV

WITH A SHOUT OF ADRENALINE, Heru launched himself at Bharam. The man let out a cry of shock as the Xanan landed on his back. Heru landed a punch to the back of Bharam's head, causing it to jerk forward. The Nem Pahlan's head nearly struck the cobblestones from the force of the blow. Twisting on his back, Heru felt his knee connect with the Nem Pahlan's ribs. The man let out a grunt as the air was knocked out of him once more. Readjusting his position on the man's back, Heru threw a few punches at the back and side of Bharam's head. Pleas for forgiveness went ignored as Heru continued to unleash his frustrations from the last few days upon the fallen Nem Pahlan.

A flurry of curses streamed from Heru's lips as he struck Bharam. Somewhere in the background, he heard a few voices calling out. Heru thought he heard Deylan's, but he ignored his comrade. All he saw at the moment was a blinding rage.

In the back of his mind, his master's voice floated in between the anger induced haze. *"Control yourself, young master. We sons of Xan do not let our emotions get the better of us. We are feared for our deadly control. You will never become an elite like your father if you continue to act on your emotions."*

Back then, the words infuriated Heru. His rage was fuel to his strength. Without the ever-burning emotion, his power would peter out. This time, the words gave him pause. How could he grow if he didn't have something to push him forward? With a growl, Heru pushed his doubt away and slammed his elbow into Bharam's head. The man turned his head just as the blow struck, cutting a gash on his cheekbones and causing blood to spill forth.

A pair of arms wrapped around Heru's midsection, pulling him up and away from Bharam. More voices, not panicked like Bharam's, sounded behind him. A few even chuckled. He resisted the person picking him up, but hearing Deylan's voice calmed him.

"Heru! Stop!"

Deylan tugged Heru to his feet. The Xanan's arms hung limply at his side. His eyes, however, remained locked onto the Nem Pahlan cowering on the cobblestones. Blood stained the street, pouring out of Bharam's nose, mouth, and the gash on his cheek. A small surge of pride swirled in Heru, pushing the last remnants of anger away. Seeing the results of his rampage was rewarding.

The silver-haired man released a steady stream of words in an attempt to calm him. Heru didn't pay much attention to what Deylan was saying. They mirrored what his master told him years ago. He began to wonder if perhaps his master had been right all along. It would be another matter for another day.

"Next time you'll apologize," Heru spat between ragged breaths.

A few men stood outside the Scourge's tavern watching the scuffle. No one moved to help Bharam as he slowly got to his feet. Blood dripped from his face onto his clothes and the cobbles. Deylan continued to restrain Heru's now relaxed body. The silver-haired man's grip remained tight around Heru's chest under the armpits despite there no longer being any resistance from the Xanan.

"You're a mad man!" Bharam cried out. The Nem Pahlan's eyes scoured the group, looking, almost pleading, for someone to take his side. When no one moved to help him, his eyes widened unnaturally. "Fools! When the gods smite you for your disrespect, I will be looking down as you burn."

"Shut yer yap," one of the men behind Heru drawled. "Get yer stuff and head onto the *Fury*."

"We don't have time for this shite," another piped in.

"Next time I won't be so nice." Though Heru's rage was gone, he knew the next time the two met would be the last. People like Bharam could not be trusted.

Bharam spat a curse at the group, but slinked away. His eyes burned and muttered a never-ending slew of Nem Pahlan under his breath. The others who came out with his friend commented on the situation, their dislike of Bharam evident, before slipping back into the Scourge's tavern. When Bharam finally retreated around the corner, Deylan let Heru go. He clapped the Xanan on the back, squeezing his shoulder reassuringly.

"We're going to need to work on your people skills," Deylan said. His voice was light and barely concealed the chuckle fighting to break free. "I know now not to get on your bad side. What happened?"

Shaking his arms to release the adrenaline that still flowed through him, Heru faced his friend and guided him towards the tavern. Bharam would figure out eventually that the *Graak's Fury* was behind the tavern. The Scourge did not abide by the Bone Coast's laws.

"It's not important," Heru said with a shake of his head. "I don't like him."

He met resistance as they neared the door. Deylan stopped, preventing Heru from entering as well.

"I have to ask," he said seriously. "Is this common? I remember how we met, and I know not everyone is as understanding. I would hate for you to run into the wrong person."

The question caught Heru off-guard. Deylan's words resonated within.

"Not exactly," Heru muttered.

Amber eyes bore into Heru. He felt as though they were peering into his soul. They weren't disappointed or accusatory – they seemed to be searching for something hidden within the recesses of Heru's very essence. Deep down, he knew that Deylan didn't believe him, and if he was going to trust the silver-haired man, he needed to be honest with his new companion. And to himself.

"I've had some encounters with my friends," he grumbled.

Admitting to his past brought an uncomfortable feeling to his stomach. Heru wondered if it was shame. Taking a moment, the young Xanan pushed away the unwanted sensation. He was a strong fighter, the son of the Great Heart. He would not let his actions rule him, not like this.

"I have a legacy to live up to," Heru began, his voice growing stronger with each word. "I cannot allow my family to be made a fool of. My friends know this, and yet they chose to test the limits of my patience. I am a proud member of the Qu'ari elite," Heru said. He emphasized the significance of his status. "One can only push me so far."

Moving out of the way of the door, Deylan leaned against the exterior of the tavern, his expression blank as he took in everything Heru said. Heru wondered how much Deylan even knew about the Xanan culture. Their people were renowned throughout all of Corinth as great warriors, especially the

Qu'ari elite. It was in their title, after all. No one dared to engage with one of the elite lightly. Yet Deylan had met Heru's challenge head-on. Even the coward of a pirate dared to speak brashly to Heru. Perhaps his people's reputation was not as well-known out on the coast. Or maybe just the Bone Coast.

Heru was so preoccupied with his own thoughts that he didn't even notice when Deylan's expression changed. The silver-haired man clapped him on the back, wrapping his arm around Heru's shoulder right after.

"So, you really are as impulsive as I thought," Deylan remarked. "And you've even beaten up your friends just to sate your ego."

Heru's cheeks flamed, the sudden rush of warmth startling the young Xanan, as he fought back the urge to throw who he began to consider someone akin to a friend's arm off him.

"I think we're going to be great friends," Deylan finished.

Clapping Heru on the back this time, Deylan steered the stunned Xanan back into the tavern.

〜

What in the seven hells just happened? Heru wondered.

Once their eyes adjusted, Deylan let Heru take lead and guide them down to the ship. During his time at the Feathered Plume, Heru managed to get a little information from Kayna's crew on where he would board the ship. Though their explanation sounded like that from his childhood faerie tales, Heru couldn't even begin to contain the awe he felt as he moved through the darkened tunnels behind Black Sam's bar.

It was dream-like. The long, dark path of old, water-soaked wood leading down toward the sea. With each step, the salty smell of the ocean grew stronger. Torches lined the corridor at frequent intervals, providing a dim, flickering light that proved enough for the two to travel through the hall without hurting themselves.

Yet, as breath-taking as it all was, Heru's mind was preoccupied with what Deylan had said outside. The young, silver-haired man did not seem the least bit bothered that Heru had taken his aggression out on those he considered his friends. In fact, Deylan almost seemed amused. Despite all of his training, Heru could never figure out people like Deylan – so carefree, yet when the time came, Heru knew his friend would be dangerous.

I wonder if anyone confused Father like this? Heru mused. *Great Heart said that Father's childhood friend got away with a lot, but I can't imagine Father allowing anyone to baffle him so.*

Remembering the Great Heart's words, Heru realized that the relationships were not the same. His father's childhood friend did not confuse him like Heru first thought. It was manipulation that had led to the God Wars.

Ameen and Bijhan have never left me feeling this way either, and we spent years training together. Deylan may be odd, but perhaps he is not much different than us. Time at sea will tell.

The sound of waves pulled Heru from his reverie. The roar of water splashing onto rocks and the ever-growing scent of the sea grew stronger. Beneath his feet, the worn wooden planks gave way to smooth cobblestones and sand. The darkness lessened as natural sunlight made its way into the corridor. His foot nearly slipped on the slick stone as he traveled down the now sloping tunnel.

"By the gods," Deylan breathed. "This is extraordinary."

"What?"

"They've found a way to both circumvent the government and keep their fleet safe from enemies." Grabbing one of the torches in the wall, Deylan pointed to something still cloaked in shadows. "Look. Their ship is magnificent."

Peering in the direction Deylan pointed, Heru could make out the dark silhouette of a massive ship. The ship was perfectly hidden from the outside world inside what Heru now realized was a cave. Water lapped on the rocks, spilling onto his boots and the sand that now crunched underfoot. The same waves struck the side of the ship, the white sea spray providing an indication of just how large the ship truly was. The cobbles and other stones gave way to pure, white sand. The grains were so smooth that Heru couldn't even hear the sound of the other pirates' feet as they walked about getting ready to set said.

Large rocks dotted the sand, natural breaks in the otherwise flat of the cave. As his vision adjusted to the bright light of the outside world, Heru began noticing more – hidden things that would otherwise have been easily missed if he let his awe get the better of him. Leaning against one of the monoliths, he noted a stash of weapons. Swords and morningstars were far away from the incoming waters, the rock they waited behind faced the tavern-side of the cave.

As men moved wooden crates onto the ship, most likely rations and other necessities, he watched as others removed empty chests. Back home, the seafarers were rumored to find great treasures, the likes of which would make even the wealthiest of kings jealous. Seeing these men remove the empty boxes made Heru question the stories he'd heard as a child – granted, they were few.

Turning his attentions back to the cave, Heru caught several flashes along the walls. Letting Deylan continue on, Heru made his way to one of the sections of the wall that he'd noticed moments before. He ran his fingers over the rocky surface, letting the bumps and grooves of the stone guide him. Nothing glinted within that stone. Feeling deflated at being unable to find anything, Heru moved to rejoin Deylan when another sparkle caught his eye. Not more than an arms-length from where he stood, Heru saw a second sparkle.

As he observed the stone closely, Heru found tiny specks of pink-red embedded within. The stones looked familiar, but he couldn't place them. The more he searched, he found along this stretch of the cave a little line of the pink-red stones. They flowed down the wall like a river – sparkling as the sun caught their surfaces.

"Ruby," Deylan murmured, causing Heru to jump.

"What?" Heru asked, his voice coming out a louder than he anticipated.

"The stones," the silver-haired man said, tracing the line of pink-red embedded in the rock. "This is what you're looking at, right?"

Humming in confirmation, Heru tried to find more deposits of the precious stone. Unconsciously, his finger scratched at a chunk of the gems as though he were trying to prise them from where they rested. The beautiful stones reminded him of a pendant his mother wore. The pink-red gem had been worked until it became a dainty heart wrapped in a brilliant piece of gold. Heru's breath caught in his throat as he remembered his mother. He probably should have told her he was leaving two weeks ago.

"If things go well," Deylan said, breaking Heru's reverie, "we will be able to bring a few of these back to our families." His hand rested gently on Heru's, stopping his finger from digging the ruby from the cave. "These stones are not for us."

Heru stopped his scratching. Turning to the wall, he took in the gem one more time before forcing himself to walk away. He couldn't explain the hold the rubies had over him, but he knew that his heart suddenly craved one of the stones to bring back to his mother.

The weapons had disappeared by the time Heru made his way to the middle of the cave. The steady line of pirates loading the ship with provisions had dwindled, leaving only a few stragglers organizing the remainder of the supplies. Aboard the ship, men tied the ropes in knots and inspected the boat for anything they may have missed. Voices called out, shouting words of respect to a newcomer. Spinning to face the tavern-side entrance of the cave, Heru saw Kayna approaching.

Dressed in a white blouse, black underbust corset, brown pants, and brown boots that went halfway up her calf, Kayna barked orders to her crew. Her fiery hair was tied in a high tail, the tiny circlets of gold encircling sections of her hair catching the light. Behind her, the remainder of her crew followed. Dhruvasht and Bharam were some of the last to enter the cave.

Bodies moved furiously as the final stages of preparation were complete. Those who had already completed their duties began climbing aboard, lining up as they awaited their leader's next orders. Deylan nudged Heru, motioning towards the ship with his head. Taking his friend's lead, the two clambered aboard the *Graak's Fury*.

Leading the way before them, Dhruvasht spoke to Bharam in rapid Nem Pahalese. Occasionally, words from the Common Tongue were interspersed into their conversation. Judging from the tone and few words Heru could pick up, it seemed as though Dhruvasht was displeased with something. The ramp to the ship trembled suddenly, causing Bharam's head to spin as he tried to find the source of the disturbance. Heru couldn't help but grin as the Nem Pahlan's eyes widened as he noticed Heru and Deylan for the first time. An unbroken stream of Nem Pahalese poured from the man's mouth as he spoke to his captain. Dhruvasht glanced over his shoulder, dismissing Heru and Deylan with a roll of his eyes.

Getting Bharam alone would be more difficult than he hoped. The idea of not being able to finish his business with the coward left Heru's spirits feeling deflated.

"Take the opposite end of the line," Deylan whispered. "Away from those two."

Nodding so Deylan could see, Heru continued his trek upwards towards the deck of the ship. As he crested the ramp, the Xanan observed that every soul aboard the ship stood at attention, waiting for their captain to board. The quiet respect these people afforded their leader impressed Heru. The men he'd come to know were raucous and didn't take much seriously, but now they were as disciplined as the best Xanan warrior.

Scanning the deck, he noted how Dhruvasht and Bharam made their way towards the stern. Much to the displeasure of the crew, Dhruvasht elbowed his way in between a couple of the men so that he was closer to the helm. The large man ignored the scowls of those near him, his eyes turning down on the group in disdain. Taking advantage of the Nem Pahlan captain's actions, Bharam squeezed in between the group, a smug look of satisfaction now plastered on his face. The expression left Heru feeling conflicted. He couldn't explain to himself why, but Bharam's self-satisfied grin caught him by surprise because there was no reason for the man to act like that, but it also left Heru's jaw clenched to keep himself from commenting on the feeling of entitlement the Nem Pahlan appeared to be enjoying. The desire to strike the man grew, but he couldn't figure out why. It would be like striking a common drunk – Bharam wouldn't be able to defend himself and come out of the altercation unscathed.

The gentle pressure of Deylan squeezing his forearm distracted Heru from glowering at Bharam and Dhruvasht. As he glanced up at the silver-haired man, Heru noted the reassuring look his friend gave him. Deylan nodded slightly to Heru. He was right. Taking a deep breath, Heru made a concerted effort to pull his gaze from the two Nem Pahlans.

I will not be broken, Heru told himself. *I am a Qu'ari Elite. It will take more than a pathetic layabout to destroy my years of training.*

In less than a heartbeat, Heru accepted the fact that this journey would test every ounce of his resolve. The most minute lessons he'd learned as a child – the subtle changes that he'd made growing up, all of it would challenge him to become a man more than his Trials ever could. It wouldn't be his father who he had to worry about. Like an egg cracking over his head, Heru felt the cold realization hit him. A somber chuckle threatened to break free.

The gods have decided to test me. I will not fail.

XV

Watching Kayna's flaming red hair bob as she climbed aboard the ship almost felt mesmerizing. Back home in Ro'thre, people did not have hair the color of the setting sun. Then again, the people of Ro'thre didn't have silver hair. No matter where he went, Deylan stood out from the rest – for better or worse. Focusing on the arrival of his new captain, Deylan wondered how much weight Dhruvasht's words would now carry. Back on *Death's Rose*, the man broached no fools and left little room for anyone to question his authority. Deylan couldn't imagine the man relinquishing that kind of control, even if it was to one directly under the Scourge. Whatever happened, it was bound to be entertaining.

What little conversation remained on the deck vanished instantaneously as Kayna's head crested the side of the ship. Though they were not law-abiding seamen, there was still a level of decorum these men observed amongst themselves. Those who could stood a little straighter, but none stood at attention or removed their hats. Glancing out the corner of his eye, Deylan tried to see what Heru was doing. True to his military background, the young Xanan was the only one who stood at full attention, his body stiff and alert.

He's putting us all to shame out here on the Bone Coast, Deylan mused. *I'll have to teach him our ways or he'll give us away.*

Ignoring the men lined up in front of her, Kayna spoke to someone over her shoulder. Unlike Dhruvasht, the red-head wore an easy smile, her flesh sun-kissed from the years of traversing the sea. As she turned to face the crew, Deylan caught the glint of her emerald-like eyes standing out against the backdrop of the dreary cave that hide the ship and her surroundings. A moment later, Maya's face emerged over the crest of the ramp. A bemused smile tugged at the woman's lips as she followed her captain onto the ship.

"Morning!" Kayna called out. Her sultry voice carried an almost husky tone to it. A tone that commanded respect while still leaving room for the playful expression that she wore.

Along the deck, her crew roared back in unison, "Good morning!"

A few of the older men added a little flourish that clearly was personal to their relationship with the daughter of the Scourge, drawing pockets of laughter from the line. Beside him, Heru appeared to be struggling with how to address the captain. The intricate hierarchy of the warlords seemed to leave the young Xanan baffled on how to respond properly.

"As you know," Kayna said without any preamble, "some of us are already at the Eastern Isles. We had to break up the crew to avoid our dear baron now that he has decided to ban travel over these waters."

Grumbles broke out on deck. Though Kayna didn't seem too bothered by the baron's actions, clearly, he had angered a few of her men.

"Luckily for us," she continued, "we follow a higher law. The Scourge has left me in charge to run the Eastern Seas, and I will not lose out on an opportunity to make some money. Tan'quao's flowers are ready to be picked.

"So, we will meet up with the other half of the crew in three days and we will merge together on the *Fury*. Though the baron has forbidden travel, we will not be the only ones at sea. Now fuck off and find your post. If we're caught, the last thing you'll see is the underside of the *Fury* before the baron's men can board our ship."

Deylan found his throat suddenly dry. No one challenged her words, and she said it all so casually. The only ones who seemed concerned were Heru and Bharam. The young Xanan's face was a mask, his knit brow the only indication that his mind worked furiously to understand the implications. In stark contrast, Bharam clutched his pendant once more. Deylan hoped that the man was not put on any sort of duty that would put anyone else in danger – especially his own life. Deylan had a feeling that accidents were quickly forgotten on this ship. To his dismay, Dhruvasht almost appeared relaxed.

That smarmy bastard, Deylan thought. *He can't even be bothered to think that her words even apply to him. Gods, I can't wait to see what this crew makes of him.*

With a shout of excitement, the men darted off to work. In short time, the anchor was raised and the sails were unfurled. A gust of wind caught the fabric, causing it to fill in the same direction of the open ocean with a snap. The ship was so big that Deylan didn't even feel it begin to move. From where he stood at the bow, he could hear someone shouting as the men furiously worked to maneuver the *Graak's Fury* out of the cave. Waves lapped against the sides of the boat. Occasionally, flecks of white sea spray crested the *Fury.* The mist cooled Deylan, leaving him refreshed despite the cool early morning weather.

"Keep the flags down," someone called down from the crow's nest.

"What do you see?" Maya replied.

Leaning over the edge of the crow's nest, one of the lookouts lowered their telescope to better look at the second-in-command.

"Unidentified ships scanning the horizon," he replied. "We need to be quick and quiet."

"You heard 'em," Kayna said as she joined Maya under the nest. "Keep yer yaps closed."

It was as if a cloud passed over the ship. As one, every soul aboard stopped talking. Deylan had to assume that whoever was leading the helm and navigating the ship could get them out to sea safely and avoid confrontation. Tall, jagged rocks passed by precariously close to the sides of the ship. Though he trusted Kayna's crew, he had to wonder if the hidden parts of the rocks scratched at the bottom of the ship under water. He hoped that the mighty ship wouldn't spring a leak. Those who remained above deck stood tensely, not wanting to draw attention to themselves despite sailing on a massive ship.

Once out of the cave, Deylan was blinded by the sun. He didn't remember it being quite so bright earlier that morning. The pain from the light forced Deylan to keep his eyes closed for several long moments before he could open them again without them watering. By the time he did, the *Graak's Fury* was smoothly moving through the open waters.

The sea was a beautiful cerulean, the whites of the waves breaking the solid line of color that surrounded him. Gulls cawed overhead and the sails snapped crisply as they caught the wind. The day was absolutely breath-taking. It was the perfect day to be at sea.

Then he saw them. To his left, the slim mast and yellow flag bearing the black circle of Baron Ciadpach came into view. Deylan couldn't stop his breath from hitching in his throat as he observed the smaller ship approaching. He didn't doubt that if it came to engaging with the baron's men, Kayna's crew would far outman the ship. What concerned him, however, was whether they could out-maneuver it. As Deylan focused on the incoming ship, he noticed out of the corner of his eye a length of rope drop down from the crow's nest. A piece of red fabric was tied to the end of the rope.

Kayna also noticed the rope and went over to inspect the small bit of fabric. Glancing up at the crow's nest for a brief moment, she sauntered over to the helm and took over the captain's wheel.

"Hold," Kayna instructed as she wrapped her fingers around the wheel.

The man at the wheel remained standing nearby, awaiting her instruction. She gave the wheel a gentle turn before handing it back to him. The few souls who remained above-deck returned to their duties, ignoring the now quickly approaching ship. Deylan found himself inching closer to Kayna. The redhead intrigued him, and he wanted to watch her in action. Beside him, Heru also mimicked Deylan's movements.

I wonder if they have women like this at Xan, Deylan mused. *I can't imagine the warlord women are especially dainty. Hells, they probably would be welcomed on a ship like this.*

After speaking to the man at the captain's wheel for a little longer, Kayna strolled off, making small comments to those she encountered on her way to the edge of the ship. Deylan tried to follow discretely, leaving behind a perplexed Heru. He had to ignore the Xanan's quiet exclamation in order to keep himself close enough to Kayna without appearing too obvious. Still, Deylan thought he saw a rogue glance or knowing smirk as he passed men by. Stealth had never been his strong suit upon ships. The confined spaces weren't good for sneaking around during the day.

"Do you have any questions?"

Deylan froze. Though Kayna's back was to him as she leaned against the side of the ship, she obviously spoke to him. There was no one else around.

"I saw the others starting on their chores." Deylan's mind raced as he fought back the knot that formed in his chest. He thanked the gods that his answer didn't come out in a stammer. He worried his words would be as rapid as his pulse. "I wanted to make myself useful to help downplay any suspicion before my shift."

He thought he heard her snort. Patting the railing she leaned on, Kayna beckoned him over.

"Stay by me for a bit," she said.

With sweaty hands, Deylan took his place next to the redhead. The baron's ship was nearly upon them, yet she stood so poised, almost unconcerned about what would happen next. He didn't dare look directly at her, not wanting to upset the redhead, but he couldn't help sneak a peek out of the corner of his eye.

Kayna's eyes were closed and a faint smile played on her lips as her hair tickled her face. She truly was content. Deylan knew the feeling. The sea had a way of calming even the most frayed nerves.

The ship was unexpectedly larger than Deylan first imagined. The thin mast was comparable to the *Fury's*. Thick planks held the ship, the *Crowne Glory*, together. She was indeed smaller than *Graak's Fury* instead of dwarfed by it. On the prow, an elegant woman's bust, her long hair covering her otherwise exposed chest, was carved into the wood. Her face was exquisite – from the fullness of her lips to the dainty curve of the nose. She clearly would be the masterpiece for whoever added her to the *Glory*.

The plainness of the flag confused Deylan, however. After taking in the extravagant front of the ship, seeing the simple yellow flag fluttering atop the thin mast seemed underwhelming.

Why create such a magnificent ship and stop on your flag? Surely, your coat of arms would be better than just a black circle?

Deylan wondered if Kayna knew the history of this strange flag. Probably not, he reasoned. Her kind did not venture into the mainland much. They wouldn't be familiar with the finely detailed flags of the other nations. He nearly commented on the stark contrast between them, when he noticed a tiny man walk to the edge of the ship. Dressed in what Deylan imagined to be a fine navy-blue coat, the man faced where they stood on the *Fury*.

"Stop in the name of the baron!" The voice from the other ship sounded far away as the two ships closed the gap between themselves. The man must have quite the voice to be heard from this distance. "Haven't you heard of the travel ban?"

"Haven't you heard that it's bad for business to delay the Scourge?" Kayna called back as the ships pulled next to one another.

"Oh, Lady Kayna," the man said upon recognizing her. "Out on business you say?"

"Aye. And it would best if we weren't bothered."

Tossing a piece of silver at the man, Kayna tilted her head in the same, charming manner as a puppy. The man caught the coin and quickly pocketed it. Turning from the *Fury*, he called out to his crew.

"All right there. This ship has clearance. Let's check the western-most side of the port."

The baron's crew hurried to obey their commander's order. Checking over his shoulder, the man nodded his head in Kayna's direction, and with a wave of his hand, the baron's ship changed its course in the opposite direction of the *Fury*.

Several minutes later, the *Crowne Glory* became nothing more than a speck on the horizon. Life aboard the *Fury* returned shortly after the ship moved on and raucous laughter could be heard. The difference between being crammed inside the tavern and out in the open air was astonishing – the men somehow managed to be even louder outside than they were inside. Kayna kept her position at the side of the ship enjoying the gentle breeze and hot sun against her skin.

"Not many can say they've got the baron's men under their thumb," Deylan said, closing his own eyes. Even with his wide-brimmed hat, his bangs managed to tickle his face. He'd been on several ships in his day, but something about the *Fury* felt familiar. There was an odd air surrounding it. "And for such a reasonable price."

"Aye. And not many can say that they are above the minor lords. Having the Scourge for your father can really motivate people to ignore some things. Although, it makes finding a suitable partner a little more difficult." She flashed him a coy smile. "But we make due and enjoy both the positives and the negative."

Deylan found his face rapidly growing warm as a brilliant flush took over. Kayna proved to be much bolder than he originally imagined. Endless possibilities opened up at that moment, and though he was uncertain, Deylan knew he didn't want to miss any of it. He would have to keep an eye on the red-headed captain.

"I can only imagine," he replied. If he played his cards right, this trip would turn into something much more lucrative than he could have ever dreamed. "If you ever find yourself looking for a sympathetic ear, mine is always listening. I have been told before that I am exactly what they needed. I guess I have a knack for being a good source of comfort."

"I'll keep that in mind. You better find your spot below deck quick. By now, all of the good ones will have been taken."

Without another word, Kayna pushed off the side railing and headed off towards the center of the ship. Deylan could have sworn that the captain put a little extra sway into her walk

– her hips moved in a way that captured his attention more obviously. Leaning back against the side of the ship, Deylan rested his elbows on the smooth wood, enjoying her departure. Maya approached Kayna, and the two spoke briefly before Deylan thought he saw the captain nod in his direction. The more stoic woman shot the red-head a bemused look before beckoning the captain to follow her.

By the time the two women disappeared to the other side of the ship, Deylan found himself taking in the commotion that came with traversing the sea. Men called out to each other, a bark of laughter breaking the otherwise soothing sound of lapping water against the hull and the raucous cawing of gulls. Five years ago, Deylan found these sounds obnoxious. Now, he closed his eyes and let the gentle sway of the ship take him away to a time where he could be free.

～

He always shouted.

Ever since Deylan and his mother arrived in Ro'thre thirteen years ago, Xi made it his mission to make their lives miserable. At first, he had been their hero, providing a safe space for Deylan and his mother after they fled their home country. When Deylan's mother felt safe that no one had followed them, he finally allowed himself to relax. But he was only four. He didn't understand how true evil could be everywhere.

It took only a year for the shouting to start.

Dzaria, Deylan's mother, found herself with child six months after they met Xi. The first of Deylan's sisters. The first of four. Xi married his mother shortly after Mei was born.

Then came the beatings. Deylan couldn't stop them. All he could do was watch in horror as the man who became his father struck his mother over and over. Many a night Dzaria would cling to Deylan, her body bruised and bloodied, after Xi returned home drunk. Deylan pretended not to notice her tears or the way her body shook as she cried silently. He just held her in his tiny arms, hoping that he could heal her pain with his hugs.

But there was always shouting.

Lan was born after his eighth birthday. By then, Xi started hitting Deylan. He continued to beat Dzaria as well.

Deylan didn't stay home much. He took Mei and Lan out whenever he could, but on the days that he had to sneak out, Deylan found himself wandering the streets. If Xi hadn't returned home, Deylan could usually find him at the local tavern, shouting boisterously with a group of men.

Qiu and Li were born by Deylan's tenth and thirteenth year. He was quite adept at sneaking around by then. Xi started bringing his friends around after Qiu was born. They looked at Mei and in a way that made him uncomfortable, so he took her with him whenever he could. He didn't want to leave Mei at home with his mom and other sisters.

It wasn't long until they began looking at Lan in the same way. He quickly learned how to sneak the three of them out.

He could never save his mother.

Soon, she began crying.

On the outskirts of the Woods of Lingora, Deylan found a copse of trees. Underneath one of the trees, there was a den carved into the trunk, as though a fox made her home there. It was a tight squeeze, but Deylan and his sisters could all fit inside. He gradually brought a few blankets and stored them inside. They used their little hideaway as a makeshift home often, and the blankets helped shield them from the biting cold of the woods of the north.

It wasn't all bad times. Under the light of the stars, he would sit in their little home while the girls frolicked about. They would spin around, the skirts of their dresses fanning out as they held their arms out wide. They felt free. Safe. They could finally be little girls and giggle again.

No one ever bothered them. The Woods were rumored to be home to a group of mercenaries. He'd rather take his chances with them.

Mei began teaching Lan how to make grass dolls, and the two would spend hours weaving the blades together. In the spring, they all would search for wildflowers to braid into the dolls' hair. Mei even made dolls for their younger sisters and Dzaria. The women of Deylan's house cherished those dolls – never letting them be too far from their sight.

Still, there was shouting.

A year after Li was born, Deylan had had enough. One by one, he gathered his sisters and the five of them climbed out of Mei's window and onto the lush grass outside. Xi had returned home late that night and after beating Dzaria unconscious, he turned his attention to Deylan.

"Scrymman scum," Xi spat, nearly frothing at the mouth. "Filthy bastard."

Deylan's parents had been married. His father had been worse than Xi.

Xi passed out right in front of the door before he could go get his friends. Dzaria's limp form, bloodied and tear-stained, was still passed out in the kitchen.

So, Deylan took his sisters to their special place, the hidden grove on the edge of the Woods of Lingora. The darkness of night, only broken by the myriad of diamond-like pinpricks of the stars, provided them with the perfect cover as they fled. Even the moon did not betray them. They ran fast, stopping often to hid from city guard and the occasional drunk who happened to be out.

Qui began crying, her soft sobs barely more than a whimper as she clutched onto Mei's hand. The young girl held on for dear life, unsure of what was going on. Blessedly, Li remained asleep in his arms. Several times during their escape, Deylan glanced back. He was met with Mei's determined gaze, and Lan's silent tears as she furiously tried to brush them away.

He hated Xi.

Finally, the five made it to the edge of the woods. Deylan found their little tree, a well-placed ribbon marking a tree a few yards away from their tree. He tied the ribbon on the specific maple years ago to draw people away from their little sanctuary. When they got to their copse, he urged his sisters to hide. Mei and Lan crawled in, pulling Qui in behind them. Lastly, Deylan handed the still slumbering Li to Mei. The four sat cramped and huddled in their safe spot. Three pairs of eyes stared up at him in fear, their little chests heaving as they struggled to catch their breath.

"Hurry," Mei urged, waving Deylan in.

She scooted over, attempting to make room for him inside. There was no room.

"Stay here," he instructed. "Don't come out until I tell you. If I'm not back by morning, make your way to Pharn. Travel only at night. It'll be safer."

Lan and Qui began crying, their sobs echoing in the stillness of the Woods. Even Mei cried silent tears. It broke his heart.

"Keep them safe," Deylan said. "I'll be right back."

He'd spent five years trying to save money to buy his family's freedom. Many nights he lay awake, wondering where they ended up. He hoped that they were free of evil men like his father and Xi. Five years of robbing pirates and stealing their plunder. Over the years, Deylan became quite adept at what he did. Only once did he make a mistake. That mistake almost cost him his life.

Unconsciously, Deylan touched his chest. Underneath his tunic and the strips of cloth bandaging his wounds lay a scar – a reminder of the dangers of letting his guard down. He never made a mistake like that again.

"What are you doing?" Heru asked, sidling up next to him.

Glancing behind him at the open sea, Deylan closed his eyes and took a deep breath. The tangy sea salt cleared his mind and left him feeling at ease. Remembering his past in such vivid flashbacks left his heart racing and hand clammy. It also filled him with a profound sense of loss. He didn't want to leave his mother and sisters in such a predicament. He had to get back to them soon.

"Nothing," he replied.

Heru raised a brow. The Xanan didn't believe Deylan, not that he blamed Heru. To his credit, Heru didn't push Deylan any further. The Xanan's stoic nature worked out for Deylan, who didn't feel like talking much, even if it raised further suspicion.

"We need to get a spot to sleep," Deylan added after a few beats. "Kayna said that all the good spots are probably gone, but if we go now, we might still find something."

"Let's find where the coward is," Heru said.

"Why? I don't want to be near him."

A wicked grin crept across Heru's face. Deylan almost swore that this was the Xanan's playful side coming through, mischievous or not.

"If it's any good, we'll take it from him. No one will say a word."

Excitement filled Deylan like a bubbling spring at the thought of inconveniencing the Nem Pahlan. He wondered if this was how children felt when they tricked someone. The emotion was so intense, he almost felt his feet do a little dance, he was so giddy.

"Let's go."

Deylan's voice came out higher than he'd ever heard it. Even before he became a man, his voice never reached this octave. The sound embarrassed him. He hoped Heru didn't notice. If he did, the Xanan didn't react. The two shared the boyish energy that radiated between them.

Oh gods, Deylan thought. *It's almost as though we're drunk.*

Not wanting to draw any attention to themselves, the two tried their best to casually saunter below deck to claim their sleeping area.

XVI

T HE SLEEPING QUARTERS were crammed. Blankets and rucksacks marked where men claimed their spots. Thick swaths of fabric were tied in corners, creating beds that hung from the ship's rafters. Those must have been claimed first because no one bothered to place their belongings in the makeshift beds. Instead, their bags sat on the floor nearby. Heru and Deylan traveled light as well, a small bag of essentials and weapons were all they needed. But Bharam, neither knew what he brought aboard with him.

"We might have to ask someone," Deylan suggested.

The ship lurched to the left, throwing the two off-balance.

"By the gods," Heru swore as he nearly fell to the ground. "What in the seven hells was that?"

"We must have hit a big wave," Deylan explained.

"Damn," the Xanan muttered.

Deylan shot him a sympathetic look. Blood pounded in Heru's ears and he clenched his jaw, biting his tongue. It had been a long time since someone looked down on him, and Heru didn't take the pity well.

"What?" Heru snapped.

"I hate to tell you, but this won't be the last wave that shakes the ship," Deylan explained. "Once we get further out to sea, we're going to encounter plenty of rough waters. Right now, these smooth waters are uncommon."

Heru's mouth dropped in shock as the *Graak's Fury* was hit with another wave that threw the pair forward once more. Heru stumbled a few steps further than Deylan, who was obviously used to maintaining unstable footing.

"What have I gotten myself into?" he murmured through clenched teeth. "You should have told me about this."

"I thought people understood the dangers of the sea," Deylan replied. "It's not like we're traveling on solid ground. I remember my first time at sea."

A wistful gaze crossed his eyes. The way Deylan spoke, it almost were as if he were reliving a fond memory. Heru could feel his stomach start to protest as the motion of the waves got increasingly rougher. If Deylan's first time was as peaceful as his expression suggested, Heru was going to have to smack the man. No one should have to feel this much unease while just standing around.

"I spent three days in bed, sick as could be. May Graak afford you finer winds and smoother waters."

"What is that?" Heru asked. "Some kind of prayer?"

Deylan nodded, turning to look for something amongst the crew's belongings. The words left Heru feeling nonplussed. He didn't think that Deylan was a particularly religious man. Graak clearly was a powerful being – the Scourge named his ship after the god after all. Perhaps it would be best to offer obeisance to the elder god than the one he'd grown up acknowledging, Freyna.

"I hope he does."

The two spent a few moments carefully riffling through the sacks in the room. Nothing they found gave them any more information about the contents' owner. Heru began to wonder if Bharam would even be sleeping in the main quarters. He pushed the thought out of his mind after a few heartbeats. Bharam was a man who would not be inconvenienced, even if he were part of a crowd like Kayna's crew. There had to be soft pirates that sailed the seas, letting others do their dirty work. Just like there were back home.

"Damn," Deylan muttered as he dropped the last bit of clothing into its bag. "I can't find his shite anywhere."

"Wait," Heru said, his body swaying as they hit another large wave. Keeping his knees slightly bent, he was able to better maintain his balance. A surge of pride welled up as he realized he was getting the hang of the rocky sea. "Why don't we ask someone. Hold on."

Darting out of the room, Heru didn't have to wait long before he found one of the men, a scraggly one with a face so grizzled and covered in hair that he almost didn't even look human. He bore more of a resemblance to one of the childhood horrors his mother used to tell him about. Pushing away the uncanny resemblance to the undead, Heru cleared his throat.

The man fixed him with a blank stare. One of his eyes appeared to be glassy, as though it had been blinded long ago. Heru tried not to stare. He'd seen the old men and women back home, their eyes milky with blindness, but he'd never seen someone with an eye like that before.

"Where does the Nem Pahlan sleep?" Heru asked.

"Which one?" the man spat back.

Even his voice carried the gravelly rasp of death. Heru fought the urge to take a step back. This man surely wasn't human.

"The soft one. He's close with that second captain who lost his ship."

"Ahh," the man said faintly. "The one who's marked for death."

The man's bluntness startled even the young Xanan. Being honest and upfront about his words, not covering them with saccharine to soften the impact, was something Heru prided himself on. To be flowery like Deylan could lead to confusion. Heru sought to be understood. Understood and to the point.

Even Great Heart Pram was too indirect for his liking. The Great Heart called it diplomatic, Heru called it insubstantial.

"For death?" Heru found himself blurting out.

"Aye. Neither Graak nor the captain can save 'm. We know what he did on his last ship. Your friend wasn't the only one who survived that wreck."

The man gave a knowing nod, his gnarled fingers coming up to scratch his temple. Heru noticed the thick knobs that made up the man's joints. They looked like the roots of a great tree. Again, he found himself questioning if the man was even human.

"He's hiding away, hoping that we forget. But we know that he's sequestered himself in the galley. Death will not stay her hand much longer."

Heru dipped is head half in bow and half in agreement as he slowly backed away. The man returned to whatever he was doing, promptly ignoring Heru as the young Xanan took in everything he just heard. There would be no need to steal his spot. From the sounds of it, it wouldn't be a very nice one to begin with. By the time he made it back to the sleeping quarters, he found Deylan lounging in one of the hanging beds, eyes covered by his wide-brimmed hat.

"How can you sleep like this?" Heru asked.

"You learn to rest where you can. Besides, what else do we have to do? Bharam and Dhruvasht have disappeared into thin air and until they tell us when our shift is, we have nothing to do. It's better to rest in the event they want us to take night watch."

Sliding his hat up, Deylan sat up in the bed. Heru wondered how he didn't just flip over. The bed seemed so unstable as it rocked with every movement. He found himself praying for the day when he no longer felt nauseous and could wander around the *Fury* without feeling off-balance.

"What did you find out?" Deylan asked.

"Do your people believe in dīv?" Heru asked.

The confused expression that he received made him regret the question. A little pang of disappointment bled into everything else he'd been feeling. Heru had come to think that Deylan was one of the most worldly people he'd met, having been familiar with his culture and all that the silver-haired man had learned sailing the seas. Heru knew he shouldn't be disappointed, the undead fiends - dīv, were stories specific to the Qu'ari. Most didn't know about these monsters.

"Forget I mentioned it," Heru said quickly. "It's not important now. But," he motioned for Deylan to get closer and lowered his voice. Though he didn't think it would be an issue, he didn't want anyone overhearing what he was about to say.

Deylan scooted out of the hanging bed and quickly crossed the room. The Xanan noted his nimble gait – the two would have to get in a little sparring practice he decided with a grin. Following his friend's lead, Deylan leaned his head in to Heru's mouth.

"The coward is in the galley. I think you're right, he knows that he hasn't been accepted by this crew."

"The galley?" Deylan whispered.

"I don't know if he's aware, but his time is limited. They have marked him for death. Do you think this puts us in harm's way?"

Deylan paused. Heru could see him thinking – calculating the odds to see if fate had turned against them. The Xanan found himself wishing he had consulted a shaman one last time before boarding the ship. His last reading one concerned finding his father. In that one, he had been successful. Heru waited for several long heartbeats until he noticed that he'd been holding his breath in anticipation. He let out a slow, quiet stream, trying not to disrupt Deylan.

"I don't think so," Deylan finally said. "You would know. If what Black Sam said was true, they seem to like you. We just need to be careful so as not to give them a reason to change their mind."

Satisfied with the answer, Heru crouched down and leaned back against the wall. Setting aside time for sparring was looking like a good idea. Learning to move while on the swaying ship would only benefit him. Despite the ban on the Bone Coast, Heru had no illusions that other pirates would follow it any more than Kayna and her crew did.

"Do these people train during their down time?" Heru asked.

"I'm not sure. None of the ships I traveled with really did much. Some did exercises, but no organized sparring or anything like that."

The heaviness that came with a big disappointment settled over the young Xanan. His inability to quickly acclimate to sea life would be a fatal disadvantage if he couldn't adapt. One way or another, her would need to figure out how to overcome this weakness.

"Perhaps you and I could find a quiet spot and work together."

The unexpected suggestion from the silver-haired man snapped Heru from his reverie. Turning to Deylan, Heru scrutinized the man's face. He had proven himself more than capable during their first encounter. Was this pity? Or did he truly want to train with Heru.

"Let's help each other," Deylan added.

Help – a concept Heru couldn't quite grasp. It must be pity or respect. Needing assistance was for the weak. Heru wasn't weak.

But he needed help.

"I would appreciate that," he replied softly. "I think we could both learn from each other."

Clapping Heru on the shoulder, Deylan joined him on the floor. He sat close to the Xanan, his shoulder gently resting against Heru's. The familiarity of the contact, the relaxed demeanor of the man, both provided a sense of comfort that

Heru had rarely encountered. Back home, Heru did not have many close friends. His efforts to become stronger prevented him from pursuing the young women of his village. None of the one's he'd bedded chose to stay with him – his determination to become an elite proved too much for them to handle.

The closest he'd had to a relationship like this was with his older sister, Bermet. Or his mother. The age difference between Arezou, his little sister, and himself made it difficult for the two to form a close relationship. But his bond with Bermet could not be broken. The two shared too much, suffered disappointment one time too many to not be connected.

This felt like that – almost.

Letting his guard drop, Heru relaxed and let his body melt into Deylan's. The two sat in the contented silence that two life-long friends could enjoy. He closed his eyes and imagined his sister hovering over him. Her smile filled him with warmth. Perhaps some day, he could have the same thoughts about Deylan. If he didn't mess it up first. The moment did last long. A rough wave followed by a shout outside the sleeping quarters broke the spell.

"Do you want to take his spot in the galley?"

A mischievous, almost childlike smile danced on Deylan's face as he turned to Heru. Without a moment's hesitation, Heru nodded. The two popped up and made their way down to the galley.

XVII

THEIR TIME AT SEA passed quickly. Bharam miraculously disappeared on the albeit grand ship. Word traveled quickly, and by the time he discovered that the spot he'd chosen to sleep had disappeared, and that Heru and Deylan claimed the spot in the galley near the singular cooking pot, the Nem Pahlan made himself scarce. The boys' prank earned them a disapproving stare from Maya, but Kayna couldn't stop the corners of her mouth from twitching up. The other members of the crew didn't speak on the matter. Whether he slept in the galley or somewhere else on the ship, Bharam's days were numbered.

Every day after their morning meal, Heru and Deylan disappeared to the bow. They started by just working on their footwork. Heru found at first that making a sudden turn or jumping out of the way left him feeling disoriented as he caught his balance. The rocking of the ship got rougher the farther out into sea, but the *Graak's Fury*'s sheer size helped reduce the swaying greatly. Large waves splashed against the sides, their spray sometimes cresting onto the deck.

The first few days had the two practicing hand-to-hand combat. Heru quickly noted how nimble Deylan truly was. Like a cat, the silver-haired man could twist and spin in an instant, his body moving out of reach of Heru's strikes and giving Deylan an advantage several times during their practice. The two never landed heavy blows against each other, especially since Deylan still took his featherfew to treat the headaches he occasionally experienced.

Deylan's ribs still hurt. Each sudden movement or blow to the body sent a jolt of agony shooting through him. Not wanting to take advantage of while Deylan was injured, Heru usually allowed a small pause during their sparring, giving Deylan time to catch his breath. On the occasion when the two were lost in the dance of their fight, he either ended up thrown to the ground by the Xanan or received a punch to the face, which stopped their training.

Heru tried not to hit Deylan too hard, and Deylan reciprocated. He also tried not to end up on the ground. Apart from being nimble, Deylan demonstrated surprising strength in ground combat. His knowledge of how to manipulate his opponent's arm or wrist won him many a sparring session. Heru walked away several times, gnashing his teeth as he nursed his sore wrist or arm.

They repeated their training in the evening after dinner. Their attempt at hiding their efforts resulted in members of Kayna's crew watching the pair whenever there was a lull in the day's duties. A few would place bets on them, wagering a pint of ale from the Eastern Isles or a copper on who would win. Ignoring the grizzled crew became tougher as the days passed.

The Xanan proved to be an adept learner and they soon moved to combat with weapons. By day four, they were moving quickly, darting and twisting as though they were on land. To Deylan's relief, Heru only used his scimitar – although it was the blade he favored. Deylan occasionally pulled his dagger, but most times he borrowed a sword from the armory. Steel clanged on steel as they traded blows. Their battles never got too intense, but they did test Deylan's skill.

After each training session, the pair walked off breathing heavily and covered in sweat. Though he never wanted to show it, Deylan noticed how his hands trembled, his legs feeling like jelly and threatening to collapse beneath him. He was afforded a few precious hours to eat and rest before starting their shift on the night watch where Deylan often found himself wandering around to avoid nodding off. The combined hours of their efforts left both in a state of exhaustion that only comes from militant training, the likes of which stretch the mettle of even the King's Guard. Like a rock, Heru never showed his exhaustion, but Deylan still saw it. Deylan knew that Heru felt as miserable as he did.

A week into their daily routine, and Heru finally felt comfortable enough that he would no longer be thrown to his feet or overboard and into the ocean. When a stronger than usual wave slammed into the ship, he no longer fell forward, grasping wildly about for something to help him keep his footing. Now, he widened his stance and bent his knees to keep himself grounded. The difference between when he first joined the crew and his newfound confidence was stark.

During the day, whenever he wasn't training with Deylan, Heru found himself wandering the deck. He used the time to take in the ship, taking note of his surroundings and what tools he had available to him should they fall under attack.

No one really bothered him. Most of the crew left him to his own devices, allowing Heru the opportunity to acclimate and study. He never ran into Bharam either. After taking the Nem Pahlan's sleeping spot, Heru expected the man to confront him or try to reclaim his position. The lack of a response disappointed Heru. Surely, it would be better to try to fight for respect.

I'll never understand men like him, Heru told himself on more than one occasion.

During the day, Deylan disappeared. For their first few days on the ship, Heru tried to find the silver-haired man. When his efforts proved fruitless, he gave up and continued on his exploration of the *Fury*.

The Xanan also spent a lot of time watching the sea. Staring out into the endless blue waters calmed the young man. There was a serenity unlike any other in those azure waves. He noted the gentle flow of the currents, occasionally broken by a wave. No matter what happened, the water always returned to the benign seas of rich blue.

Though he managed to keep his exterior tranquil, a storm of uncertainty swirled within him. In a short while they would be docking at the Eastern Isles and Heru could continue his search. Somewhere out there, his father waited. Heru had waited for twenty years for a chance to spend time with his father, and fifteen years to ask his father why he hadn't been good enough. Heru spent years of his life training in his father's shadow – hearing how much like the former Great Heart he was. But Heru wanted to be his own man.

The façade he'd developed over the years threatened to crack, and underneath, the confused little boy cowered behind the shadow of his father's legacy. Heru wondered if his father would be proud of the man he'd become – he never wanted to be a fighter, but he trained hard and became an elite, just like his father.

The very idea of being so close to his father sent a wave of shivers through him. His pulse quickened and he struggled to keep his hands from trembling. In the back of Heru's mind, images of him throttling his father for abandoning him and his sisters years ago flashed by in rapid succession. For years, he'd dreamed of confronting his father, and now that he was so close, Heru found himself faltering. The sensation left the young Xanan feeling a little agitated – a concept that was completely foreign to the young man.

So, to keep himself occupied, Heru watched the waters.

Standing in line for his afternoon meal, Heru managed to catch Deylan heading out of the galley, apple in hand. Heru wanted to call out to him, but seeing the silver-haired man's attentions were turned inwards, the young warrior held his tongue. Taking his portion of dried meat and bread, Heru darted down the hall in the direction Deylan had gone, his curiosity piqued.

His feet echoed against the wood despite there being a number of people moving around below deck. The morning rotation neared its end, and the evening watch prepared to go above-deck. A few glares and curses were thrown his way as Heru wove through the narrow area. Several times he slammed his shoulder into the wall, but he didn't care. Shouting would draw attention to the pair. Though he ran the risk of getting into a fight, it was better to race through the tight corridor and take a few knocks from the ship instead of his crewmates. His focus always remained on his silver-haired friend.

Taking the stairs two at a time, Heru found himself above-deck in the blistering sun. The day was uncharacteristically hot without a cloud in the sky. More than one man's flesh aboard the *Fury* turned a painful shade of red, even if they spent just a few minutes in the sun. Deylan had insisted their morning practice take place before the sun rose, as if he anticipated the sweltering heat.

Glancing about, Heru found his silver-haired friend sitting under a thin blanket draped over a few barrels and held down at the corners as a makeshift tent t keep him protected from the sun. His wide-brimmed hat, Heru noticed, was nowhere to be found. Seeing the young man without the hat was strange to Heru. The hat was just as much a part of Deylan as Heru's blades. Seeing him without it felt like he was seeing his friend vulnerable, exposed. The feeling nearly made Heru chuckle at the absurdity of it all.

Seeing his friend approach, Deylan waved Heru over and scooted to the side. Slipping under the blanket, Heru handed Deylan a bit of his meat as he sat. Pulling his knees close to his chest, Heru made sure that his entire body was covered from the sun. He'd been burnt enough times and didn't think there was any salves aboard to soothe his blistered skin. At least he hadn't seen any of the crew treating their burns.

Deylan took the bit of meat with a word of thanks, offering the Xanan a bit of the apple in exchange which Heru turned down.

"Fancy seeing you," Deylan said with a smirk before taking a bite of his apple.

The crunch rang in his ear, tempting Heru and making him wonder if he should have accepted the proffered bite. A bit of juice dripped down Deylan's hand. The silver-haired man slurped it up before it ran down his arm. Taking a bit of his dried meat, Heru hoped to distract himself. He expected to lose a bit of weight and muscle while on the seas. The food rations were not what he was used to and he often found himself sitting up at night with a rumbling stomach.

He wondered how his father managed to look as healthy as he did despite spending so much time on the ship. The brief moment that he saw his father, Len looked robust – not the shadow of his self like Heru felt.

"I could say the same," Heru pushed his mind away from his hunger and onto the reason he pursued the man. "I thought I would be seeing more of you on this trip. There aren't many places to hide on a ship."

"I've found the *Fury* to have a few secret places," Deylan replied with a wink. "All ships have at least one if you know where to look."

The comment caused Heru to make a non-committal hum as he mulled over Deylan's words.

What has he found?

"Clearly," Heru said at last. "That coward has done a good job of keeping his bedroll hidden from the rest of the crew."

"Oh, they know where he sleeps. They're just biding their time to lull him into a false sense of security. When the time is right, they will strike. We'd be wise to steer clear."

As Heru opened his mouth to respond, Deylan held up a hand.

"You'll know. The air on the ship will change. I'm sure your people have a similar feeling when justice is about to be meted out. I've noticed that it's a common sensation no matter where you go."

Heru wanted to discuss Deylan's whereabouts, but the statement gave him pause.

"How many people have you seen killed?"

Taking another bite of his apple, Deylan shrugged his shoulders. "Apart from the one by my hands, I've seen two or three people meet an unfortunate end."

"Your own?" Heru's brows threatened to disappear into his fringe. "Despite how much you talk, you really are a man of many secrets."

This brought a chuckle from Deylan's lips.

"I suppose I have a few surprises of my own. Don't we all have our own demons?"

His words did not carry his usual lilt. To Heru's dismay, Deylan's gaze dropped and he stared at the apple cradled in both of his hands.

He wanted to speak up, but he noticed the Nem Pahlan captain skulking by. The man spent the majority of their time at sea in his quarters – he'd insisted on his own chambers away from the rest of the crew, even his own. The former captain of *Death's Rose* eyed the two as they sat under the blanket sharing lunch. Heru returned the man's gaze, holding it with the steely resolve of a Qu'ari elite ready for combat. The man quickly broke contact, turning his head as he continued on to wherever he headed. He would need to keep a closer eye on that one as well.

Turning his attention back to his friend, Heru felt his hand twitch towards Deylan as though he wanted to give the man a pat on the arm. Heru pushed away the subconscious movement. He couldn't be sure that that was the correct action to take. Instead, he sat there awkwardly, trying to figure out how to proceed.

"I didn't mean," Heru began. "What I was trying to say..."

"It's nothing," Deylan interrupted. "I apologize for making this uncomfortable. There's no reason for this conversation to become so serious. Besides, I get the feeling that you want to discuss something of your own."

A smile forced its way onto his face. For those who didn't know the man, it would seem genuine; but to Heru, who had spent a little bit of time in close contact with him, he could tell it was insincere. There were no crinkles at the corners of the silver-haired man's eyes or the little twinkle of mischief subtly masked behind his gaze. He would need to have another conversation with his friend if he wanted to pursue the matter further.

"I apologize for making you uncomfortable," Heru murmured. "I think this is a discussion for another day, if you are up to it."

Heru paused, giving Deylan a chance to respond. A small nod – his answer.

"But you're right," Heru continued. "I had an ulterior motive for hunting you down today."

This produced a snort from the silver-haired man. He took another bite of food, the subtle motion confirming to Heru that Deylan was ready to move on. Heru took a bite of his own before continuing on. Wanting to further alleviate the tension between them, Heru leaned over his knees and dropped his voice conspiratorially.

"Where have you been hiding these last few days? There is no way you can disappear so completely."

Ignoring the question, Deylan finished his apple before wiping his hands on his pants. He studied the men completing their duties for the remainder of the day watch without a word. Sure, they called out to each other, chatting about what they wanted to do when they reached the Eastern Isles. A good portion of the conversation consisted of them discussing which girl they wanted to spend their money on. Heru noted a woman named Delli being brought up several times.

"Have you met this Delli?" Heru asked.

"I haven't," Deylan admitted. "She seems to be quite popular though. I don't know if I have enough to afford her company."

"Like that would stop you," Heru said with a snort. "I've seen what you managed to do with the women at the Feathered Plume. You can talk yourself into anyone's bed." Shooting Deylan a sidelong glance, he added, "Or stable."

This brought a full-bodied laugh from pair. It had been a long time since Heru found someone to laugh with. He told himself he would have to do it more often.

"I see you've met a few of my consorts," Deylan replied.

No one paid the two any mind, leaving the men to sit in relative quiet as they observed the smooth handling of the duties aboard *Graak's Fury*. The sun moved closer to the horizon, the day cooling. Men shuffled about as the day watch moved below deck and the night watch took over. The heat still lingered about the ship, no doubt leaving those who toiled all day in it ready for a good night's sleep.

Deylan's head rested on Heru's shoulder as they took everything in. Heru scanned the deck, keeping an eye out for Dhruvasht or Bharam. Somehow, both succeeded in keeping their presence relatively obscured.

"How does that bastard not have to earn his keep on here?" Heru muttered to himself.

"The time will come for him to earn his safe passage," Deylan replied. "Everyone has to give something to secure their spot onboard. Time, money, some captains don't care."

The answer caught Heru off-guard. He wasn't expecting an answer, Deylan's heavy, rhythmic breathing leading him to believe that the silver-haired man had fallen asleep. He moved his head as much as he could since Deylan didn't move. Deylan must have felt the Xanan's body shift because he finally sat up.

"They will call on us as well," Deylan stated. "Don't think that our debt is forgotten."

Leaning his head back onto the barrel behind him, Heru closed his eyes. He'd overlooked his own responsibilities. Having been asked to join the crew by Dhruvasht, a part of Heru figured that he would be immune to ship duties. He would gladly lend a hand, but no one had asked. Perhaps they were showing him a kindness by letting the Xanan get his sea legs, but now that he thought about it, Heru knew that they would be coming to him for his due soon.

Soon, night would be upon them and the torches would be lit. By the time dinner was served, the weather would be more tolerable. Heru wanted to make the best of his time aboard the ship before meeting his father, and what better way to hold his anxiety at bay than to engage in mock combat?

"Are you comfortable with two blades?" Heru asked.

The delay in Deylan's response was answer enough. Of course he wasn't. He would learn why the Qu'ari elite were regarded as the masters of combat shortly. The giddy butterflies of excitement took flight within him as he prepared to showcase some of his true strength.

XVIII

LIMPING OFF THE DECK gasping for breath, Deylan's hand rested on the small of his back. Sweat soaked his arms, causing his tunic to stick to his flesh. The dagger in his hand quivered as his muscles shook from exhaustion.

"That bastard," Deylan puffed, "enjoyed every damn minute of that."

Their practice that night drew quite a crowd. Even the members of the day watch climbed up to take in the spectacle. Weaving between Deylan's attacks, Heru's battleaxe and scimitar spun in deadly arcs. The blows rained down with frightening accuracy. It was only by the grace of the gods and Heru's over ten years of training that kept Deylan from becoming a smear on the deck.

He'd managed to do well for himself, dodging between the strikes and getting a few good kicks in on Heru's leg, but the Xanan held the upper hand for the majority of their engagement. Seeing the progress Heru made with his balance in the seven days since they left the Bone Coast startled Deylan. The Xanan proved to be a lethal opponent.

How did I survive our first encounter? Deylan wondered. *I should be dead.*

By the end of their session, it was all Deylan could do to limp off while Heru took his break above deck. A cool breeze rustled their hair, picking up in intensity during their practice battle. The small gusts pulled at Deylan's tunic – Heru had removed his halfway through their training.

"He's nearly as good as the other one," a lanky man said as he squeezed by Deylan on the way below deck. "I reckon he'd even give Len a run for his money. Both use the same weapons."

"Have you seen the other Xanan in action?" Deylan asked.

"Oh yeah," the man replied. "He's like a demon from the seven hells. It's no wonder that he hasn't killed all he comes upon. If you think that youngin' had good self-restraint, wait until you see Len."

"I'll have to remember not to practice with him," Deylan said, the pitch of his voice rising as though he were concerned for his safety. While he was worried, he had no intention of doing anything to cause the former Great Heart to draw his blade.

The lanky man slapped Deylan on his back nearly sending him tumbling to the ground. By some act of fortune, he managed to keep his balance well enough that he didn't fall down the stairs. Ignoring the stumble, the lanky man bumped into Deylan and continued on with his business.

"Damn arsehole," Deylan muttered as he reached the bottom step. "It's always a game with these people."

Straightening up, Deylan made his way into the sleeping quarters. Thankfully, there weren't too many people in the room. Most were under their blankets, snoring soundly. A few sat quietly in their spots talking to themselves. Deylan often wondered if they were praying; he'd met a few religious pirates. The beliefs that came from a life at sea tended to affect their thoughts on at least the God of the Ayr. Even Deylan did not tempt Graak – that would be foolhardy.

Massaging his arms, Deylan felt the almost instant relief of his muscles relaxing after an evening of strenuous activity.

This should be getting easier, he mused. *I thought sea life would have at least given me more of a fighting chance.*

Moving to massage his back, Deylan also stretched his legs. To his credit, the tension he usually experienced after each training session appeared to be lessoning. His body still ached, but it was nowhere near what he first felt.

After several long minutes, he finally felt well enough to move on. His hands stopped quivering and he was able to take a drink of water from the skin without spilling. By the time he left, everyone lay asleep on the floor or in their hanging makeshift beds. Unlike during the day, the passages below deck were silent as the night watch all worked above. Deylan hoped he would find a couple people in the galley who would let him sneak a snack. Supplies were getting low, and he didn't know if they would be as relaxed right before they docked.

"Jolly, how are you this evening?" Deylan asked as he strode into the galley.

A grizzled pirate, his face pockmarked and leathery from a lifetime at sea grunted at Deylan, but did not look up. His hair and beard, more stubble than hair, had turned white long ago, leaving no trace of its former glory. At the same time, his body remained lean yet hard. Deylan could see the muscles that lay ready in wait should the need arise. White scars marred his arms and the side of his face. Jolly was no stranger to battle.

"I was hoping that you might have a little morsel I could take with me to bed."

"I told Kayna it was a bad idea bringin' extra people on this trip," Jolly groused. "Always wantin' to eat."

Bringing his hand to his chest, Deylan knit his brows in mock surprise, his tone rising as he spoke. "Why Jolly, surely you don't mean that? I thought we'd developed a little relationship here."

"Heh," the grizzled cook spat. "Ye shouldn't be gettin' any strange ideas. Friendships are earned. Ye can't buy 'em with pretty words an' a smile."

"Oh, come now, Jolly. You've seen how that Xanan brute beats me. I need something to help me keep my strength."

The room echoed with laughter. Deylan could see the few remaining teeth in the seasoned pirate's mouth as he shook with mirth. Jolly stopped his cleaning and finally glanced at Deylan, who watched the grizzled man with a smile. Even the toughest of shells could be broken, Deylan learned that long ago.

"Go on now," Jolly said, pointing with his middle finger towards a barrel in the corner. His missing finger no longer a shock to Deylan. "Ye know the rules. Never a word."

"My sincerest thanks to you, Jolly," Deylan replied as he pulled a soft apple from the bottom of the barrel. "I'll make sure that I treat you to the best dinner when we return to the Bone Coast."

"Been a long time since I had a good meal. I'll kill ye if ye try an' swindle me."

"I would never dream of doing that," Deylan replied with a wink. "Duty calls. Hope the night treats you well and Graak blesses you."

By now, Jolly returned to his cleaning. He grunted in response, but Deylan could see the shadow of a smile playing on his lips. Seeing the old man brought Deylan a measure of joy he hadn't expected to find on this trip. If he had known his grandfather, Deylan imagined that he would have the same relationship with his grandfather as he did with Jolly. One day, he promised himself as he took a bite of his apple, he would learn Jolly's name.

<center>~~~</center>

"What kept you?" Kayna asked.

Her red hair that she usually kept tied in a high tail was down and spilled over her shoulders. The freckles that kissed her shoulder stood out on her lightly tanned skin. Her cream-colored blouse that hung off her shoulders managed to remain clean despite their time out on the waters, a testament to her meticulousness.

"Heru beat me soundly," Deylan admitted.

"Hopefully not as badly as you think," she purred.

Turning to face him, Kayna put down her hand mirror and sauntered over to him. Her hands traced his jaw, moving down to his chest with a familiarity the way only lovers could. Her light touch sent a thrill through Deylan's body. There was a reason why the Scourge would make it difficult for her to keep a partner. Kayna knew how to control her men – years at sea ensured that. The few men lucky enough to share her company must have regretted the time when they separated. Deylan knew he would.

"I'm sure I could put up a fight in a pinch."

A jolt of excitement shot through Deylan once more as her soft lips brushed against his. The feeling was unlike anything he'd experienced with a woman.

"Good," Kayna replied softly.

One hand ran over his bicep, the other moving to his trousers. Deylan felt himself stiffen in anticipation at her touch. His hands moved to her waist, pulling her in closer. Kayna's lips brushed his once more. Her breath smelled fresh, and her hair smelled faintly of flowers – a combination he never expected from someone in her trade and one that still left him pleasantly surprised.

Pressing his mouth more firmly against hers, Deylan brought her body in closer. He could feel her melt into him, and their kisses became more passionate. Her teeth bit his lower lip, sucking on it for a moment before her tongue moved past his lips. Before he knew it, the two were on her bed.

The only true bed Deylan had seen so far, Kayna's bed was unexpectedly firm. Instead of sinking into it like he would a normal bed, their bodies rested on top while their hands explored each other. He was used to sinking into beds, letting the mattress act as a cushion.

Her hand found its way into his trousers and began moving in a stroking motion. Deylan felt himself completely stiffen as she caressed his body. His own hand found its way into her black pants. He could feel the smile on her lips while they kissed as he too began his own stroking. His free hand slid under her blouse and cupped her breast. Though it wasn't much of a handful, he found her soft flesh and petite size more to his liking.

Deylan's fingers went deeper. As he did, her hand moved a little faster. He felt her open up as they got more passionate with each other, letting him explore her body with abandon. Her hand stopped and she motioned for him to reposition himself. Deylan then pulled her closer to him and allowed himself to enter her fully. Her body felt so familiar to him at this point – they now spent a week learning about each other in the privacy of her room.

As they moved more into their act of passion, Deylan had a fleeting thought.

The Scourge better not find out about this.

The idea nearly gave him pause, but he was able to move past it and continue on. It was a problem for another time, and he didn't have the energy to entertain the notion that moment.

Kayna's body trembled around him, breathy gasps escaping her lips in between kisses. Each time her body squeezed around him, Deylan found himself getting closer to release. Their bodies became sweaty and Deylan found himself tiring as the minutes dragged on. The continual exercise each morning and evening followed by the secret visits to Kayna once or twice a day tested his stamina.

At last, the two collapsed in a heap with Deylan laying on top of Kayna as they panted for breath. The two exchanged short kisses, and Deylan rolled off of her. His arm, however, remained wrapped around her, pulling her in closer to him as they cuddled on the bed.

Kayna's finger traced the side of his sweaty face, her eyes sparkling at him. She looked beautiful. Her lithe body and sun-kissed, freckled skin glowed as they basked in each other's presence. Deylan almost found himself wishing they could remain together after their journey to the Isles and on to Tan'quao to harvest the purple flowers.

"Would you consider staying with the *Fury* after we finish this trip?" Kayna whispered. She held his gaze as she spoke.

Blinking at the unexpected question, Deylan took a minute to think. He hadn't planned on remaining on the Bone Coast for much longer. He could create a life with Kayna, or Nefeli, but his options were limited. A life as a thief who takes from pirates would never end well – or with a long, happy life. Soon, Red, or one of the other ships he'd stolen from, would come looking for him. Thinking of the scar on his chest, Deylan knew that next time Red wouldn't miss.

But beyond all of this, deep down, Deylan missed his mother and sisters. He wanted to go home and pay off his debt to Xi's family. He wanted to live a quiet life with his family – to feel the safety of the home he never had growing up.

But he couldn't decide if he would say no.

"I..." he stammered, his voice almost a whisper. "I don't know."

Beneath his arms, Deylan felt Kayna deflate at his response. Seeing such a strong woman withdraw after being so vulnerable with him caused a pang of sorrow to spike through him. He could see himself spending eternity with Kayna, but he couldn't devote himself to the sea. Not yet.

"No, please," he begged. "It's not you. I... I have some business that I need to take care of before I can answer."

Pressing her lips to his once more, Kayna disentangled herself from Deylan and sat up to get dressed.

"I understand," she replied as she slipped on her top. "Life as the Scourge's daughter has accustomed me to a life most would not want. Not many are ready to take to the sea, just as I cannot leave her."

With her blouse covering her nudity, Kayna reached out and pat Deylan on the cheek. A wan smile spread on her face, but Deylan noted how it did not extend to her eyes. She was tired, he could see. Tired of the constant rejection, and probably more. His hand moved to cover hers, resting lightly on her slim hand.

"If I could, I would," he said softly. "Maybe after I finish my business that brought me to the Bone Coast to begin with, we can return to the sea. If I could pull you from her, I would bring you with me in a heartbeat."

A snort of laughter escaped Kayna as she closed her eyes. When she opened them once more, she looked younger, as though his words refreshed her and washed away her exhaustion.

"We will see," she said.

An hour passed by the time Deylan exited Kayna's quarters. His shirt was still rumpled and his hair sat mussed on his head, but a wistful expression replaced his previous exhaustion. Not wanting to interrupt those who slept, Deylan fought the urge to whistle. The cool night air would give him the space he needed to clear his mind.

As he made his way to the stairs, Deylan bumped into Bharam. Seeing the Nem Pahlan out of whatever hiding place he managed to secure startled Deylan. He remembered that the man had been assigned night watch on Dhruvasht's ship, but he didn't think Bharam would want that this time. Accidents happened in under the cover of night.

"Fancy seeing you here," Deylan said.

The way Bharam's eyebrows disappeared into his dark hair-line quicker than Deylan could get his greeting out told Deylan everything he needed to know. He fought to push back his amusement as he watched the man. Bharam looked like a child caught stealing one of their mother's cookies. Bharam moved to touch the pendant hidden under his tunic around his neck, but stopped himself. The change from his usual affect left Deylan nonplussed. He'd never seen the man resist his impulse to touch his religious artifact.

"What are you doing in the captain's quarters?" Bharam asked, ignoring the question. His voice did not sound like his usual mild tone. The pious disdain that he made some effort to hide now dripped from his words. "Shouldn't you be minding your watch?"

There was something behind his tone that set Deylan on edge. He couldn't explain why, but something about the sharpness, the almost accusation layered within the question, coupled with the glint in the man's eye.

"No reason," Deylan replied. "Just having a meeting with the captain to discuss our next step once we reach the Isles."

Bharam took a step closer, his eyes hardening.

"No you weren't."

XIX

"**I**'M SORRY?"

"I said no you weren't." Bharam took another step forward until there was barely any distance between the two. "You were sharing her bed."

As Deylan took a step back, he felt the wall of the ship pressed against his back. Bharam took one more step, his eyes flashing in the darkened hallway of the ship. His head swiveled side-to-side, as though he were afraid someone would walk up on them.

"You should be ashamed of yourself," Bharam hissed.

"It's not as big of an issue as you are making this out to be," Deylan replied. "The captain and I engage in a nice conversation now and again. There's nothing wrong with that."

"You find time to talk to her twice a day every day?" he said, raising his brow. "Why would a captain like her want to speak to you so frequently? You never even spoke to Dhruvasht on the *Rose*."

With every word, Bharam's voice rose, his voice starting to shake as he spoke. Deylan felt his cheeks warm as a flush crept over them. Indignant at the accusation that he was gaining undue influence over the captain, Deylan found himself taking a step forward. All thought of formality or pretense of civility was dropped. Deylan would not let Bharam paint him out to be a swindler.

"I would watch my words, if I were you," Deylan said softly.

"I know who you are," Bharam sneered. One hand went to his neck, clutching his religious icon while the other hand went to his hip and he squared his shoulders. His eyes darted about, only resting on Deylan when he once again found no one else in the hall. "My uncle figured out that you were the one who stole from Red. And now, you use your gilded tongue to deceive the captain, but I know your secret. You placed this curse over my head – I haven't slept since we set sail. Before I die, I will have peace."

Before Deylan could respond, the Nem Pahlan rushed forward and wrapped his arms around Deylan's waist, tackling him to the ground. Deylan let out a grunt as he hit the ground, the wind knocked from his lungs. In a heartbeat, Bharam scrambled on top of him, the man's hands squeezing his throat. Deylan tried to gasp for breath to replace what was knocked out of him, but couldn't.

Hands scrambling, Deylan sought to free himself. His fingers gripped Bharam's hands, digging into the man's flesh as he tried to dislodge the death-grip around his neck. Propping his feet on the ground, Deylan prepared to thrust his hips up when he saw the glint of steel in the low corridor light. The sight of the blade sent his pulse racing. He hadn't even noticed when Bharam removed one of his hands to go for the dagger.

Without thinking, Deylan's right hand shot up palm first. He felt, more than heard, the sound of Bharam's nose breaking. The Nem Pahlan let out a shout, his body rearing back as he cupped his face. The clatter of the dagger dropping to the ground echoed in Deylan's ears – every sense unnaturally heightened as he gasped for breath the moment Bharam's hand left his throat.

A stream of curses flooded the hall as Bharam clutched his face. Deylan didn't wait for the man to recover. Lifting his shoulder off of the ground a couple inches, Deylan's hand scrambled frantically to find the weapon on the ground. Every grain in the wood stood out like a mountain range as he searched for the blade. When Deylan touched the cold steel, another surge of adrenaline flowed through him.

Spinning it around with his fingers, Deylan's hand wrapped around the hilt and he brought it up. Not looking where he struck, Deylan felt the momentary resistance as the blade pierced the skin and buried itself deeply into Bharam's neck. The howling stopped, replaced by a singular gasp that rang out in the corridor. The sudden intake of breath hung in the air hauntingly – as if a specter dangled over the two of them. Deylan slowly pulled his hand away from the Nem Pahlan, his fingers tight around the hilt, pulling the blade free from the neck.

The seconds crept by with the beating of his heart. After three or so seconds, a guttural gurgle escaped the Nem Pahlan. Warm droplets of blood dripped onto Deylan's face between Bharam's fingers as he grasped his neck in an effort to staunch the lifeblood that oozed out of him. Somewhere in the distance, the sound of boots thumping on wood broke through Deylan's haze as he stared at Bharam's ever increasingly pale face. Everything seemed muffled, as though a bubble had engulfed his head.

Bharam's eyes stared at some unseen horror – wide in disbelief and mouth hanging open. His lips moved in silent prayer, unable to form the words he so desperately wanted to speak. Blood seeped through his fingers and out from the corners of his mouth, a few stray drops landing on Deylan. In what felt like an eternity but barely took more than a few heartbeats, Deylan saw the last vestiges of life fade away from Bharam's eyes.

Waiting for the body to fall on top of him, Deylan felt a pair of strong hands reach under his arms and pull him up. The shadow of a figure stood behind Bharam as well, holding the now limp man up and keeping him from smothering Deylan.

Countless eyes stared at the two, both covered in blood, from the doorways. Even from above him, Deylan could feel the stares as those on deck ceased their duties and observed what happened below. The hands holding him up gave him a little shake, silently prompting Deylan to stand on his own. He obliged.

It was all so surreal. Deylan didn't expect their exchange to escalate so quickly.

A strong grip seized his forearm. The adrenaline had vanished, leaving Deylan exhausted and wanting nothing more than to melt into his bed roll. If it weren't for that hand – Heru's hand, he would have just stumbled off.

"I got you."

Heru's voice sounded so far away.

The crowd parted as Deylan was led back to the sleeping quarters. As he passed Kayna's chambers, he saw the redhead peering out her door. The two locked gazes. Her crystal blue eyes stared deep into his own, studying him as he stood frozen before her. Before Heru could pull Deylan along, Kayna broke the connection by turning and disappearing into her room.

A low rumbling rang in his ears with each step. Deylan couldn't understand what people were saying, but he knew they were talking about him. He just focused on walking.

In the back of his mind, Xi's face stared up at him, ashen and lifeless.

"Oh gods," Deylan muttered.

He'd worked so hard to push away that image.

The warmth of the galley hit Deylan unexpectedly like a wall of flame. The modest fire crackling in the corner hurt Deylan's eyes after the darkness of the corridor.

Roughly pushing Deylan down onto his bed roll, Heru quickly followed by shoving a cup of water into Deylan's hand. Deylan took a sip. His stomach clenched and the unpleasant sensation of saliva filling his mouth right before he voided his stomach left him feeling nauseous. The cup tipped over onto the ground as Deylan grabbed his head with his hands.

"Oh gods. Not again."

XX

"DEYLAN," Heru said, placing his hands on Deylan's shoulders. "What happened?"

Mind racing, Deylan paused for a few deep breaths. He fought back the wave of nausea that threatened to overwhelm him. With each breath, his world came back into focus. The blistering heat he'd felt upon entering the galley suddenly vanished, leaving his body cold. The bubble that settled over his head, drowning out all other sound, popped and he was hit with a wall of noise. The wood snapped as the flames licked them clean and the night's meal bubbled in the tiny cauldron hanging over it.

"He attacked me," Deylan mumbled. "He caught me leaving the Captain's Quarters and accused me of..." Deylan swallowed the lump that formed in the back of his throat. "Impropriety."

"Dammit, Deylan," Heru hissed. "Can't you stay away from the one woman who controls our fate?"

"She invited me," Deylan protested. "Besides, her friend wasn't nearly as receptive."

"Oh gods," Heru breathed. "Are you serious?"

"Let's focus here. The little shite attacked me. I just wanted to have a nice walk on the deck and watch the heavens. Oh gods, what are they going to do to me?"

Heru took to pacing around the cramped galley with his hands clasped behind his back. He continuously muttered under his breath as he circled. In the background, Jolly appeared from behind a stack of boxes. In the cook's hand, a half-consumed bottle of wine sloshed about. The grizzled man's flesh took on a ruddy hue and his eyes were glazed over.

"I think we need to pull ourselves from attention," Heru said slowly. "We should stop our practices and just keep to either one side of the deck or to our room."

"What did you do, boy?" Jolly slurred, plopping down on the ground next to Deylan.

The wine got dangerously close to spilling out of the bottle from the sudden movement. Deylan couldn't help but smell the strong spirits on the man's breath. This probably wasn't his first bottle of the evening.

"I killed someone." Deylan felt small as he confessed to the grizzled man.

Beside him, Heru leaned against the wall, watching their exchange. Deylan hadn't had the opportunity to introduce the two. He wondered what Heru thought about the cook.

"'Oo?" Jolly asked.

"The Nem Pahlan, Bharam," Heru cut in. "The one we chased out of here when the ship first set sail."

Heru's arms rested against his chest, crossed, as he stared down the grizzled cook. His body stood tense. Deylan wondered if he could draw his blade before Jolly did anything to him. He glanced back up at Heru and saw the man calculating something in the back of his mind. To his credit, Jolly didn't appear to notice the intensity of the Xanan's stare.

"About fuckin' time," Jolly said, slapping Deylan on the back. A bit of wine spilled out of the bottle and onto Deylan as Jolly's body lurched from the motion. "He's been a right pain in the arse."

Jaw dropping, Deylan turned from Jolly to Heru. This had to be a joke.

"Are you serious right now?" Heru asked, moving away from the wall. "Deylan's just put a target on the both of us."

Jolly stared at the two with the glassy eyes of one who is three sheets to the wind. His body swayed in a way that was almost opposite of the ship. Yet he did not seem the least bit perturbed by what he said. In a way, Jolly stood tall behind his words.

"They said he was marked for death," Deylan admitted. "You said so yourself when we first boarded. You had a conversation with one of them."

"I didn't actually think it would happen," Heru protested. "Let alone by you. I thought I'd kill him before you did."

"By the gods," Deylan groaned, pressing his palms into his face. "What am I going to do? I can't exactly disappear on this damn ship."

"Doesn' matter 'oo kills him," Jolly replied. His statement provided a welcome break to the tension that had been building. "So long as he's dead. The ship will be happier because of it."

"Dhruvasht won't be pleased," Deylan muttered.

"That old fool can jump off the ship," Jolly spat. "Or take it up with Kayna. His choice. I have a feelin' though he'll keep his mouth shut."

The two shared a glance, trying to piece together the truth from the drunken cook's words. Surely, the former captain would not let the death of his only remaining crewman go unanswered. The man had been livid when one of them deserted him, running away after the *Death's Rose* washed ashore two weeks ago.

Jolly, apparently satisfied with how the conversation went, got up off the floor, spilling a little more drink in the process. He then proceeded to stagger out of the galley, and hopefully, towards his hammock. Deylan couldn't imagine what would happen if the inebriated man managed to find his way on deck. He'd heard tales of more than one man who got a little too drunk and toppled off the side of a ship. The thought always sent a shiver down his spine.

"You should probably stay here until we reach shore," Heru said once the pair were alone.

"Sorry?"

"We don't know how people will react. I'd rather not be murdered in my sleep just for noticing you. Lay low and we can sneak out when the time is right."

"No," Deylan said with the shake of his head. "I have to face my punishment like a man. If I hide, I'll put a bigger target on myself. Better to at least die with dignity."

His mother's face flashed in his mind. Her silver eyes stared back at fifteen-year-old Deylan wide with fear. He could feel her hands upon his shoulders once more. "Live your life," her words echoed in his head, a haunting lilt to her message. The panic he'd felt as a child washed over Deylan, constricting his chest and making it difficult to breathe.

Deylan found himself praying to every god he could think of, hoping against hope that Kayna would be merciful once she'd discovered what he'd done.

Suddenly struck with an indescribable fatigue, the kind that made every limb, and even his eyelids feel heavy, Deylan yawned and curled up on the ground. He wanted to take the time to sort out his feelings, but his body demanded that he sleep. There was a good chance he would regret not unwinding the night's events tomorrow. But that was a problem for another day.

Now, rest.

"Good night, Heru," Deylan said through another yawn. He felt like he'd been crying for hours.

There was a part of him who needed to know if his companion would stay with him, or if Heru would leave him by himself for the night. To Deylan's relief, Heru sat down nearby and pulled his knees to his chest as though he planned on taking a night watch over the galley.

"Perhaps we should pass on our morning work out?"

Deylan hummed in agreement. He wanted to find Kayna and talk to her. He needed to know that he was still welcome aboard the ship. Otherwise, he would find his way back to the Bone Coast.

XXI

"Brother, why does Daddy hit Mommy?"

Five-year-old Mei looked up at Deylan with her big, brown eyes. Thick lashes framed them, giving her the appearance of one of the porcelain dolls he'd seen the affluent children in town carrying. Her dark brown hair sat braided into two buns, one on each side of her head. She looked the epitome of innocence.

His fingers touched his cheek. Deylan could feel the bruise that would be forming before morning. His flesh was tender, and even the slightest touch made him wince. He found himself turning away from his little sister. He couldn't let her know that Xi had begun hitting him too.

"His work is difficult," Deylan repeated the words he'd told her, that he'd told himself, countless times. By now, they sounded hollow to him, but he didn't want to scare her. "Sometimes, when he argues with Mom, she may say something he doesn't like."

"But why does he hit her? Doesn't he love her?"

The words stung. He could feel the hot tears threatening to leak out of the corners of his eyes, just as a flush crept over his face. One day, he would no longer allow for Xi to hide behind his image. One day, Deylan would no longer cover for the man and pretend that he was a flawed yet good person. One day.

"Why does Daddy hit Mommy?"

The words hung in the air, a haunting question with no answer.

"Doesn't he love her?"

"Why does he hit her?"

Over and over again. Each time the question echoed in his mind, blocking out all else. The very words vibrated within his body to the core.

The same answer passed through his lips. Each time Deylan heard himself say it, his words became more muffled and harder to hear. Time moved strangely. He seemed to be aging, yet the question still came from his five-year-old sister.

The world went black. Deylan stood alone in a realm of emptiness. A white light illuminated where he stood, but other than the single light, there was nothing. He took a step, the sound of his boot echoing in the void.

"Why does Daddy hit Mommy?"

This time, the question reverberated in his mind, filling his soul. It hit him so hard that he nearly toppled over from the weight of it. He struggled to breathe, gasping for air against the invisible hand that squeezed his throat. The question that he'd heard for an eternity finally threatened to overwhelm him and deny him of life. If Deylan could not find a proper answer, he would suffocate.

The sound of Mei's voice faded away, replaced with a heavy silence. The silence didn't last long. His heart raced. With each frantic beat, Deylan could feel the vibrations shaking him. The whole room shook, as if mimicking the panic within. Below him, a small spot of light intensified, growing larger. It wasn't the brilliant pure white he'd been looking at moments before. It glowed with a warmth like a roaring hearth.

Xi's lifeless body lay before him. Red stains covered his body, pooling on the ground at his feet. Deylan gripped a kitchen knife tightly in his trembling hand. His knuckles went white around the handle. He couldn't let go.

The darkness crept in around the light, causing it to fade. However, Xi's prone figure wouldn't disappear. At some point, the sound of his beating heart stopped. In the back of his mind, Deylan heard his voice break the silence.

"Mommy won't be hurt anymore."

A sudden jolt threw Deylan against the wall, waking him. Tin cups and plates rattled in their crates on the ground with each lurch of the ship. His back stung from the impact. Before he could do more than rub his sore body, another rough wave sent him into the wall once more. This time, Deylan struck his head against one of the wooden panels, creating white stars in his mind's eye. Beside him, he heard Heru bark out a curse. A groan escaped him as he closed his eyes, willing the stars to disappear.

"What in the seven hells?" Heru spat, a hint of discomfort tinging his words.

Disoriented, Deylan wondered if the Xanan also slammed against the side of the ship. He thought he'd heard another thud, but wasn't sure if it was just the throbbing of his head. Everything felt so real only moments before. His heart still raced as he saw Xi's bloody body lying on the floor next to him. Nearby curses to Graak and his damned swells from the hall sounded muted through the wooden wall of the galley. Deylan's fingers ached from clenching the handle of his dream knife. He hoped he had a little more featherfew to treat the pain in his head, but the last few days his bottles felt woefully light.

"Good morning to you too," Deylan murmured. "Perfect way to start the day, right?"

The iron pot Jolly used for cooking somehow managed to remain upright, although a decent amount of thin soup had spilled over the rim. Boxes lay toppled over. The god of the seas must have been very upset to send a wave that strong into the ship.

"Shut up," Heru muttered, rubbing his head. "I'm going to check above deck."

"That's a wonderful idea. You should be able to tell if the water is a bit rough today."

The Xanan glowered at Deylan. The disgruntled look brought a smile to Deylan's lips. It was only a dream, after all. Outside the galley, shouts could be heard in the passage.

"I guess everyone is awake," Deylan remarked. "Might as well join you on deck." Noticing Heru's concerned glance, Deylan forced himself to adopt his charismatic persona. "It'll be fine," he lied. "Besides, I already failed to show up for night watch last night. I don't want to give them another reason to be angry."

Leaving the warmth of the galley behind, the pair headed out into the tightly-packed corridor. Men staggered out of their sleeping quarters, many still rubbing the sleep out of their eye while others shouted out to those above. No one said anything to Deylan as he made his way above-deck. In fact, no one seemed to notice him.

Out on the deck, water sloshed onto the deck as a wave slammed against the ship and sent it tilting sideways. Even though he and Heru found their balance, the sudden arrival of waters this rough was enough to send them staggering into the captain's wheel. Dark grey clouds filled the heavens and a cold drizzle fell from above.

"Strange weather," Deylan noted to Heru. "I'm surprised no one else seems bothered by how rough it is."

The scowl he received from the Xanan amused him.

Pleasant as ever, he thought to himself.

Deylan rubbed his arms as goose flesh appeared on his bare torso. He wasn't the only one who felt the chill. Despite his best attempt to appear unfazed, Deylan could see Heru's teeth chattering and goose flesh raising on the Xanan's exposed body as well.

"It's colder than Dhruvasht's teat," one of the men exclaimed as the drizzle hit him.

Deylan felt himself shrink as he neared the group of men. He purposefully left his dagger under his pillow. He didn't want to give the men a reason to think he was on guard. Heru shot Deylan a look, one of reassurance perhaps. The damned Xanan still didn't understand how to properly convey emotion.

A round of laughter erupted on the deck. Deylan found himself grinning along with everyone else as he spied the disgruntled former captain of the *Death's Rose* slinking around the deck. He seemed to be the only person fully dressed amid the sea of bare torsos. Dhruvasht shot the man a withering glare, but the man didn't even notice him. By chance, Dhruvasht noticed Deylan by the wheel. The glower that he fixed onto Deylan caught him by surprise. Dhruvasht never showed any emotion while Deylan was on his ship. Losing all authority did not suit the Nem Pahlan well. Another wave of bodies emerged from below deck, allowing the former captain to disappear.

Deylan glanced around at the men on deck. No one seemed to pay him any mind. Not wanting to let his guard down completely, Deylan allowed himself a moment to relax. The lack of open hostility seemed a good sign, but he couldn't be sure if there were whispers about his fate when his back was turned.

The sea's anger gradually subsided, her waves no longer slamming into the *Fury* with the force of a battering ram.

"All right you lot," Kayna's voice sounded over the general din. "You all need to take your spots. We should be seeing El'Lenan soon. I'll not have the *Fury* crashing on her rocks. Get to it lest I keel haul you."

A resounding "Yes ma'am!" rang out over the fury of the sea. A moment later, everyone rushed to their tasks. Deylan found himself standing awkwardly by the wheel with Heru as people moved around them. Despite the hurried nature of their duties, no one bumped into the pair.

Kayna maneuvered through the bustling crew, giving an occasional order to one of her men. Deylan thought he saw Dhruvasht sneak down below deck. Deylan noticed that she glanced at the Nem Pahlan's retreating form, but she didn't say anything. Only a shake of the head expressed her displeasure. Now was his time to gauge how much trouble he was truly in.

"Meet me down below," Deylan said to Heru. "We should help Jolly."

"Where are you going?" Heru asked. He seemed taken aback at being left behind during such a critical moment.

"I need to talk to Kayna."

"Now?" Heru asked. "Is this really the right time?"

Taking a few steps towards the redheaded captain, Deylan quickly turned back to his friend. "I'll be right back. I promise. Play nice."

Heru rolled his eyes and turned with a grunt. Not wanting to waste the opportunity, Deylan jogged over to Kayna. The rocking of the ship and the moving sea of bodies made it a difficult task. He danced on his toes around a bear of a man carrying a barrel towards the portside. The man lumbered on, not bothering to acknowledge the slimmer man who tip-toed around him.

"Nimble," Kayna smirked, nodding as if in approval. "Where's your friend?"

The ship got knocked to the starboard side, causing Deylan to stutter-step to maintain his balance. Even Kayna took an extra step to widen her stance and brace herself against the rocking. The man nearest to the two barked out a curse, grumbling to Graak that they had an accord.

"I sent him to help Jolly in the galley," Deylan replied. "I'll be down there shortly. I just wanted to talk to you a little... about last night..."

The words hung awkwardly in the air. Deylan found it hard to meet her gaze, but he didn't let that stop him from staring into her crystalline blue eyes. The smirk left her face, replaced with something soft. Pity perhaps? Deylan couldn't tell.

"There's nothing to talk about," she said stiffly. "I enjoyed our time together. We can continue as long as you want, but I cannot leave her." Her attention shifted towards the tumultuous sea, a twinkle of longing shining in her eye. "Or my men. It is my duty to uphold my father's rule. After the Gods' Battle, he's been away from the sea; unable to keep order on her demanding waters. I will die out here." Turning back to face Deylan, a wan smile pulled at the corners of her mouth. "And I'm at peace with my place. It's lonely, but I don't want you to feel trapped in a life you don't want. You're young and deserve a happy life."

The redhead reached out and gently took his hand. Her touch still electrified him. Deylan found himself forgetting the real reason he approached her. He almost wanted to tell her that he would stay – that he would spend his life with her on the ship as long as she would have him. But his sister's face flashed in his mind. Then his mother's. He couldn't let them think that he had abandoned them forever. With a heavy sigh, Deylan knew he couldn't stay.

"I need some time to think about it," he said, not wanting to make his decision official by speaking it into reality. "I want to."

Kayna gave his hand a squeeze, pulling him into her as another wave struck the side of the boat and almost throwing her off balance. As the two crashed together, Deylan's arms wrapped around her slender body, his hands resting on her waist as he finally found his footing. The two shared a glance, Kayna's head craning up to meet his amber eyes. Her lips twitched up once more, acceptance etched onto her face.

"Take all the time you need," she replied.

Though she spoke normally to be heard over the crashing waves and drizzle, it sounded little more than a whisper to Deylan. He felt himself being drawn forward towards her. His head tipped down. The thick lashes that framed her eyes were beautiful – a light shade of brown that almost appeared red in the light. Kayna pushed up on her toes until her nose lightly pressed against his. Deylan felt her body touch his. They fit together so well.

"And about last night," she added, the words causing panic to rise in Deylan's chest. "Keep your eyes peeled for that piece of scum, Dhruvasht. You have my protection on my ship. You have no debt on the *Fury* for your actions."

Tension broken, Deylan blinked in surprise. The two separated, taking a step back to put some distance between them. Around them, the crew carried on, ignoring their moment next to the captain's wheel.

"I'm not in trouble?"

Kayna shook her head. "I've spoken to several of my men, and they said that he attacked you. I didn't expect it to be you. They were set to follow my orders before we reach El'Lenan. I'm sorry you got caught up in it all."

Stunned into a rare moment of silence, Deylan gaped at the redhead for several heartbeats. A voice called out from the crow's nest, pointing out a landmark that they spotted despite the grey gloom overhead.

"Go," she said, pushing him gently away from her. "Jolly will appreciate your help. Besides, if you're not careful, Jolly's infectious personality will rub off onto our little Xanan."

And like that, Kayna spun on her heels and headed towards the bow the ship. Her voice rang over the now dying roar of the water, the waves starting to calm as the morning wore on, for her spyglass. A man darted in the direction of the stairs to retrieve her spyglass below deck. Deylan counted to ten before following the man below.

XXII

THE WARMTH OF THE GALLEY washed away the chill that had seeped into Deylan's bones. He hadn't realized just how cold he'd been until the heat of the hearth engulfed him. The clink of tin plates and cups reminded him of a high-end clock merchant he ran into on his way to the Bone Coast. The constant clanking of their interior mechanisms had intrigued him. It reminded him of some mystical chorus of birds. Deylan hoped to find that shop once more.

In the corner, Heru and Jolly worked wordlessly side-by-side. Watching the older man move as nimbly as the young Xanan preparing the morning meal, Deylan realized that Jolly was a good ally to have on his side.

You never anger your cook, he told himself.

"I'll have Kayna leave you some silver so you can restock," a deep, feminine voice said.

Deylan straightened up as Kayna's first mate, Maya, emerged from behind some barrels along the wall. Unlike most of the ship, she was immaculately dressed, her clothing crisp and clean, much like Kayna's. It was a testament to the two women that they managed to maintain an image of power and authority despite their rough lifestyle. Deylan knew firsthand how difficult it was to keep his own belongings pristine to uphold his carefully crafted image.

As soon as she noticed him, Maya's gaze roved over him, taking in his disheveled appearance and bare flesh. Where Kayna would have raised her brow or twitched the corner of her mouth in approval, Maya kept her thoughts concealed behind a mask of indifference. Making her way to the group, Maya handed a bit of dried meat and a couple of plums to the grizzled cook.

"Have them brought to my chambers later," she instructed. "We should be arriving shortly and I still have a few things to attend to."

Not looking up at his superior, Jolly grunted in acknowledgement as he poured a ladleful of thin broth into the worn tin cups. Steam danced off of the surface of the meager soup – at least it was aromatic. Maya didn't seem bothered by his lack of attention. Deylan caught her glancing over at Heru. He wasn't sure if it was his imagination, but he almost could have sworn that he saw her head dip into the slightest of nods, as if pleased with what she saw. As she turned to him, she dipped her head once more and exited the galley.

"You heard her," Jolly grumbled. "Take them to her room. And grab the silver."

Sharing a glance with Heru who shrugged his shoulders, Deylan picked up the small bundle of food and wrapped it in a cleanish cloth he found atop one of the barrels. He hoped that the stains weren't from cleaning up some recent spill. Jolly and Heru worked in silence, the two maintaining a harmony in their motions despite not looking at each other. Deylan wanted to talk with the Xanan, but pushed his desire aside. They would meet up once they reached land.

"Wait for me when we dock?" he said, leaving the question hanging between the two of them.

"I'm ready for a good meal," Heru said without looking up. "And a strong drink."

"The Anchor is where ye'll want to go," Jolly interjected. "Best food an' drink in Last Call."

"Last Call?" Deylan asked.

"Aye, that's the town where we get our supplies. It's the last stop before ye reach the far eastern lands. Most don't make it far past Last Call."

"The Anchor it is then. Wait for me."

The tiny passageway inside the *Fury* bustled with bodies deftly dodging each other. In the few adjacent rooms, Deylan could hear people talking brusquely as they packed up whatever essentials they needed before they reached land. The sound of rushing feet above deck created an ominous air in combination with the occasional sharp rocking of the ship.

"At least the seas died down," Deylan heard someone remark from inside the sleeping quarters. "Graak must've finally calmed them."

A muttered consensus from the others in the room voiced their agreement. Though he could make out some other voices, Deylan kept his steps purposeful as he made his way to Maya's chambers. He hadn't seen Kayna's first mate much during their journey, but he assumed that her room would be near the captain's.

Once he arrived at the door, Deylan paused a moment, unsure how to proceed. All around him, the organized chaos continued. The efficiency of the *Fury's* crew greatly impressed him. Not wanting to take any more time, Deylan raised his hand and knocked three times against the thick wooden door. His body suddenly lurched forward as someone pushed past him in their effort to run upstairs. Deylan's hand flew forward to stop his head from smacking against the wood, the blow causing his hand to sting from the sudden impact. A hurried apology from the man could barely be heard before the man disappeared above deck.

Muttering to himself, Deylan decided to forego formality and cautiously pushed the door open. As he suspected, the room was empty. Maya remained with Kayna on the main deck organizing their arrival to the port. Taking a moment to inspect her quarters, Deylan noted how neat it was. A small desk with a pot of ink and quill sat ready, a stack of parchment neatly bundled in the center of the desk ready to be written upon. Curiosity got the better of Deylan and he opened the single drawer on the right side of the desk. Inside, he found a crumpled cloth covered in black ink. At least the desk wasn't stained, though Deylan wasn't sure exactly how she managed to do that. Beside the soiled cloth, the edge of a letter peeked out. Picking it up, Deylan saw it was closed with a burgundy wax seal. The urge to turn over the letter to see who its recipient strongly tempted Deylan, but he forced himself to close the drawer and walk away.

Part of him wondered if it was worth the risk to find out, but reason got the better of him. These were not a group that he wanted to anger, and he got the impression that Maya's wrath would be dire should she let it loose upon him.

The rest of the room was rather nondescript. A simple bed and quilt lay crammed in the corner. A pair of chocolate-colored boots rested under the desk, and a wooden chair sat pushed under the desk. For some reason, Deylan was disappointed. He expected to find her walls papered with maps and possibly even a small shelf with old leatherbound tomes detailing their travels or some other scholarly work. Seeing such a modest room left him wanting more.

Both she and Kayna couldn't be content with such barren rooms? Could they? Not knowing where to leave her little snack, Deylan placed the cloth containing her requested rations on her bed and quickly exited the room.

A commotion on the main deck caught Deylan's attention before he could begin making his way back towards the galley. Following the lead of several men as they made their way above deck, Deylan found himself climbing the stairs to see what was going on.

The skies were dark and overcast. The winds had died down, but still pulled at his trousers and froze his bare flesh. A shiver ran down his spine and his arms unconsciously closed in a self-hug, his hands running up and down his arms as he attempted to warm himself.

"Put a shirt on before ye freeze yer tits," a voice called out. The comment was promptly followed by a slap on the back. In the chilly weather, the strike stung Deylan more than it should have. "Ye have time."

Not wanting to welcome another slap, even if it was in good humor, Deylan scurried below deck to the sound of raucous laughter. Inside the galley, Deylan nearly ran into Heru as the young Xanan finished pulling on his shirt.

"Cold?" Heru asked, a momentary twinkle of amusement flashing in his eye upon taking in Deylan's trembling form.

"No, I'm fine," Deylan tossed back, making a beeline towards his clothes. "Just thought I'd see how long I can go before I frost over."

This brought a chuckle from Heru. Deylan continued to throw on his clothes. With each layer, he gradually felt a modicum of warmth, coupled with the heat from the small fire over which the cauldron cooking a thin soup bubbled, bringing forth a sigh of relief.

"It's a bit chilly out here in the East," Jolly mumbled matter-of-factly. "Wouldn' recommend goin' outside without yer clothes very often."

A glower of annoyance broke Deylan's usually chipper façade. The grumpy cook paid him no mind as he moved about with his business. Emotion simmered within Deylan, rising almost to anger until he noticed a rare smirk on Jolly's face.

"If I didn't know any better, I'd say you're mocking me," Deylan said, the negativity that boiled inside quickly extinguishing and becoming replaced with amusement.

The sight of the normally cantankerous man's mirth brought him joy – it had been a hard-fought battle to form a relationship with the cook. Deylan counted it as another success thus far on this journey.

Ignoring the comment, Jolly finally turned to face the two. "Get on above deck," he commanded. "I can handle the rush for food. Grab yers now. Might as well have somethin' to keep you warm up top."

～

Steam wafted from the small wooden bowls of soup in the frigid air. Translucent strips of carrots and the tiniest specks of potato floated through a broth so pale it could almost be mistaken for water. Sipping directly from the bowl, Deylan quietly thanked Jolly for suggesting that he take the hot drink with him. The wind had picked up since he last stood on deck and bit through to the bone.

The crew milled about, more relaxed now that the main duties in preparation for docking had been completed. Heru stood silently by Deylan. His dark gaze took in the horizon in between sips of his soup. On occasion, his brow twitched together, as though he saw something that caught his attention.

"We should reach Last Call before mid-day," Kayna called out.

The ship quieted down at her words. Standing behind the wheel on the helm, Kayna cut an impressive figure against the dark grey sky. Her red hair flew freely in the wind like the flames of a fire. Her white ruffle-sleeved blouse and black bodice along with her black hose and boots elongated her naturally petite form.

"A few of our men have already arrived and are awaiting our arrival. Get your desires out now because come tomorrow we sail for Tan'quao. Don't make me regret my arrangement with their baron. It's already getting more costly to make these runs."

Approaching from behind, Maya made her way to wait patiently for Kayna to finish. Dressed like her captain, Maya's already statuesque figure looked even more imposing. Atop her head, a simple black hat rested on her closely shaved head. Her hands rested behind her back, almost in a militaristic posture.

Kayna's warning from earlier echoed in Deylan's mind. He almost expected there to be a small shift in the tension, but her word must be law because the crew did not seem the least perturbed. Deylan found himself unconsciously looking around for Dhruvasht and Bharam. Surely the little weasel of a man would betray his emotions whether he meant to or not.

Right...

How he forgot that not even a day before he and Bharam fought to the death stunned him. His conversation earlier with Kayna still resonated in the back of his mind and he wanted to tell Heru.

As he mulled over his final moments with the Nem Pahlan, Deylan found Dhruvasht standing away from the main crowd. Dressed in his pressed copper coat, the former captain of *Death's Rose* maintained his superior air and kept his distance from the grimy members of Kayna's crew. Turning back to the helm, Deylan didn't want to risk making eye contact with the man.

"Those of you who I spoke to earlier today will wait until I leave the ship," Maya's voice rang out. "We do not have time for frivolities, so don't keep me waiting."

"Land ho!" a voice from the crow's nest called out. "The current is bringing us in faster than expected."

Kayna spun to face the horizon. Deylan noticed a large land mass quickly approaching. What had been a small strip of land, a shadow in the distance, gave way to what appeared to be a heavily populated coastal town with a mountain range hovering behind. He could almost make out the buildings that lined the coast through the fog. The cool wind blew the low-hanging clouds past them, leaving drops of condensation on his flesh and dampening his clothes.

"Looks like we'll have a hard time finding the Anchor," Heru said.

His words startled Deylan. He'd forgotten that his friend stood right next to him. Taking a deep drink to finish that last of his soup, Deylan felt that momentary rush of now lukewarm warmth flowing through his body. The disappointing heat still felt better than nothing.

"A place like the Anchor should be easy enough to find," Deylan replied. "It sounds to be quite popular – or at least one of their maids does. Delli, I believe. I'm sure someone will lead us to it."

Watching the coastal town grow ever-closer, Deylan found a rush of excitement flow through him. He'd never been this far from the Bone Coast. There were so many opportunities for him to take advantage of. First, he would need to find a few dolls for his sisters.

XXIII

T HE PLANK HIT THE WOODEN SLATS of the port with a resounding thump. Men scurried down the long, thin
board as deftly as a pack of rats, not one of them losing
their balance as they rushed down to the port. Lengths of rope
were thrown over the side and the men who just disembarked
tied them to the thick round beams that stood at waist level on
the pier. The waves sloshed against the stones of the port, a bit
of white foam occasionally cresting the ledge and splashing
those who got too close to the edge. The fog had not lifted, and
between the tangy sea air and the dense, low-hanging clouds,
the port was pleasantly warm. The winds died down, adding to
the most welcome change in atmosphere. It must get quite hot
when the sun came out.

In small groups, the people aboard the *Graak's Fury* made
their way onto land. A small contingent accompanied both

Kayna and Maya reminiscent of a king's retinue. Heru and Deylan followed a short while later, taking note of the two groups before they split up to head out on their respective business. The wind picked up a little, pushing away the dense clouds of fog that blanketed the ship and making the walk down the thin plank a little more precarious. Thanking the rope that now served as the only railing to hold on to, the two cautiously made their way onto land.

"It gets a little easier each time you do it," Deylan told Heru. "But it still takes time. Go slowly."

The closer they got to the pier, the more stable the descent felt. As they stepped onto the pier, a splash of chilly water sprayed their legs. To Heru's relief, the water didn't fill his boots and soak his feet. He still struggled adjusting to the cold.

"Let's find that tavern," he said to Deylan. "I'm ready for a drink and proper meal."

Walking into the town, Heru marveled at the diversity of the buildings. Closest to the water's edge, tens upon tens of little makeshift merchant stalls lined the roads. Many of the merchant shops carried a variety of fruit – mangoes, cherries, peaches, plums, coconuts, and figs piled higher than Heru thought possible. The mangoes, cherries, peaches, and plums sparkled like gems in the sunlight, their skins practically perfect.

Other stalls held fish, urchins, and clams, while others sold kebabs with thick chunks of meat and savory vegetables. Dotted amongst the main food stalls were ones that sold sweets and honeycakes – their sugary aroma somehow breaking through the salty and savory air and making Heru's mouth water. The booths that did not sell food items had modest pieces of jewelry and elegant combs displayed. The simple silver combs and brilliant golden necklaces sparkled despite the clouds blocking the sun. Behind them, the true shops loomed large and impressive.

Heru took his time walking through the merchants' stalls. Seeing the many vendors calling out to him and the others wandering about reminded him of home. Even the honeycakes brought back childhood memories of his time with his big sister while clutching his mother's silk pants. One of the vendors with brightly colored candies caught his attention. The young woman selling them perked up as he stopped to check out her wares.

"How can I help ya, love?" Her voice came out high-pitched and mousy. "Are you looking for something sweet, or maybe a piece of candy?"

Looking up from the sweet display, his raised brow caused a fit of giggles to erupt from her. Running her hand through her hair and flashing a seductive smile his way, the young woman leaned forward a bit. To his side, Heru noticed Deylan standing back, taking in the whole exchange with a bemused expression.

"Not now," he replied. "I'm trying to find the Anchor."

For a brief moment, the woman's face fell, but she quickly covered up her disappointment with another of her brilliant grins. Bringing her arms together to push out her chest, she leaned forward and beckoned him closer.

"Won't you try just one?" she whispered. Her lips were so close to him that they tickled his ear. "I promise that you won't be disappointed. Everyone likes my treats."

"I think we will stop by on our way back," Deylan interjected.

The unexpected response startled the two, causing the young woman to pop up and move away from Heru. He found himself grateful to his friend for extracting him from that awkward conversation. A pout formed on her lips, but Deylan motioned for Heru to follow him. The silver-haired man flashed the young woman one of his smiles and touched the rim of his hat in respect before hurrying Heru along.

They put several booths between themselves and the enthusiastic candy vendor before Heru found his voice.

"Thanks," he grumbled. "That's not a situation I'm used to being in."

"No problem," Deylan replied airily. "I'll consider it as payment in exchange for my lunch."

Brows knitting, Heru held his tongue as they continued on. The number of merchant stalls began to thin as they moved further into the town and away from the coast. The permanent establishments stood two and three stories tall. Many were finely decorated with balconies covered in bright orange and white flowers or colored ribbons dangling down. The façades of many were made of brick, but a good number also appeared to be made of some sort of dark clay. Their windows stood brightly lit, illuminating their wares and beckoning people in off the streets. The shops carried both exquisite and exotic fashions.

At one point, Deylan remarked, "Why, these shops rival even Alocar's fashion."

Unsure of the nations outside of Xan, Heru could only mumble a non-response as they passed a large window housing elaborate gowns dyed in rich colors. In Xan, they dressed more humbly, more practically. The women wore silks and simple dresses, the silks making up voluminous pants and modest tops. Their clothes fit their figures and were not embellished with petticoats and underskirts. The extravagant gowns beckoning from the windows struck him as impractical and almost intimidating with their strings and ribbons cinching everything together.

They didn't have to travel far before they heard a couple of familiar voices up ahead. Having wandered down one of the main roads by chance, the two spied a few of the *Fury*'s crew ambling in down the street. Their voices carried as they leered at the local women, making lewd comments. For their part, the women didn't appear too bothered by the pirates' banter. One pulled a fan from her bodice and fanned it, a coy smile playing on her lips as she bat her lashes. Her friend clutched her arm with a giggle and the two carried on, not responding to any further comments from the men – who, to their credit, didn't seem to care that the women moved on.

The small group carried on at their leisurely pace, commenting on every woman that crossed their path. To Heru, it almost seemed like they had a friendly relationship with the people of Last Call. Growing up, the stories always painted them as an unsavory bunch, constantly getting drunk or into fights and living as outcasts of society. The juxtaposition between what he'd always been told about pirates and what he saw left him confused.

He glanced over at Deylan. Though he didn't consider his silver-haired companion to be one of the sea-faring folk, Deylan had spent a considerable amount of time amongst them, blending in with them and their kind. Heru couldn't help but wonder if a part of the pirate life seeped into Deylan's personality.

"There it is," Deylan said, nudging Heru with his elbow.

Blinking in confusion, Heru nearly stopped in the middle of the street. Checking his surroundings, he noticed that the men they shadowed turned into a pristine store in the middle of the street. A wooden sign with an anchor painted on it announced the tavern from so far away. A golden flourish around the tavern's name reminded Heru of the Feathered Plume. This must be where the wealthy went – yet Kayna's crew also seemed to frequent it with no issue. Again, another question that he didn't know if it was worth worrying about to answer.

The front of the tavern was indeed immaculate. Just like the Feathered Plume, all traces of grime and wear from the salty sea air could not be found. The exterior, though varying shades of natural brown and occasional lacquer, had the same beauty it must have held when the doors first opened. The name "Anchor" had been engraved into the wood and painted over with an indigo dye in a fine script.

"Strange," Deylan mused. "I would've thought they'd go for a more dilapidated appearance."

"The almost handwritten look confused me too. With a name like Anchor, I thought it'd be more like the Scourge's personal tavern."

"This is almost too nice for our kind. It matches the coastal market, however." After a pause, Deylan turned to Heru, his hand resting on the doorknob. "Shall we?"

The inside of the Anchor hosted a mixture of rough and rowdy pirates from Kayna's crew and the locals. The people of Last Call kept themselves rather fashionably dressed, though a good number of them spoke just as crudely as the pirates. Here, the laughter flowed just as freely as the mead and ale. Barmaids dressed in stylish yet alluring dresses, their breasts pushed up as their corsets were cinched up especially tight rushing about with both tankards and plates of food.

The room was almost completely packed as everyone enjoyed their afternoon meal. A few tables sat open amid the otherwise packed room. Despite the chaos, everything moved smoothly and with an efficiency that impressed Heru. There was almost a militaristic quality to the order. Tankards weren't left empty for long and empty plates didn't clutter the tables. In the corner, an elderly woman, her braided grey hair tied loosely down her back, sang an aria. Her powerful soprano rang throughout the room. It didn't overwhelm the general conversation – people still spoke freely without needing to raise their voice, but it still sounded over the din so others could enjoy her music.

Nudging Deylan with his elbow, Heru pointed to an empty table close to the singer as she finished up her song. Without waiting for a response, he wended his way through the tables and bodies to take a seat facing the door. Having the window a few tables behind him at his back left Heru feeling exposed, but he bit down his discomfort and rested his blades against the side of his chair. No sooner did Deylan join him did a young woman with thick curly hair flounce over to greet them.

"Welcome to the Anchor." The alto of her voice bounced with every word. The implicit pride she felt for herself not only expressed itself with her greeting, but also in the sparkle of her eye. "What can I get you?" Her gaze roved over the two of them, drinking them in. "You all are new here."

It wasn't a question.

Removing his wide-brimmed hat and placing it on the chair next to him, Deylan gave her a little wink. The exaggerated movement reminded Heru that everyone he'd met on his journey thus far was not who he expected them to be. Returning his attention to the barmaid, he tried to put on what he believed to be a pleasant smile. However, it didn't feel right and he was sure he looked more bemused.

The barmaid didn't seem bothered.

"You're so observant," Deylan replied, his tone light and ready for banter. "What are the favorites here?"

As the barmaid lit up, prepared for a spirited exchange, Heru couldn't help but marvel at the ease of their interaction. Growing up, the few he considered to be friends never joked so easily. They'd been focused on earning the title of Qu'ari Elite and mastering the art of using two blades in combat. At twenty-one, had he missed out on forming proper relationships with others? Is this how others communicated, or were Deylan and people like this barmaid an anomaly?

"We have a whitefish with a nice sauce and tomatoes, or my personal favorite – a long-grain rice dish with local spices and a nice slice of lamb. Both are very delicious, I just prefer the lamb. We have blackberry or apple honey mead, as well as a nice blonde ale if mead doesn't work for you."

The barmaid crossed her arms, almost unconsciously, and pushed her chest up. She shifted on her feet, jutting her hip out as she glanced from one to the other. Heru couldn't help but wonder what went on in her head as she observed them so keenly. Clearly, she was scrutinizing them, but for what?

"I'll take the fish and an apple honey mead," Deylan said after a moment's thought.

Her attention shifted to Heru. He almost swore that she winked at him as she shifted her weight once more.

"I'll take the lamb and blonde ale," Heru said at last. "Do you have honeycakes as well, or are they only available at the port?"

"Absolutely." Her voice pitched up as though she were excited to tell them more about their options. "We also have a nice glaze and fresh strawberries that add as a topping. Would you like that?"

It sounded divine.

Heru nodded his head, the forced smile on his face becoming more natural as he thought about enjoying the rare treats from his childhood without having to stop by the very forward woman's merchant stall once more. There was something about her playful aggression that was off-putting to him in a way that the usual advances of a barmaid did not.

"I'd love one as well," Deylan said.

"Very well," the barmaid said with a soft clap of her hands. "One fish, one lamb, one apple honey, one blonde ale, and two honeycakes. Who knows, maybe you'll have room for some dessert after."

Once again, the barmaid winked at the two before spinning on her heel. Her skirts fanned out momentarily before her hips became center-stage and attracted the attention of the Anchor's patrons with each step. Heru found it difficult to not stare at her retreating form.

"I see she intrigues you," Deylan said. His brows wiggled in a bemused way as he held Heru's gaze. "I don't think I've seen a woman who has caught your attention like that before."

"It's not something to make a big deal about," Heru mumbled. He felt his face flush and hoped that the red creeping over it was too noticeable. The sensation made him uncomfortable.

A heavy thump sounded next to them.

"Well damn," a weathered man said, slapping his hand loudly on the smooth lacquered table.

Heru recognized the man as one of the deck hands on the *Fury* named Zavian. His heavily tanned skin and clean-shaven head caused him to stand out amongst the rest of Kayna's crew. Although, seeing him with a shirt on for the first time made the pirate appear out of place.

"We should have known that Delli would prefer a younger partner."

Behind Zavian, a few others voiced their agreement over the general conversation and powerful vocals of the elderly woman. Heru couldn't help but notice the hungry expression in the man's eyes. Spending most of time on a ship with a group of men must really take a toll on them.

"She was just being polite," Heru muttered.

"Oh, come now," Zavian pressed. "Before your meal is done, she will make her move. Delli isn't shy about her wants."

"Give him some space," Deylan said, his amber eyes narrowed slightly, eliminating the usual twinkle that played behind them. "He doesn't think of women like we do. He's new to this life."

Zavian and his table gave a laugh, but left the two alone. Heru watched the man return to his table. He couldn't help but be on guard despite the man's retreating form. Something about the casual aggression set his hackles on edge.

"Are they all like this?" Heru asked.

A piercing note from the soloist broke through the Anchor's din, earning her a resounding round of applause from almost every table. Heru noted how Deylan joined in, not quite paying attention to her musical gifts.

"More or less," he replied with a shrug. "Some are better, some worse. It all depends who you happen to join."

The answer didn't sit well with Heru.

"What about you?" the Xanan asked.

"What about me?" Deylan replied. His tone carried a hint of steel, as though he dared Heru to challenge him further.

"I've seen you enjoy the company of a few women. Is she one you'd bed?"

"Absolutely." There was no room for argument. There was no shame. "Over the years, I've learned how to take advantage of situations and turn them into my favor. I'm not always proud of what I do, but I do it to survive."

The soloist finished another song to a round of polite applause. Deylan and Heru sat in awkward silence, watching each other. Deylan proved to be one to never shy away from his feelings. Heru remembered when the two of them sat in the shade of the cloth out of the harsh sun on the *Fury*. Deylan had no qualms about resting against the Xanan when others would consider that a sign of weakness. Heru wondered if he insulted the man by implying, he was too impulsive.

His thoughts were interrupted by the delicious smell of lamb and spices as Delli slid their plates in front of them with a cheeky grin. Heru's mouth watered as he stared at the first proper meal he'd had in over a week. All of the training and the lack of substance left his body lean and demanding nutrition. Even Deylan's fish smelled amazing.

"Here you are," she said with a wink. "I'll be right back with your drinks. If you need anything else, ask for Delli."

And with that, she sauntered off with a swish of her hips, leaving the two men to watch her retreating figure back into the kitchen.

XXIV

I T WAS HARD NOT TO STARE at Delli as she made her way to the kitchen. She knew exactly how to work her full hips, and knew that if she did it right, she would find herself with a little something extra after each patron left. Deylan sometimes wished he had it so easy, but he knew that if he wanted that little something extra, he had to take the next step. Watching Heru follow the barmaid so intently filled the silver-haired man with a warm feeling of contentment. He'd seen the shadows that threatened to overwhelm the young Xanan. Deylan wished for Heru to find peace.

Tucking into his fish, Deylan nearly slammed the table – the taste was phenomenal. The explosion of lemon, butter, rosemary, and sage in combination with the flakiness of the fish and the garlic and paprika infused rice filled his mouth with the best flavors he'd ever experienced. He ate greedily and didn't even notice when Delli returned with his flagon of mead. It wasn't long before his spoon scraped against the bottom of the plate in one spot.

"By the gods," Heru breathed. "Did you just not eat on the ship?"

Looking up from his plate, Deylan realized that he'd completely blocked out the world as he ate. The realization that he somehow managed to ignore all of his surroundings, something he'd never done before, brought an uneasy feeling to his stomach. His pulse quickened and Deylan found himself scanning the tavern, a practice he'd been doing for the last five years.

"I can't believe I just blocked everything out," Deylan muttered. Giving himself an internal shake, Deylan managed to push away the discomfort that began creeping in. "This is the best thing I've ever eaten." Pointing to Heru's partially eaten bit of lamb, he asked, "How is yours?"

Pushing a chunk of lamb around on his plate, Heru flashed a wan smile. "It reminds me of my mother's."

The revelation stunned Deylan. Other than their first few conversations, the two had kept their lives relatively personal and gave only cursory information. He observed a cloud pass over the Xanan's face, darkening his features, yet it also gave him a vulnerable quality that was so foreign to the silver-haired man.

"She used to make lamb kebabs or lamb and barbari bread when father came home. It wasn't often, but they were my favorite meals growing up."

It was hard to tell whether he should break Heru's train of thought or if he should stay silent. Deylan found himself reaching for his flagon and taking a long draught of the apple honey mead. The drink washed away the lightness of his fish and filled his mouth with an unexpected sweetness.

Heru reached for his own tankard and took a sip of the ale. If he liked it, his face didn't show it. The cloud of emotion still hovered over him.

"He used to come home more often when I was younger. After my sister Arezou was born, he stopped visiting as much."

Unsure what to say, Deylan took another small sip of his mead. "Maybe his arrival was disrupting your people?" Deylan offered.

His knowledge of Xan's politics wasn't the best, but he did now the generalities. Formed of six separate clans, the Great Heart was the epicenter of the nation. The Great Heart led the other groups, making the main decisions for the benefit of the nation. Other decisions were decided by vote from the six chiefs. As son of the previous Great Heart, Heru's family would be under tight scrutiny and any disruptions would be highly looked-down upon. The pressure to maintain the image of the Great Heart and juggling the shame of having him abandon their family would be immense.

"After all, if the leader of a nation runs off to chase a dream, how would the other chiefs handle the change? Even if the new Great Heart is a good man, I can't imagine that the arrival of his predecessor would go unnoticed by those who respected him. The Great Heart may have asked him not to return."

The thought upset Deylan. He couldn't even imagine what Heru felt upon hearing those words.

"I don't care!"

The outburst caught Deylan off-guard. Such raw emotion from the young Xanan seemed out of character. At least he didn't strike Deylan.

"He could come home and live a quiet life with us. My Trials were a disgrace. I was the only one without... without someone to guide me." Heru's voice trailed off and the two sat in silence for a bit.

After a minute or two, Deylan realized that the soloist had finished her performance and walked off a while ago.

Hopefully nobody heard that, he said to himself. *Vulnerability like this will be to his disadvantage on the ship – and word will definitely get back to his father, if that man is his father. That could lead to complications of their own. Gods, this is getting more complicated.*

"I'm... I'm..."

Heru struggled to get the words out. Likely, this was one of the rare times he actually attempted to apologize. He didn't even apologize for his attack at their very first meeting.

"No need," Deylan said with the wave of his hand. "I would be nervous if I were about to meet the man who ruined my childhood too."

Downing the rest of his flagon, Deylan finished off the last bites of his meal. He noticed Heru's shoulders relax and the cloud finally leave his face. The Xanan looked down at his plate and began eating with a renewed vigor. In between bites, he took long draughts of his ale until he too had an empty tankard before him.

As if sensing their empty plates and mugs, Delli sidled up to their table and laid two small, white porcelain plates. In the center of the plates were two honeycakes each. A drizzle of red glaze and small chunks of strawberries topped the dessert.

Looking up at Heru, he saw the Xanan staring fondly at the treat. A childish twinkle flashed in his eye that could almost have been mistaken for a tear if Deylan hadn't noticed the corners of Heru's mouth turn up as well. The expression was fleeting, only there for the briefest of moments, but Deylan caught it. It warmed his heart to see his friend so vulnerable.

"How was your meal?" Delli asked. She placed her hand on Heru's shoulder, causing his head to snap up and meet her gaze. "I hope everything tasted delicious."

The bounce that usually filled her words vanished and was replaced by an uncharacteristic softness. Deylan watched as she focused her attention on Heru. She hovered over the Xanan with a sisterly affection – her hand gently rubbing his shoulder. The two shared a look that spanned over several heartbeats, oblivious to the rest of the world. Deylan thought he saw a flash of longing cross Heru's face.

"Very good," Heru muttered, not breaking his gaze. His voice caught in his throat, giving it a hoarse quality Deylan hadn't heard before. "Reminded me of my mother's."

"I'm glad to hear that," Delli replied. "It's an honor to be considered as good as mom's. I'll let our cooks know." Turning to Deylan, Delli fixed him with an expression that asked. "Well?"

"Same," Deylan replied in a muted tone. "I've never had anything so delicious. I can't wait to try these." He motioned to the honeycakes in front of him. "Might I have another mead? One for me and one for my friend?"

"Absolutely." Giving Heru's shoulder a squeeze, Delli fixed him with a gentle smile and a wink, this one playful in a way that didn't come off as expecting banter. This one showed her spirit as good-natured. "Apple honey goes well with these. I'll be right back."

When Delli was beyond earshot, Heru finally spoke.

"She reminds me of my sister. It's been a long time since I've seen Bermet."

"She's your big sister, right?"

Heru nodded. "She could have been an elite like me. I wish she'd never left."

A lump formed in Deylan's throat. *Is she dead?*

Struggling to say anything, Deylan took a bite of the honey-cake. A few strawberry bits rested on this piece, adding a sweetness that didn't overpower the cake. He couldn't' respond. This moment would be for Heru to get out whatever he needed to say at his own pace. Without ignoring the Xanan, Deylan continued to nibble on his dessert.

The mead arrived to a silent table. Delli rubbed Heru's back without saying a word before walking off to continue serving her patrons. Heru didn't say a word. He himself was lost in his own memories and dessert.

Is he ready to meet his father? Deylan wondered.

⟋⟋⟋

An uncomfortable tingling around Heru's eyes, coupled with his face warming, brought back a familiar and unwanted memory. The same hollow pit he'd felt the first time he lost Bermet settled into his stomach. Thinking about her right now brought back all of the pain he'd originally felt. He'd spent the last few years purposefully trying to forget his sister. It was easier that way.

Before taking a bite of his cake, Heru took a sip of the apple honey mead. Deylan had been right. It was wonderful.

Maybe I'll switch from ale to mead after all. Damn.

He took another sip, this time a bigger one. The ale had been stronger, but it wouldn't be hard to find himself drunk after a couple of these.

Time for the cake.

His fork went through the soft pastry with ease. They weren't dense like some cakes, letting him know that if the honey and strawberries were added correctly, it would be a masterpiece of a dish. Wiping a little of the glaze that rimmed the plate and scooping a few strawberry pieces on top, Heru took his first bite.

"Damn, that's good," he muttered.

Just like home.

"It's fantastic," Deylan agreed softly.

Though he didn't look up, Heru felt a jolt of panic as he realized that he'd lost himself in his own thoughts yet again. Just as Deylan had disappeared into his own plate earlier, Heru experienced the same. It was deeply unsettling how easily both of them lost track of their surroundings.

The two finished their dessert in quiet contemplation. By now, the chatter of the full tavern became muted, Heru having blocked out the extraneous noise and only listening for raised voices or other signs of trouble. Out of habit, Heru tapped the hilt of his scimitar and battleaxe. The familiar touch of the worn leather of his weapons brought him comfort. For now, he would push Bermet to the back of his mind. He would deal with that another time.

XXV

BELLIES NOW FULL and their heads slightly fuzzy from their drinks, Heru and Deylan exited the Anchor. The abrupt switch from quiet after the loud and crowded tavern proved to be a welcome change. It almost felt stifling – but the sudden appearance of a small group of people walking through the streets broke the mood, returning everything back to normal.

As they left, Delli approached them once more. She held Heru's gaze as she thanked them for their visit and wished them well. As she turned to Deylan, she added that she hoped it wouldn't be long before their next visit. Her flirtatious demeanor returned as she spoke with Deylan, only to be replaced with the twinkle of lust in her eye as she grabbed Heru's hand and gave it a squeeze.

Outside, the midday sun hung high in the sky as clouds still obscured it. The fog had disappeared by now, but the air still retained the cool, an almost-drizzle-like feeling despite the halo from the sun against the clouds.

"We should probably start heading back to the ship," Deylan said.

Glancing over at Heru, the Xanan remained pensive, but not dejected. Deylan wondered if the Xanan's mood would improve after having a talk with his father. It carried the potential to be a complete disaster. Deylan almost hoped the two wouldn't find time to catch up, although the likelihood of that happening was next to none.

"Do we have time to stop at the market? I might want to pick up a few things to keep in the galley. I'm not going to starve myself until our next stop."

A small snort escaped Deylan. The joke most certainly was unintentional, but after such a long trip and the uncertainty of the future, he couldn't help but agree. The world beyond the Eastern Isles was largely unknown. Only the most seasoned seafarers ventured out into those open waters. None of the crews he'd joined in the last five years went anywhere near the Eastern Isles. Most just stayed to the small islands a few days away from the Bone Coast or patrolled the waters up and down the coastal shores of Corinth – just like they didn't go much further past the Isles of Corin on the western coasts.

There were some places you just didn't go – not even Jyalla, the pirate leader who dared try and defy the Scourge.

"That's a great idea," he replied. "I haven't lost this much weight before, and when going into the unknown it's probably best to make sure we're getting enough to eat, especially while we continue training. I don't know how much we'll get that can go bad over a long trip."

"We better buy dried meat and fruit then. That soup will last forever and I assume we'll catch fish as well."

"First, let's look for an apothecary. You never know what they have that we may need. There might be some salves we need to treat wounds or poisons we've never seen in Corinth." Deylan suggested.

With a nod, Heru stood on his tiptoes to look over Deylan and at the street behind. Spinning around, Deylan noted that fewer shops appeared to specialize in clothing. At that moment, he noticed a few people entering and exiting the shops. They didn't appear to be searching for an outfit for the next big event at the baron's estate – just everyday locals enjoying a quiet day of shopping. With a flick of his head, Deylan motioned for the Xanan to follow him.

Further into Last Call the atmosphere shifted. Away from the wooden stalls with simple cotton cloths thrown over for shade that carried mouth-watering food and fruit as beautiful as jewels and the prominent shops carrying elegant gowns and dapper suits for men, the storefronts became more muted. The buildings were still massive with delicate carvings into the exterior and bouquets of flowers lining the windows, but their windows were now smaller and the lights did not shine quite as bright.

Shops filled to the brim with thick tomes and simple leatherbound books or meticulously crafted pocket watches, hand scopes, and compasses became a little more frequent. Occasionally, they spied a building with larger windows and gowns that made the ones displayed in the port appear plain. These had little crystals sewn in, delicate white lace, and fabrics so vibrant that even the bejeweled hummingbirds appeared muted.

The two took their time wandering through the streets. At one point, they even found a sweet shop and picked up a small bag of sweets each.

"Better than dealing with that forward woman again," Heru had said as they walked out of the shop, bags of brightly wrapped candies in hand.

Deylan couldn't help but agree. When merchants pushed too hard to sell their wares, he always wondered if there was a reason for the added effort.

A worn wooden sign at the end of the road caught Deylan's attention.

Odd, Deylan noted. *This is out of place amongst the opulence surrounding it.*

The faded paint on the sign, not engraved and embellished like nearly every other shop, stood out like a stray dog amongst the king's hounds. As they got closer, Deylan noticed that the image was of a mortar and pestle.

"Looks like this is it," he said, pointing the sign out to Heru.

As they neared the shop, Deylan felt a blow to the back of his head. White stars flashed before his eyes and he staggered forward, almost falling to the ground. As his knees buckled, he heard Heru calling out nearby.

///

The bag of candies flew out of Deylan's grasp and landed on the cobbles with a muffled thump. Heru threw out his hand to help stabilize his companion and keep him on his feet. As he turned to help his friend, Heru saw the Nem Pahlan captain, Dhruvasht, standing behind Deylan, his hand raised and poised to strike him once more.

"What in the seven hells?" Heru asked, his hand twitching for his blades. He had to fight the urge to grab them until he felt confident that Deylan could remain on his feet.

"Stand aside," the Nem Pahlan snarled. "I have business with this jhafti."

"For the last time," Deylan gasped, straightening up and holding his head. "Don't call me jhafti."

Dhruvasht spat at him. "You mainlanders are so sensitive. Sensitive and traitors."

Deylan stepped forward, but Heru threw out his arm and stopped him. Heru glowered at the former captain who gnashed his teeth. His hair and normally pristine clothes were disheveled, adding to his deranged appearance.

The former captain listed to the right the tiniest bit before swaying back to the left in an effort to regain his balance. Taking advantage of the pause during the attack, the Xanan scrutinized the Nem Pahlan. Though he swayed in place, his eyes didn't appear to be glassy, indicating that he hadn't had too much to drink. Dhruvasht had had at least one though. There was a reason he suddenly acted so bold. The captain gnashed his teeth and glowered at Deylan. To Heru's surprise, Deylan stood firm despite being struck from behind without warning. The silver-haired man's eyes glinted, his hands resting by his side.

"I should have dealt with you after you killed my nephew," Dhruvasht spat.

An unfamiliar feeling formed in Heru's chest, tightening and sending his heart racing. The hair on his arms stood on end – the strange sensation left Heru unnerved. Glancing over at Deylan, Heru noted the confusion that crossed over his face.

"Bharam?" Deylan's incredulity raised the pitch of his question higher than usual.

"The coward?" Heru asked at the same time.

A range of emotions flashed across Deylan's face – confusion, surprise, dismay, and then confusion once more, all in the span of a heartbeat. His mouth opened as if he were going to speak, but he closed it quickly and remained quiet.

A vein throbbed on the right side of Dhruvasht's jaw at their exclamations. Heru almost swore he heard a low growl come from the man. The Nem Pahlan's fists clenched, but he did not move forward, his eyes darting from Deylan to Heru and back.

He's afraid, Heru realized. *A coward like his kin.*

Taking a step back and crossing his arms, Heru made sure he held the former captain's gaze before speaking. "Two on one is not a fair fight. Handle it like men."

Deylan's head swiveled in Heru's direction, incredulity written all over his face. The expression was mirrored by the Nem Pahlan as well. A moment later, a feral grin spread over the captain's face. He began cracking his knuckles as he stared Deylan down. To his credit, Deylan maintained his stance, eyes locked onto Dhruvasht and his hands resting by his side.

Sparing one more glance towards Heru, the former captain of the *Death's Rose* launched himself at Deylan. His speed impressed the Xanan. The Nem Pahlan's build wasn't much to boast about, but Dhruvasht moved with an agility that belied his form.

However, he wasn't nearly as nimble as Deylan.

Just before Dhruvasht's hands could grasp Deylan, he stepped out of the way, landing a knee to Dhruvasht's stomach as inertia continued to propel the Nem Pahlan's body forward. A bit of spittle flew from his mouth as Dhruvasht gasped for breath, his arms grabbing at his stomach. Deylan swiftly followed up his strike with a hammer fist to the base of Dhruvasht's head. The Nem Pahlan dropped to his knees, holding his stomach and gasping for air. His head teetered forward from the force of the blow to his head.

Quick as a snake, Deylan's arm wrapped around Dhruvasht's throat, seizing the front of the wrinkled coat, the other hand grabbed a handful of dark hair. Heru continued to watch the spectacle, a bemused expression on his face. Aboard the *Fury*, Heru learned Deylan's fighting style, but seeing the silver-haired man in action impressed the Xanan.

Whispering something into Dhruvasht's ear, Deylan released the clump of hair he'd been holding tightly and grabbed the other side of the captain's coat, giving the Nem Pahlan's heavier body a shake. Possibly to emphasize whatever message he had for the man.

Dhruvasht's mouth hung opening, still gasping for breath against the forearm that pressed on his throat. His eyes raged like a madman's, which, combined with his disheveled appearance made him look more deranged than he had when they first laid eyes on him. Gradually, Deylan removed the pressure against the Nem Pahlan's neck and the man's face morphed into a snarl.

Finally, with a shove, Deylan pushed the former captain away. Dhruvasht's caught himself with his hands on the smooth cobbles. This time, Heru definitely heard a growl escape the man.

"You'll regret that," Dhruvasht spat.

Faster than Heru could react, Deylan's leg slammed into the Nem Pahlan's head, knocking the man out and leaving him sprawled out on the road. Turning to face Heru, Deylan smoothed down the back of his tunic, his hands moving over his backside several times. He leaned over and rummaged through the fallen man's coat, pulling out a tattered piece of parchment with a self-satisfied grin. Stashing the paper into his waistband, the mischievous twinkle that usually sparkled in Deylan's eye returned once again.

"Are you ready?"

The question came out as casually as though Deylan asked him whether he wanted a drink. His head spun to look at the unconscious man on the ground once more. Without waiting for an answer, Deylan began making his way to the port, and ultimately the ship.

"Are you going to talk about what you grabbed from this cur?" Heru asked.

"All in good time," Deylan replied with a wave of his hand.

Picking up the bag of candies with a snort, Heru spared one last glance at the fallen man before following in Deylan's step – his respect for the silver-haired man growing.

XXVI

THE SUN HAD NOT BROKEN THROUGH the grey clouds overhead despite the chill of impending rain having disappeared. The now muggy atmosphere brought an uncomfortable sticky sheen to Heru's flesh. His clothes clung to his body and he couldn't wait to leave the island. The weather left him missing the dry heat of Xan. A few steps ahead of him, Deylan moved briskly in silence. He didn't stop to check out any of the merchant stalls like they had planned over lunch. Instead, he moved with purpose towards the still docked ship. The unusual quiet concerned the Xanan and he wondered if the attack against him had shaken his confidence.

"Did you still want anything?" Heru asked.

As Deylan turned around, Heru motioned towards the wooden stalls where merchants continued to sell their wares to those wandering around the port. He watched as Deylan's gaze roved over the nearby booths. Many sold fruit, breads, or dried meats. A look of longing flitted across the silver-haired man's face, but he shook his head.

"I want to get back to the galley and rest," he said softly.

With a nod, Heru pointed back to the stalls. "I'll get some food for the both of us. Go inside and get yourself checked out. Looks like he hit you pretty hard."

As if remembering his injury, Deylan rubbed the back of his head, his eyes fixed on something within that Heru couldn't see. Without a word, the silver-haired man spun on his feet and continued trudging back towards the plank to climb aboard *Graak's Fury* once more.

Watching his friend depart in such a dejected manner left the Xanan with an unfamiliar feeling he couldn't quite place. Moments before, he marveled at the skillful way Deylan had handled his attacker. Now, it felt like the time his little sister, Arezou, asked him why their father was never around – a mixture of sorrow and disappointment that settled heavily into his stomach and refused to go away easily.

Heru found himself wanting to do something nice for his friend. Glancing over his shoulder, he took in the crowded market just off the port. With a sigh, Heru turned and headed towards the vendors. It wouldn't kill him to engage in a little light conversation if it helped both himself and Deylan have a more enjoyable journey at sea. The two bags of candy rested lightly against his hip next to his woefully empty coin pouch.

It was worth it, however.

The sheer variety of food available overwhelmed Heru. He wanted to buy food that wouldn't go bad quickly, yet he knew that his body would want fruit or some meat to supplement the meager soup they'd no doubt be eating for breakfast for the majority of the trip. The thought of slurping down the thin liquid with a few shavings of carrot and onion left him feeling hungry despite the hearty meal he'd just eaten. No, Heru would do whatever he could to ensure he didn't consume the insufferable broth longer than he needed to.

The first merchant Heru approached had a wide array of fruit sitting on his booth table. Small pockets in the display showed where people already picked through his wares, but there was still plenty available. Picking up three mangoes, Heru paused as he realized that he had no way to carry the produce back to the ship.

Seeing that his customer faced some internal struggle, the merchant, a well-fed woman with dark curly hair tied up in a high bun, addressed him. "What's wrong, my dear? Surely, you won't find better fruit elsewhere. I know others sell similar fruits, but mine are touted as the sweetest."

Still staring at the mangoes in his hand, Heru held them up as if they could solve his problem. "I don't have a way to carry them," he muttered. "I wanted to get some for my friend as well."

"Not a problem," she said, with a grin. Reaching under the table in her booth, the merchant pulled out a large chunk of dark and dirty cloth, waving it triumphantly in front of him. "If you buy enough, I will give you this bag to carry everything in."

Handing over the mangoes to the woman, Heru continued to browse the produce. With a little disappointment, he put down several of the softer ones in exchange for some firmer ones that would last longer while out at sea. To his delight, they were all pleasantly heavy, letting him know that there was a lot of sugar inside and would be sweet. After picking out a little over a dozen mangoes, Heru moved onto cherries and peaches. Just like the mangoes, he chose a variety of soft and firm peaches for the two of them. The cherries he picked by the handful, throwing the blood and ruby red fruits into the bag that the merchant woman offered him. Lastly, he picked out five coconuts. Not only would their meat be a delicious treat, but after a long day of training on deck under the scorching sun, the milk would be most refreshing.

He gave the woman a mixed handful of silver and copper coins with a couple of gold ones thrown in from the small leather pouch at his hip. After grabbing the bulging bag from the merchant woman with a word of thanks, Heru continued on through the market in search of another stall.

The closest merchant booths carried gold and silver jewelry as well as some household trinkets like mirrors, hair clips, and chalices. After five booths or so, Heru found what he was looking for. Loaves of bread, both circular and long braided loaves begged him to buy them. Some had herbs baked in while others were topped with cheese baked on them. A small corner section of the booth carried savory buns with meat baked inside. Heru's mouth watered looking at everything.

Resting his hand on his nearly empty coin pouch, Heru debated whether he could afford anything or if he should just move on to the dried meat. Glancing over at the meat buns once more, Heru resigned himself to a very frugal trip back home once he completed his business with his father.

The merchant, an older man with thinning white hair on the sides of his head, brightened up and flashed Heru a toothy smile as he approached – well, toothy enough considering several were missing. The man reminded Heru of the few beggars he encountered back home outside of FaTinh, his home town. Tanned leathery skin hung loosely on the man's slim frame, jiggling with each movement.

"Hello, good sir," the man greeted. His voice wobbled with each word. "What can ol' Henrei do for you?"

"I am looking for something to take on my voyage for me and my friend," Heru said.

He debated on whether to mention that he was heading out to Tan'quao or if he should pretend that he would be returning to the Bone Coast. To his knowledge, not many made it out to Last Call, but even fewer went out further east. He wondered if the man would give him a good price if Heru told the truth, or if the man would try and overcharge.

"I see you have a pretty sizeable bag of fruit," Henrei noted. "Looks like you're going on quite the journey. Might you be heading out east to the unknown lands?"

Again, Heru balked and considered lying, but something told him to tell the man the truth.

"Um...yes. We're going further east. This is my first trip at sea, and I don't know what I will need."

Feeling rather childish, Heru admired the different breads in front of him so he wouldn't have to face the man. A couple braids with what looked like rosemary baked in caught his attention, as did a large circular loaf and a smaller, long dark brown one.

"How much would these be?" he asked, pointing to the loaves he'd just been admiring. "And what is this dark one made out of? Oh, and some of those meat buns? How much for those too?"

The old man looked down at the bread Heru pointed out. His eyes darted from piece to piece.

"This dark one here is a honey wheat with molasses baked in. It's much softer than it looks, and quite delicious. As for the ones you asked about, I ask for three silver."

A heavy price, but not outrageous for so much. Digging into his ever-dwindling purse, Heru pulled out three silver coins and placed them into the man's weathered hand. Quicker than Heru would've thought possible, the man made the coins vanish. Next, the man began pulling the breads from his display and handing them to Heru one by one.

Four rosemary braids, the large circular bread, three honey wheat, and eight meat buns. The additional honey wheats were a pleasant surprise to Heru. He didn't expect the man to be so generous.

"Thank you," he muttered to the man. Slipping the final loaf into the now overflowing cloth bag, Heru dipped his head in a semi-bow to the elderly merchant.

"My pleasure, my boy," Henrei replied. "You take care of yourself. The eastern waters are no place for a young lad like yourself. Especially if you're inexperienced. There are rough waters out there – Graak doesn't look favorably upon those who intrude in his realm. You keep your thoughts right and you'll be all right."

Standing at a loss for words, Heru shifted on his feet before slinging the bag over his shoulder. The weight of its contents pulled down on him. Heru wondered briefly if the thin cloth would hold long enough for him to return to the ship. He wanted one more stop, but his time at Last Call was nearing an end.

"Are you looking for anything else?" Henrei asked.

"Meat."

Giving Heru a knowing look, Henrei said, "Wait right here," before slipping out from his stall and wandering off into the market.

Heru waited for the man to return. To pass the time, Heru leaned against the wooden booth and took in the market. People still meandered about – mostly locals based on how they dressed, but there were still some of the seafaring folk mixed in. He hadn't noticed it earlier, but there was one other ship tied to the dock.

"*Thuul's Redemption*," he murmured. "Wonder if anyone's named a ship after their sister?"

Unbidden, a memory from his childhood flashed before him.

During one of his father's last visits, the former Great Heart pulled seven-year-old Heru aside with Bermet. Their mother worked in the kitchen, making their favorite dessert, honeycakes with fresh berries. The warm evening air blew through the open windows. The cicadas chirped, their song floating on the summer breeze.

"I've talked to Pram and he's going to let you begin your Elite training on your ninth year," Len told Heru. "Normally the training begins after your Trials, but he's doing this as a favor to me."

Heru looked up at his father with big brown eyes. The innocence of youth and the baby fat on his face did not mark him as one destined to be a Qu'ari elite. Heru cocked his head like one of the stray dogs when they did not understand.

"Father," Bermet interjected. "Heru hasn't even begun basic training. They will hurt him if he practices with the Elite."

Their father's eyes flashed dangerously and his mouth tightened to a thin line. Heru had never seen his father look like that before and it scared him.

"You will hold your tongue," Len hissed to Bermet. "My son will not be kept from his destiny. I have spoken to the shaman and she told me that Heru will one day surpass even me."

"But Father," Bermet implored.

"Quiet!" Len snapped. "Freyna will protect him, just as she protects you and your mother."

Bermet opened her mouth to protest once again, but Len fixed her with a glare.

"You will not question my decision anymore."

Without another word, Len got up and left the two sitting in stunned silence. Heru glanced from his sister to his father and back, his mouth opened in a small O of confusion.

"I don't want to be an Elite," he muttered after his father moved out of hearing distance.

Bermet's arm snaked around his shoulder, pulling him closer. A tear rolled down his cheek as his father disappeared into his room. In the kitchen, their mother continued to bake in rigid silence. Slowly, gently, Bermet's fingers moved through his hair, stroking his face and tussling his hair in a motherly fashion.

"Don't worry, aziz," she whispered.

Heru loved how she called him dear just like his mother. Though she was only three years older than him, Bermet acted older beyond her years.

Pulling him in even tighter, Bermet planted a tender kiss on the top of his head.

"I will watch over you." Her words were so faint, almost imperceptible. "You will be greater than Father. Freyna will bless you in ways Father can only dream. The Ayr is strong in ways most cannot understand. Soon, you will earn the blessing of Freyna and her brothers."

～～

"Thank you for waiting."

Henrei's voice startled Heru from his memories. The elderly man reappeared behind his stall with a thin package wrapped in brown cloth. Spinning around, Heru's mouth dropped at the sight of Henrei. The images of his father and sister were so vivid. He could actually feel Bermet's arm on his shoulders even now – just as the kiss on his head lingered. Her words still echoed in his ears. They had just been there.

"I know someone," Henrei continued, not noticing Heru's reaction. "Who sells a variety of delicious dried meats to your kind. They're so well-seasoned and cooked to perfection – you'd almost think you're eating regular meat. I got you some for a great price. Two silvers."

The elderly merchant opened up the cloth and displayed the dried meats for Heru to see. Wrapping everything up, he then pulled a separate piece from his breeches hidden along his waist and broke off some for Heru to eat. Taking the proffered morsel, Heru found himself pleasantly surprised as the smoky taste of the meat left him wanting more.

Henrei nodded in approval at the Xanan's silent approval. Sliding the package across the booth's surface, Heru felt the need to accept the man's assistance and grudgingly handed over two silver coins. The man seemed to have gone through a lot of effort for Heru and he hoped that he wasn't being taken advantage of.

Bidding the merchant farewell, Heru took his bag of food now nearly bursting at the seams and headed towards *Graak's Fury* as small drops of rain began falling from the sky.

XXVII

THE LIGHT DRIZZLE came up quickly, the rain coming down almost like a fine mist that could have been confused with fog if it hadn't been for the thick, angry clouds that blocked out the sun. By the time Heru boarded the ship, his body was coated with a layer of precipitation that left him feeling chilly. The moment his feet touched the deck, Heru breathed a sigh of relief. The bag hanging from his shoulder threw him off balance and caused the plank to buckle more than it had when he first disembarked. After accidentally looking down and watching the waves crash against the rocks below, Heru kept his gaze fixed straight ahead at the hull.

The clouds darkened and Heru struggled to figure out what the time of day was. They couldn't be docked here much longer. Judging by the casual activity by those aboard, it couldn't be too late, but there was no way of knowing. Making his way to the stairwell, Heru spotted Deylan standing by the captain's wheel hanging up a bit of cloth to act as a weak protection from the precipitation.

"All settled?" Heru asked, sidling up to his friend.

The question felt awkward as it left his lips, but he couldn't find a better way to express his concern. To his relief, Deylan flashed him a tired smile and motioned for Heru to follow him. Taking a seat on a barrel behind the captain's wheel, Deylan patted the top of the one next to him.

"That could have turned out worse," Deylan said with a sigh.

"That couldn't have been your first encounter like that," Heru said, dropping the bag of food to the ground.

Bread and coconuts spilled out of the bag, forming a small circle of deliciousness around it. Grateful for Deylan having the foresight to hang up the cloth, meager though it was, Heru didn't rush to pick up the spilled bread. It would not spoil at this time and he could afford to wait a few minutes.

With another sigh, Deylan bent down and picked up one of the meat buns and took a bite. The fragrant aroma of curry powder and coriander wafted between the two, making Heru's mouth water. Deylan raised a brow and gave a small nod, impressed with the quality of his snack. Not wanting to miss out, Heru rummaged through the bag and pulled out a meat bun of his own. The two sat in silence as they consumed their food, the light drizzle becoming a little heavier. Raindrops hit the cloth with a dull thud. Heru wondered if the thin fabric would leak, but so far it held the water at bay.

"I suppose we both have been keeping our secrets close to us," Deylan began. "If we are going to survive this, I think we need to be honest with each other."

Pausing mid bite, Heru locked gazes with the silver-haired man. He had been honest with Deylan, but he'd also been keeping some secrets. Going into the unknown would be risky. Taking the trip with a group of seasoned sea-faring pirates with a penchant for violence, albeit under their own code, was dangerous. Could he trust Deylan enough to help them return to the Bone Coast, and eventually leave this world of self-sanctioned justice?

Taking a bite, Heru nodded. As a man of his word, this agreement aboard *Graak's Fury* carried more weight – almost as though he were conforming to the pirate's code himself. Satisfied, Deylan stared down at the remnants of his bun. The stain of meat juice on the soft, white interior of the bread stared back at the silver-haired man.

"I killed a man," Deylan said flatly. "He spent years beating me and my mother. He would have moved to my sisters if I didn't. The laws of Ro'thre demand retribution, by any means necessary. To save me, my mother snuck me out of Ro'thre. I ran away to the coast."

The slim man did not strike Heru as strong enough to kill a man, especially before he reached his manhood. The admission caused Heru's brow to raise in a quizzical, almost doubtful expression. Deylan had said he'd been living this life for the last five years. Instead of making the Xanan more wary of his friend, Heru found himself gaining more respect. Honest and humble, at his core, that was who Deylan was, and his confession opened him up to Heru like a scholar opening a book.

"I am not Ro'thre. My mother instilled our values into me and my sisters."

Heru wondered why Deylan did not name his birth home. His silver hair reminded Heru of the people of Scrymme with their silver eyes, but they had dark hair. Nobody else in Corinth had the mark of the goddess Aria and her silver hair in their bloodlines like those with the silver eyes. Deylan also did not have the features of those in the west, or the far north. He must be of mixed blood, Heru decided.

"I've been collecting treasure – coins and jewels – for the last five years. Once I get enough money, I plan to sneak my family out of Ro'thre and seek shelter somewhere else. Possibly Alocar's capitol of Madden."

He glanced up at Heru and shoved the remainder of his meat bun into his mouth. While he chewed, Heru weighed Deylan's words. Something didn't feel right to Heru. Men were murdered for far less, and their killers weren't exiled. At least, not in Xan.

"Why not just take them away now?" Heru asked. "There's no need to live amongst these people and gather treasure like a raven." Pausing once more, Heru's brain tickled as he remembered what Deylan said when they first sat down. "And this wouldn't be a reason for you to be attacked by that Nem Pahlan or his ilk."

"I don't just steal from lonely women or sneak a few jewels buried in proverbial treasure chests," Deylan said with a wan smirk. He glanced around him, suddenly tense.

Heru craned his neck, looking to see what put the silver-haired man on edge. Not seeing anyone, Heru turned back to his friend.

"Have you ever wondered why I don't sail on the same ship for more than a few trips?" Deylan asked.

Opening his mouth, Heru froze mid-word. He hadn't thought about that.

"If you're careful, you can slip a good number of things out from under their noses. By the time they notice, I was on the next ship with a different name. It's been years since I've gone back to my natural hair color. The only thing I can't hide are my damn eyes."

Impressed, Heru nodded his head.

The man is a thief, he mused. *No wonder he fits in with these people so well.*

"About a year ago, I messed up." Deylan's voice became faint and he stared at his now empty hands. "There was a pirate who went by the name of Axe – you can guess what his favorite weapon was. Well, Axe happened to catch me in a compromising situation. Luckily, it was not with my hands in his booty." Deylan chuckled at his choice of words. "At least, not his treasure. I... uh... I was caught in bed with the woman he claimed as his."

"By the gods' mercy," Heru swore. "Can't you control yourself?"

This time, Deylan let out a full-bodied laugh. "I like how my debauchery is the worst of this." Dropping his voice as he noticed one of Kayna's crew walking within range of the pair, Deylan picked up a handful of cherries from the bag and popped them into his mouth. "If Axe knew what else I'd taken of his, I probably wouldn't be alive. Let's just say he had good taste in treasure and women."

"So, you took everything?" Heru asked.

Deylan nodded. "She was quite energetic," he admitted. "But I got careless. We'd just gotten back from our trip and I thought I could get away before anyone heard. Axe walked in and found us in a less-than-ideal situation. He called his men and they beat me pretty soundly. Then, he took me to above deck. I was lucky he only stabbed me and didn't keelhaul me. Bastard kicked me off the ship with the blade still sticking out of my chest. That was the only thing that saved me, from what the healer said."

"What happened to Axe?" Heru asked with baited breath. He found himself leaning forward, wanting more of the story. Why wouldn't Deylan give him more details?

"I've steered clear of his territory – part of why I let my hair return to its natural color. I was afraid the silver would never be the same. Last I heard, he ran afoul of Jylla, a real thorn in the

Scourge's side. Stories say he's more of a distraction, not actually breaking the Scourge's law after a run-in maybe twenty years ago. I haven't heard of Axe being seen off the Bone Coast in almost a year. But I keep on looking. If he knew I survived he would finish the job."

A soft gasp escaped Heru. The silver-haired man was like one of the tricksters in the stories his mother told him as a child. His palms rested on his knees, supporting his weight as he leaned forward in anticipation. The bare bones of this story were not enough to whet his appetite. Now, Heru wanted to hear more of his friend's extravagant tales.

"But," Deylan added, holding up a folded piece of parchment, "today hasn't been a total waste."

Heru barely glanced at the parchment in his friend's hand. Deylan's eyes flashed mischievously, the corners of his mouth pulled up in an almost boyish grin for several heartbeats. There was a secret behind his eyes – one that taunted Heru with all of his adventures.

"What about you?" Deylan asked.

Still thirsting for more, Heru tried to wave the question away. "I've told you my story," he insisted. "I'm searching for my father. I need to know why he gave up his title and family." In the back of his mind, Heru recognized that he should be upset at that, but he still wanted more from the silver-haired man. "How many ships did you sail?"

This time, it was Deylan's turn to ignore the question. "Nothing else?"

The two words finally struck Heru, pushing the eagerness he'd felt moments before to the side. They brought a heavy pain with him – the kind that lingered despite there being stronger emotions swirling around. It also brought up the image of his sister.

"I want to know why my sister disappeared," he muttered. "She disappeared six years ago and didn't say a word. She was all I had. I need to avenge her if she's fallen."

Popping a few more cherries into his mouth after spitting out the pits from the previous bunch, Deylan let out a hum. Reaching over, he patted the Xanan on the arm.

"I will help as best I can, if you would have me," Deylan said. "My sisters mean the world to me. I can't imagine what it would be like to lose one as special as yours."

Reaching into the bag for more cherries, Heru grabbed his arm. With a shake of the head he gave Deylan's arm a little squeeze.

"We don't have enough to piss them away all at once. Save some for later."

A cold splash on the back of his neck brought a startled curse from the Xanan's lips. His hand flew to the back of his neck, and at the same time he looked up at the cloth above him. In some areas, small puddles formed on the cloth and began dripping.

"Let's get this back inside," Heru said, pointing to the bag of snacks. "We can't let this get ruined."

"I heard we'll be setting sale soon," Deylan added. "When I boarded, I heard that Kayna and Maya are returning. We should sneak these in before anyone else sees them. I have a feeling stuff like this has a habit of disappearing."

Quickly gathering their belongings, the pair scrambled to get below deck before the rain soaked through their clothes or damaged the rations. The ship became busier as men rushed to prepare the ship to sail. By the time Heru reached the stairs, he noticed two men scurrying up the mast and into the crow's nest. Their speed and the strength of their hands astounded the Xanan – the rain-slicked mast looked no more difficult to scale than the trees the neighborhood cats climbed.

By the time they reached the galley, the fires had been started and the iron pot burbled. Piles of potatoes, carrots, onions, and other types of produce lay stockpiled in various parts of the room. Checking the room, Deylan casually passed the table and grabbed a handful of cherries, the one Heru had forbidden him from taking from their own bag, and shoved them into his mouth. Jolly was nowhere to be found. Hopefully he would also be none-the-wiser.

"Hide that somewhere that Jolly and the scavengers won't think to look," Deylan instructed. "If we're not careful, it'll be gone by morning."

"Where do you store your stolen goods?" Heru asked, tossing the forgotten bag of candy at Deylan and hitting him in the side of the head. "I haven't seen you visit anywhere more than two or three times. You might be better suited to protect our food."

Hushing the Xanan, Deylan snatched the bag of bread, meat, and fruit out of his friend's hands. Glancing around as he paced, Deylan chewed on the inside of his mouth. He struggled to find a suitable hiding place. Heru's comment about his personal hoard. Keeping the three extra pouches of gold in his travel bag kept him constantly on-guard, but if anyone knew he kept it buried whatever he didn't sell outside of town back in the Bone Coast, he would be robbed quicker than he could blink.

His eyes roved over the room, taking everything in. Spying a group of dirty pots, Deylan dropped the food bag into the pot. Moments later, he wrung out the excess water from the cloth over the fire causing it to hiss and smoke as the flames sputtered on the logs before shoving the cloth into the pot – though not as tightly. To complete his façade, Deylan threw his hat down by his bedroll and stripped his socks off, placing them on top of the damp cloth.

"Add yours," he said to Heru. "Now we just need to hope no one adds their dirty clothes atop our own."

With a shrug, Heru pulled off his socks and added them to the pot. For good measure, he also took off his pants and rung them out, just to add to the illusion that the pot was filled with soaked clothes.

XXVIII

S EVERAL MINUTES PASSED and Heru and Deylan warmed themselves by the low fire in varying stages of undress. Occasionally, Deylan would reach over and stir the stew inside the big iron pot. Watching the chunks of carrot and potato sift through the roux like lazy fish in the sea made his mouth water. Even though he'd had a substantial meal maybe an hour earlier, the thought of a proper dinner followed by days of thin, watery soup in the future made Deylan want to eat as much as he could at that moment to stockpile a layer of fat on his slim frame.

Lounging on one of the barrels, Heru somehow managed to keep it balanced on one edge without losing his perch. His booted feet helped prop him against the wall, providing an an-chor to keep him steady. Next to the pot, his tunic lay in a crumpled heap. The warmth of the flames licked his tanned body, reminding him of evenings back home.

The not-so-subtle rocking of the waves hitting the ship warned the pair that the weather was not improving. Or, maybe it was normal weather for the Eastern Isle and the port of Last Call. Whatever the case, it was not something either man enjoyed.

"Don' ye two have nothin' better ta do than crowd my cookin' space?" The grumpy drawl preceded Jolly's entrance into the galley. "Get yer damn feet away from my food." A thick sack thudded onto the table and Jolly cracked his back with a groan. "An' stop stealin' my food, ye little picaroon. If ye need ta busy yerself, I know of a few things ye could be doing."

Heru's feet dropped to the floor. He straightened up so quickly, one would have thought he'd been burnt by the very flames that warmed him moments before. Deylan moved more slowly, taking the time to put the little pile of cherries balanced on his lap back onto the table. Jolly scooted behind the silver-haired man and smacked him on the back of the head like a father would his young child. Though not a devastating blow, it still hurt and Deylan reached for the back of his head after the strike.

"Dammit it, Jolly," he whined, rubbing his head. "Was that really necessary?"

The curmudgeonly cook grunted in response. "Teach ye for eatin' my supplies," he muttered.

The two young men scrambled to put everything back where it belonged and redress themselves. With a grimace, Deylan grabbed his and Heru's wool socks. His were still a little damp. Suppressing a shudder at putting them back on and chilling his feet, Deylan tossed Heru's socks at the Xanan. Lunging to catch them, one landed on the ground and the other smacked Heru on the face, earning Deylan a scowl.

"Get yer asses above deck," Jolly said, sitting on one of the barrels and peeling a potato with a small dagger. Pausing to point at Heru with the tip of his blade, Jolly added, "I think you'll find somethin' especially interestin'."

Intrigued, Deylan motioned to Heru to follow him above deck.

<center>~~~</center>

The sails flapped in the wind that developed while the two were nice and warm in the galley. The ropes slapped against the mast, unfettered as the men in the crow's nest scanned the horizon. Nearly all of the crew had returned, crowding the deck and shouting orders. There were some new faces aboard that Deylan didn't recognize. Somewhere in the back of his mind, he remembered hearing something about part of the crew arriving at Last Call before Kayna and the *Fury*. Beside him, Heru quietly observed the preparations.

The sky grew to a shade of grey so dark that it bordered on black. In the distance, Deylan thought he heard the rumble of thunder. Rain fell in a steady sheet, quickly soaking Deylan in the short time that he stood on deck. A particularly strong gust slammed into Deylan. The wind chill bit through to the bone, leaving his fingers instantly chilled and sending a shiver through his body.

"Is it always this miserable here?" Heru asked, raising his voice slightly to be heard over the elements. "I can't imagine anyone would want to travel out here. Is this why no one sails past the Eastern Isles?"

"I was wondering the same thing," Deylan replied.

More men appeared on the deck as the minutes passed. Deylan rubbed his hands together, trying to breathe warmth into his stiff fingers. The people popping up and rejoining them on deck from the port below slowly trickled until no more appeared. A hush fell over the crowd, only to be broken by the howl of the wind. Heru shuffled next to Deylan, his head twisting to see what was going on. Finally, a shout from the crow's nest heralded their departure.

Men rushed to pull up the anchor and tie down any loose ropes. A bear of a man in no more than a pair of breeches and bare feet approached the captain's wheel and positioned himself behind it. Deylan watched as his large hands took hold of the wheel and leaned into a turn.

"Thank the gods," Heru said as the ship gave a small lurch and moved towards the open sea.

Opening his mouth to respond, Deylan quickly closed it as he noticed a shock of red hair followed by a distinctive black hat walking from the back of the ship towards the stairs. Beside the women, a third person followed. The imposing figure of a man with a scimitar strapped to his hip and a battleaxe on his back. The trio disappeared down below deck, but not before Deylan spied a face strikingly similar to his friend.

Elbowing Heru in the arm, Deylan pointed to the stairs and exclaimed, "I found him."

"Who?"

Fixing the Xanan with a withering stare, Deylan gestured towards where the people just disappeared into the heart of the ship.

"Who are we looking for?"

An uncharacteristic spark of excitement flashed in Heru's eyes at the news. A renewed energy vibrated through him and it was contagious. Deylan quickly found himself reciprocating the emotion. If they could resolve this, maybe they could use that same good luck to finally finish his self-imposed penance. For the first time in five years, Deylan felt hope.

XXIX

WATER RAN DOWN Len's body in rivulets, the tiny streams that coursed from his hair into his eyes irritating him despite the multitude of times he wiped them away. Below deck and out of the path of the wind, Len unstrapped his axe from his back and shook it off. Droplets rained onto the floor as they flew from the blade. Turning the weapon in his hand, Len inspected the water damage. Returning the blade to his back, Len repeated the motion with his scimitar before re-sheathing it to his hip. Cursing under his breath, the former Great Heart of Xan grit his teeth. The leather wrap on the handles would need to be oiled and the steel wiped down fully to prevent damage.

Ahead of him, Kayna and Maya strode through the passageway towards their respective rooms. Their meeting in the morning would come too soon. All Len wanted to do was have a day of quiet and rest to restore his weapons. From what he heard while boarding the *Fury*, it sounded as though Kayna managed to expand her territory, securing the lord on the eastern coast of the Eastern Isles as one of her allies. There wasn't much of a question on whether they would succeed in Len's mind. Whatever the Scourge's adopted daughter wanted she got.

The hurried sound of boots rushing down the stairs didn't even distract Len from his thoughts. On instinct, he scooted to the right to allow whoever approached from behind an avenue to pass. The rumbling of his stomach tempted him to make a quick stop at the galley for a bite to eat before returning to his room.

The sudden lack of footfall sent a tingle down Len's spine. Old habits were hard to shake. His hand went to his hip as he slowly turned to see why the men behind him didn't pass. Len was greeted with a familiar face he couldn't quite place staring back at him. A pale man with silver hair and amber eyes stood behind the first. After a heartbeat, the momentary shock passed. It wasn't every day he ran into one of his brothers from Xan.

The young Xanan, barely a man Len noted, took a step forward. A battleaxe and scimitar were strapped to his body, much like Len's. The opposite side of the blade on the battleaxe stuck out more than it normally would for providing a counterbalance. The bit of steel appeared to be the size of a fist, and was flattened like a warhammer. The advances in steelwork impressed the former leader of the warlords.

"If you're not going to pass, don't rush up behind me. That's a good way to get yourself hurt." Len narrowed his eyes, fixing the Xanan in particular with a stare.

The young man took another step forward, his face hardening as if to mirror Len's own.

"Father."

There was no question or uncertainty to the statement. The young man did not leave anything hanging – it was a statement of fact. The blunt way he approached Len left the former Great Heart speechless. Taking his own step forward, Len studied the youth's face. Stubborn clarity shone on the young Xanan. There was no doubt in the boy's mind that Len was his father.

He looks like Heru, Len thought to himself. *And Zaa'ni.* Len's throat tightened and he found it hard to swallow at the thought of the wife he abandoned. *Yes, he looks a lot like Zaa'ni.*

The young Xanan, Heru, waited for Len to respond. Len let the silence stretch, studying the boy's face and body language. A slight tremble coursed through Heru's body, one that he probably didn't even notice. His hands twitched as if they wanted to clench into fists, but remained open at his side.

It had been twenty years since Len left. There would be many questions – questions Len wasn't in the mood to answer at the moment. For a fleeting moment, Len wondered how Bermet and Pram were doing. His former righthand man should have kept Len's family safe. Heru should have been kept within FaTinh's, the capitol of Xan's, borders, possibly as an honorary member of one of the councils due to his lineage.

So many questions.

But not now.

Spinning on his heel, Len continued down the passageway towards his room. All thought of grabbing a snack from the galley were forgotten. He needed rest.

"Father!" Heru called out once more.

A hint of agony painted his cry, causing an uncomfortable sensation to settle in the pit of Len's stomach for half a heartbeat. Len learned long ago how to push away useless emotions. A leader did not allow such emotions free reign to cloud his judgement.

The sound of footsteps moving to follow him quickly disappeared. Len wondered if Heru would pursue him. The boy was smart and chose to not test fate. Len would not let his own blood impede his own goals. His quest was not yet over – the bones had spoken that Len's fate would be entwined with another's. But that had been years ago. What actions had he taken that guided his future, and possibly changed it?

～

His father's retreating figure filled Heru with a seething anger that threatened to overwhelm him. He wanted to pursue his father, to demand that Len answer his questions, but Deylan's arm held him back. Somewhere far away he could hear Deylan warning him to not follow his father. Warning him that it could end very badly. But it was all so difficult to hear. Everything seemed caught in a bubble.

"Dammit!" Heru seethed, slamming his fist into the side of the ship.

Pain blossomed in his hand. Slowly, Heru opened and closed his hand, giving it a little shake to make sure he hadn't bent his wrist at the time of the strike and broken it. The sharp pain disappeared, leaving a dull throb in its place. Manipulating his sore hand with the other, Heru didn't think anything was broken.

Punching the wall with his good hand, Heru let out a small flurry of three or four strikes, extending his rage to the ship that lured his father away from him all those years ago. A stream of curses poured from his mouth, stopping only when his last punch connected with the wood. Seconds later, the ship lurched to the side.

"Glad that happened after your little explosion," Deylan said dryly. "That would have undoubtedly broken your hand." Grabbing Heru by the shoulder, he gave the Xanan a small shake. "Control yourself. You will have your chance to speak with him. None of this will make anything better."

Heru glowered at Deylan, but said nothing.

"Come, let's sit by the fire. I'm sure Jolly can find something witty or kind to say to you."

Setting his jaw, Heru stared forward and started off towards the galley.

His room welcomed him with its dark embrace. Stumbling to where he knew his tiny table stood, Len felt around blindly for the stub of a candle and his flint. By the time he got the candle lit, his eyes adjusted to the blackness enough that he could make out the faint outline of his bed. Unstrapping his weapons from his body, Len tossed them onto his bed. The wan candle light flickered in his room. The wax was nearly gone. He'd need a new candle before the end of a fortnight.

Len moved slowly before slumping down onto his bed. His mind was so heavy it weighed his body down, draining him of what little energy he had left. The unexpected appearance of his son unleashed a flood of questions that fought to be noticed first. Instead of thinking through his thoughts logically, the jumble of questions kept him fumbling to formulate an answer.

"Damn," he growled.

Stretching for his bag in the corner of the room, Len pulled out a small, almost empty bottle of oil and a stained rag. His hands moved on instinct as his brain worked to unstick the questions twisted around in his mind.

What does this mean? Finally able to form a complete thought, Len almost sighed. *Pram was to watch Zaa'ni and them.*

His inability to say "his children" in his own mind was not missed by Len. He'd spent so long trying to detach himself from his family, and now that his family came searching for him the irony was not lost on him.

There's been no news of Xan falling. Nothing of Pram's death. Len paused, turning the rag over in his hand as he finished oiling the leathers and moved on to wiping down the blade of his scimitar. *By all accounts, Heru should be an elite. His weapons indicate as such. Why is he here unless something happened?*

Continuing to wipe the now dry blade, Len found the answer.

He didn't want to know.

Len worked in silence, moving deliberately as he cleaned his weapons. Any thought or question that dared form in his mind was pushed away. He needed peace. There would be time to address the issues later.

But it was a struggle.

I should find a shaman and consult the bones. Perhaps things have changed more than I realized.

The wax of the candle burned low in the iron candeltreow. The light flickered dangerously, threatening to sputter out and let the darkness consume him.

After finishing cleaning his battleaxe, Len placed them carefully in their spot in the corner of his room. The idea of grabbing a snack from the galley played with him once again, but he decided against it. Blowing out his candle, Len made his way back to his bed and laid down in his still damp clothes.

Closing his eyes, Len let his mind wander. It had been almost thirteen years since he'd last seen his family. His departure as the Great Heart of Xan, the leader uniting the six different tribes under a banner of discipline and unstoppable might, twenty years prior caused both scandal and confusion. Rumors of him being a disgraced leader and triggering the chaos and destruction brought on by the gods expanded past Xan's borders. On occasion during his first five years at the Bone Coast he'd overheard some traveler at the tavern talking about how the new Great Heart managed trade agreements.

Eventually talk moved to why Len had left. Sure, they sang praises about his military prowess, his status as one of the top Qu'ari elite, and of his cunning. But one thing that always seemed to be the main topic of discussion was that he'd been forced to leave by the council.

Gnashing his teeth, Len remembered how satisfying it was when Corinth found a new source of gossip. Few and far between were the discussion about his past. Kayna didn't care and neither did Maya. Their indifference dictated the crew's mood – and none were overtly curious lest they wanted to risk meeting his blade. Having fought alongside the Scourge probably helped keep the rumors at bay amongst the established pirate crews.

Few dared cross Len at this point.

His mind moved on to his wife, Zaa'ni. He missed the warmth of her body and how her arms wrapped tightly around him. The subtle scent of her body oils seemed a distant memory. He recalled a time when he found his wife standing under the young oak by their house. The canopy kept her protected by its shade, only small slivers of where the sun shone through the leaves were visible. In her arms, Zaa'ni held their daughter, Bermet.

He saw Bermet's hazel eyes vividly. More than Zaa'ni, Bermet had stolen his heart. She would follow him wherever she could, playing games barefoot in the grass whenever he was out of sight. The wind danced around her, splaying her hair out elegantly as she twirled. Ayr favored Bermet from a young age. But, despite that, she captured his heart from the moment he laid eyes on her. She was his heart, his pearl.

An uncomfortable stone settled in Len's stomach. The last time he'd spoken to Bermet hadn't ended well. He'd wanted to visit her again, but early the next morning Pram met him on the outskirts of their village. He could still hear Pram's words clearly, ever the respectful soldier, yet with a finality that came from his time as the Great Heart.

⸺

"I think it's best that you limit your time here," Pram said. *"Heru is being accepted into training for the elite, but there was some worrying talk. They think you are trying to impose your rule through me."*

"I would never insult you by making you my puppet," Len replied.

A rare half-smile twitched the corner of Pram's mouth up. Dipping his head almost by instinct in a humble bow, the new Great Heart took a step forward, closing the awkward gap between them.

"I know," he said. *"I have told them as much. Still, I worry for your son. They will not go easy on him. Or your daughter."*

Len blanched at the words. *"What does Bermet have to do with any of this?"*

With a pause of his own, Pram's face became an unreadable mask. As Len scrutinized the man who'd worked so closely with him, the man who would have given his life to protect Len, he found that there were some things Pram would not share with him anymore. Pram now held secrets of his own. Not being privy to the man's thoughts was not something Len would accept easily. Leaving now may be the best option after all.

"You will protect them with your life," Len said. He never left room for argument, and Pram knew that Great Heart or not, Len was not one to push. *"No one, and I mean no one, harms my daughter."*

A knock on the door abruptly ended the memory, leaving the rest of their conversation unsaid. A low growl passed through his clenched teeth. Whoever it was could wait. Not bothering to get up from his bed, Len didn't bother opening his eyes and slipped his hands behind his head underneath the pillow. This time, he tried to relax. Their trip to Tan'quao would only take a fortnight, maybe a few extra days if the waters were especially rough. Though he usually kept to himself while out on in that area, Len recalled seeing a few small villages with a temple in the center.

Back home, the shamans of Xan lived in a humble home with various artifacts announcing their craft. His preferred shaman was an elderly woman whose eyes had gone milky white when he was a child. She wore a corded necklace around her neck. A turtle shell adorned the wall inside her hut – as she chose to live a simple life outside the capitol grounds of FaTinh – and a strand of cattle scapulae lined the upper portion of her door frame.

Len wondered if these small villages had similar holy men to ward off evil and offer tokens for protection. If they offered those services, perhaps there may be one who would cast the bones and read Len his future. His mind went to his coin pouch that he kept hidden in a secret pocket sewn into the inside of his sirwal. His loose-fitting pants proved to be a boon time and again as he managed to travel vast distances and not draw any attention thanks to his plain sirwal.

Another round of knocks on his door, this time more vigorously, finally achieved their desired result. Len opened his eyes and gnashed his teeth. Sitting up, he fought the urge to call out and berate the person who dared disturb him.

"Get up," a voice called from the other side of his door.

"Damn it Maya," he growled. Nonetheless, Len pushed himself out of his bed and donned on his boots. "This had better be important."

Opening the door, he found Maya standing in front of him, her hand raised to knock once more. Where Kayna would face him with a bemused expression, Maya stood calmly, an almost apathetic mask pasted onto her face. After nearly twenty years, the woman still carried an air of mystery about her – yet she still reminded him of Pram. Pram had been the closest person he had to a friend during his time as the Great Heart.

"What do you want?" he growled.

"Get your ass up deck," she replied calmly. "Kayna had a barrel of good wine brought aboard to celebrate our alliance with the Duke of Hallows."

"How much is that popinjay going to pay?"

"Double what the Baron does."

Impressed, Len raised a brow. Double what the fool of a baron paid would be an almost princely amount. Fifty pieces of gold – that amount would make more frequent trips out to Last Call more worth it. Between that and the "gifts" from the locals because of their notoriety, he could find himself enjoying his life a little more.

"Will there be food?" he asked.

"Probably," Maya replied. "Jolly and the little warrior who's been staying with him have probably been busy."

"Little warrior?"

"The boy who looks like you," she clarified. "I'm sure you'll run into him soon enough. He's hard to miss. He's always with a silver-haired boy with amber eyes who looks like he's from Scrymme. The two are inseparable."

Len noted how she studied him. Her gaze bore into him in a way that no other could. She almost seemed to be prodding his mind, searching for his secrets. Shutting the door with an unanticipated force, Len started off down the passageway. Maya would follow. They didn't need to speak to understand each other.

Maya fell in step behind Len. Their boots echoed dully in the cramped corridor. A few stragglers bustled around them, never passing the pair out of respect for their rank. Len didn't consider himself one of them, but power and obedience were universal. The deference he received from Kayna's men reminded him of his past. It was something he still expected from others.

XXX

O UT ON THE DECK away from the coast, the rain let up, leaving a fine mist to coat them in the heavy fog. In the gloom, Len found himself searching for the wine. Nobel wine hit differently than even the finest tavern, and Len wanted nothing more than to lose himself in a nice flagon filled with the raspberry-colored drink. He separated from Maya as soon as he reached topside, letting her figure out whatever her next step for the day was to be.

Len spied a line forming by the captain's wheel and spotted Jolly's familiar shirtless form, his leathery skin standing out against the sun-bleached wood, passing out mugs to everyone in the queue. Making his way to the group, Len made sure to be seen, while trying to give the appearance of not standing out. Before he took a spot at the back of the line, one of the men near the front called him over, motioning for Len to take a spot at the front. No longer feigning surprise, Len quickly left the back of the queue and took his drink from the grizzled cook.

Len smirked into his flagon as he took a sip of the fine wine. He never tired of his position of power and the benefits that came with it. Never.

Making slow circles around the deck, Len sipped on his wine while the rest of the crew bustled about – most with a mug of their own in their hand. In some part of the ship, a group of men near the mast brought out instruments and began playing a spirited sea shanty. The mix of fiddle, spoons, pennywhistle, and concertina floated in the air above the slapping of the water against the hull. An unexpectedly rich tenor began singing, his lilting voice rising and falling with the melody of the tune.

In several spots on the deck men broke into dance. The hulking pirates displayed an unwonted level of rhythm as they moved about while doing their jig. Those who weren't engaged in the merriment hung around in small groups of three or four, observing the exhibition while they shared a joke or story from their time at Last Call.

Len found himself leaning against the side of the ship, his elbows resting against the ledge. The effects of the wine were starting to take effect and Len enjoyed a pleasant floating sensation that had nothing to do with the swaying of the ship. At one point, he noticed Kayna's mane of red hair bobbing around the deck. The captain wove between the groups of men, stopping to share a quick word with them before continuing on.

Unlike the rest of those aboard the *Fury*, Kayna did not carry a flagon of wine.

Time passed at the same never-ending pace that it had when Len first beheld Zaa'ni at their bonding ceremony. The minutes stretched on into eternity, yet flew by more quickly than he cared for. It was a moment of true bliss that he'd only experienced a few times in his life.

The songs flowed seamlessly one after the other, only pausing for one of the musicians to take a drink from their mug. Even the men in the crow's nest shared in the celebration. The excitement that night was palpable. Not even the light drizzle of rain that replaced the cool mist of the fog could dampen their spirits.

Out of the corner of his eye, Len spied the young Xanan meandering about with the silver-haired youth. Len snorted into his flagon as he realized how old he sounded. If it weren't for the wine, the thought would pass through his head disregarded. However, he let the pleasant feeling maintain its control over him for the moment. A part of him hoped that they wouldn't notice him.

But alas, Len would not be so lucky.

The young Xanan, his son, must have noticed him because the pair made their way towards him. The silver-haired youth glided along, his steps light as though the wine itself made him weightless. Taking a sip from his flagon, Len allowed his eyes to wander as he planned his next move.

To his left, Len noticed a group of men who joined him on the *Fury* after arriving at Last Call before Kayna and her crew. They were the few people who he'd hand-chosen to act as his retinue. They leaned against the side of the ship like Len, they were the only ones who appeared to be talking in hushed voices. Their subdued demeanor didn't fit with the mood of the ship. His curiosity now piqued, Len downed his wine in two large gulps and dropped the empty flagon on the ground. This warranted further investigation.

Stalking off to confront his pseudo-crew, Len held up a hand to stop Heru from trying to speak with him. The young Xanan's mouth dropped at the dismissal, but Len didn't care. The actions of that group sobered him up, and he now moved with purpose. Out of the corner of his eye, Len thought he even caught a concerned glance from the silver-haired youth.

At some point, Len knew he would need to have a discussion with the young Xanan. At some point, he would have to acknowledge the boy as his son.

As he passed Heru, Len heard a steady stream of curses follow him. The boy spoke like an elite, not some soft, spoiled child raised by his mother and sister. The vulgar indignation brought a smile to Len's lips.

Perhaps I'll test his mettle. I wonder who Pram had teach him.

Len's head itched to turn around and look at Heru, but he fought back the temptation. A moment later, he was glad he did. As the rainfall steadily got heavier, the group did not move to get up. Movement out of the corner of his eyes confirmed the obvious to Len, that those on the deck were scrambling below to avoid being soaked. These five, however, crouched down, squatting and continuing their conversation.

"What news do you have?" Len asked as he approached, his voice raised to be heard over the sound of the rain. "It must be important if you choose to stay out here instead of seeking shelter."

Over the splatter of rain against the deck, Len thought he heard approaching footsteps. Turning towards the sound, Len heaved a sigh. Heru quickly pursued Len, the silver-haired youth following a few steps behind. A particularly rough wave slammed into the ship, sending Heru stutter-stepping sideways. Even Len almost lost his balance.

"By the gods," Len breathed. "He's persistent."

"What are they doing here?" the leader of the group, Callum, asked.

Even in the darkness, Len thought he saw the man's eyes narrow. Len would have to speak quickly. These men were not the trusting type, and given their secrecy in front of him and the ship, Len didn't doubt that they wouldn't hesitate to continue their deception directly to him.

"Father," Heru said.

Len could feel five heads swivel in his direction. If the boy didn't shut up things could get messy. A bolt of lightning flashed in the darkness, spidering across the heavens and was quickly followed by the rumble of thunder. The winds kicked up until the rain fell to the deck at an angle. He knew he needed to act quickly.

"Hold your tongue," Len commanded, using the full power of his voice. Even in the noise of the storm, the former Great Heart's words carried to all involved. "You will not interrupt my council like some ill-natured whelp."

His son's eyes widened, his momentum faltering. Len knew he needed to seize his chance.

"You have traveled across the realms to search for me. In doing so, you have stumbled upon matters that are beyond anything you could hope to comprehend. Leave my sight, lest you anger me. It will not end well for you if you earn my ire."

Heru's mouth open and closed wordlessly like a fish struggling to breathe. Another burst of lightning flashed, illuminating the now skeletal group on deck and blinding them for the span of several heartbeats. As his vision adjusted back to the darkness, Len noticed the dark scowl on his son's face. The young Xanan's hands rested by his side, balled into fists. Len could see the boy calculating whether it would be worth it to strike him.

His bravery impressed him. A little.

"Another ship has gone missing," Callum said, breaking the tension.

Spinning on his heel, Len turned his attention back to Callum and the group. They no longer crouched down. Now, they tightened their ranks and moved closer to him. Raking his gaze over the group, Len noted that something was wrong. More than one's face betrayed their concern.

"When did you hear this? Nothing was brought up to me at the port."

"I heard from the tailor," Khaingh replied. A short, bald man, his smooth, deep bass allowed him to blend in with the mainlanders easier than the rest. Rarely would he be mistaken for the man he truly was. "That's six ships in three fortnights."

"Damn," Len hissed, his curse drowned out by a peel of thunder. "What's the cause?"

The men exchanged uncomfortable glances, almost as though they feared their response would invoke Len's fury. Len knew it couldn't be their ships. None of their men had gone missing and their fleet comprised of three ships. The final ship, *Scourge's Peace*, rarely left the harbor. It was the Scourge's personal ship – only used for his business.

"Well?"

"Locals claim the waters are cursed," Khaingh said. "This last year has been devastating. Many believe the high god of the winds has released his wrath upon those who set sail."

The silver-haired youth let out a gasp. Len's head swiveled in the man's direction. A look of understanding dawned on his face, his amber eyes suddenly turned in in self-reflection. Beside him, Heru stared at his companion with concern.

"Grab onto something!" a shout rang out.

Every head spun to the crow's nest. The two in the nest clung to their post for dear life.

"Grab something!" they warned again.

Scrambling to find something to hold onto, the group of eight raced to the mast and grasped the rope. No sooner did they wrap their hands around the stiff rope did a massive wave slam into the side of the *Fury*. Frigid water sloshed onto the deck, soaking everyone to the bone in freezing water. The sheer force of the impact knocked them to the ground. Len felt the jolt throughout his entire body.

Staggering to his feet, Len realized just how torrential the rains had become. The rain poured from the heavens sideways, stinging his body with each drop. The winds ripped at his clothes and pushed into him at the same time. The maelstrom sought to subdue Len and those aboard the *Fury* through its sheer will. It felt as though Graak himself demanded obeisance from them all.

"Go and wake the hands," Len called out. "We need to return to shore."

A gangly man with a bushy salt and pepper beard didn't wait for Len to single one of them out for the task. The man took off and disappeared below deck as quickly as he could despite the rain-slicked deck and the ferocity of the seas.

"To me," Len pointed to Heru and Deylan. "To the wheel."

As Callum, Khaingh, and the others scrambled to various parts of the ship, Len, Heru, and Deylan darted towards the captain's wheel. His feet slipped out from under him multiple times, nearly sending him face first onto the deck. Puddles formed under their feet as water continued to splash over the side of the ship. In the distance, thunder continued to get closer – its roar ever-present.

Grasping the wheel with both hands, the navigator nowhere in sight, Len attempted to brace his body against the waves. His arms strained as he pulled the wheel as far to the left as it would go – his teeth grit together as his corded muscles began trembling from exertion. Heru and Deylan rushed to help him turn the ship, the three of them groaning from their exertions.

The seconds passed wretchedly slow as they waited for the rest of the crew to emerge from down below. Mercifully, Len noticed the men toppling out from below, and a few minutes later, one of the stronger men took over and strained against the power of the wheel. Len's muscles wept with relief as they no longer struggled against the furious sea. Now, that the crew worked to regain control of the ship, Len could properly take stock of what was happening.

XXXI

THE POWER OF THE GALE reminded Deylan of the one he'd encountered not even a fortnight before. Adrenaline flowed through him, leaving his body frozen as though he swam through a river. The chill of the ocean couldn't compare to what he felt at this moment. Instead of allowing himself to seize up in fear, Deylan pushed himself to walk over to Heru as calmly as possible. The first step coincided with another wave slamming into the ship, knocking him to his knees. The blow shook him to his spine. Deylan wondered if he'd be able to regain his balance after this.

"Push," he told himself.

In the horizon, Deylan thought he saw another wave coming towards them. It was hard to tell thanks to the heavy sheets of rain that poured down onto the ship. Despite the deluge,

Deylan pushed forward. Each step brought about a sense of lightness until the fear no longer gripped him.

"Heru!" he shouted. "Something isn't right here. This is exactly what happened to Dhruvasht and *Death's Rose*."

"Get over here!" Len commanded.

Allowing Heru to pull him towards Len and the side of the ship, Deylan buried the thought of being sucked off the *Fury* by a wave deep within. Now was not the time to worry about something like that. To do so would be to plant an idea into god's head, and Deylan didn't want to tempt any angry gods – even if he didn't believe in them.

Standing alongside the former Great Heart, Deylan wondered what Len wanted them to do. There were no ropes to tie up or hold on to. The area around them was empty. Not even one of Kayna's men stood nearby. This spot was clear, free for Len and those nearby to look into the sea and watch their doom roll in.

"How many men died on your ship?" Heru asked, sidling up to Deylan.

A blinding spark blazed through the sky as lightning forked in the heavens once more. The roar of thunder was almost instantaneous. Like the roar of a giant, it echoed in the night sky over the ravenous howl of the winds.

"All but four," Deylan replied.

It felt like he whispered the words, but he knew that in order for Heru to hear them, he had to yell into the void. Though he didn't want to admit it, Deylan wondered how many would survive this time.

XXXII

THE WAVES TOSSED THE SHIP like a doll. Spray flew over all sides until the wood and every soul on board was thoroughly soaked. Len couldn't believe that such a storm would occur naturally. He'd been sailing for years and had never once faced a fury from the god of Ayr like this before. There had to be a way to stop the turbulence. Squinting against the curtain of never-ending rain, Len strained his ears. The howl of the wind and the cries of his crewmates made it nearly impossible to pick anything up. Somewhere nearby, he heard his son call for help. He couldn't do anything to help Heru at the moment, so he continued scanning the horizon.

In the darkness of the maelstrom, Len thought he saw the outline of a shadow in the distance. A crack of lightning illuminated the seas. Not too far off, Len saw a small ship sitting calmly in the storm. In the middle of the ship, a lone figure stood with his arms outstretched. The gale force winds and a heavy torrent of rain didn't seem to bother the stranger. He stood there steady on the chaotic waters.

It was hard to make out, but Len thought he saw the figure reach up to the heavens and pull his arm down, as though he were grabbing something and pulling it to the ship. A pop of lightning broke through the blackness, blinding the Xanan warrior. Throwing his arm up to shield his eyes, Len managed to make out the lone figure. The man was too far away to see, but he was there.

"God-blessed!" Len cried out. "There is a god-blessed!"

The crew, who had been scrambling to keep the ship afloat while simultaneously attempting to steer her back to Last Call, moved into position. There were no magi on the *Graak's Fury*. No one to help turn the tides against the lone god-blessed – an unknown magic style at that – attacking them. Still, they could break his concentration and hopefully stop the gale. While men rushed to find long-range weapons to pierce the heart of the storm, Len's hand went to his waist, briefly touching his scimitar.

He would need help.

"Heru!" Len called out.

From somewhere in the darkness, his son managed to hear the words that were ripped from Len's lips. It wasn't long before the young Xanan and his silver-haired friend were by his side. Deylan stood alert, his hands twitching towards the small dagger he kept strapped to his body. If it came to one-on-one combat, Len wasn't confident that Deylan would be much help against the magi.

"Stay by me," Len instructed. "We must be ready in case he tries to board our ship."

"He's going to sink us," Deylan replied. "He must be the one who's been sinking all the ships that have gone missing. I remember seeing a solitary person on a boat like this before the *Rose* was lost."

"Damn!" Len spat. "We need a god-blessed."

"Don't you have one?" Heru asked.

"No. We've never needed one. I haven't seen one since the God Wars."

A stream of curses broke from Heru's lips. The young Xanan's hand clutched his scimitar, spinning the handle anxiously as he braced himself on the deck. Behind the two, Len noticed Kayna giving directions to her crew. They struggled to find a weapon to counter attack. Bows would be ruined if they went out in this weather. Even Maya was flustered.

"We need something," Len mumbled to himself, his words lost in the screaming wind.

As if in the distance, Len heard the faint sound of a young child laughing. It reminded him of his daughter, Bermet. In the back of his mind, he saw his Bermet spinning around outside their home in FaTinh. Her dress fanned out and her dark plait whipped around as she twirled, her bare feet dancing on the lush grass. He remembered the bright smile plastered on her face. Behind her, a young girl with pale skin and periwinkle hair mimicked Bermet's every move.

The two girls giggled as they played. A profound sense of peace settled in Len's chest. The image brought a rare smile to his lips. How he missed his little pearl, his Bermet.

As suddenly as the image came, Bermet faded into blackness. Only the blue-haired girl remained. Stopping in her tracks, the young girl faced Len. Her eyes were as black as coal with no white rimming them. Her simple white dress continued to move around her, as though something tugged the bottom of her skirt.

"Freyna," Len murmured.

The youngest Ayr sibling flashed a smile at the Xanan warrior. It had been a long time since he saw the goddess. Every time he did, she offered her protection and power to him. Reaching out with her hand, Freyna grasped Len's hand. Her tiny hand felt cool in his. The strength of the wind flowed through him, whipping about and tugging at his clothes.

"Please, mighty Windstrider."

Giving his hand a squeeze, Freyna turned from Len to face the lone ship in the tempest. The sound of children's laughter sounded in Len's ears once more. It had been so long since he'd seen his daughter. He hoped that her image would pop into his mind once more, but she did not. Walking towards the violent sea, Freyna rose into the air until the tips of her toes just scraped the edge of the waves. Once she'd put some distance between herself and *Graak's Fury*, Freyna turned to Len one last time. It was almost a look of sorrow. Len wondered if this would be the last time he saw the young goddess.

Spreading her arms out wide, Freyna stilled the winds. The waters gradually became less choppy until the sea's surface was smooth as glass. The clouds cleared and a beam of light broke through. Night broke and the sun was rising. The solitary ship could now be seen. The man aboard appeared frantic. Raising his own arms, the waters reacted to his call. He sought to bring the storm once more.

Taking advantage of his moment of panic, Freyna turned and made a pushing motion towards *Graak's Fury.* Something slammed into the ship, sending her rocking. The sheer power of the blast sent her careening backwards, away from the exposed magi. A cry of surprise broke out on the ship as the sails filled with air, pulling the *Fury* back home. It was mere minutes before the enemy ship became a tiny speck on the horizon, disappearing completely moments later.

"What was that?" Heru gasped. "Did you see that?"

"No," Deylan said slowly, shaking his head. "I've never experienced anything like that."

The bedlam on the ship died down as Kayna got her crew under control. Ever composed, she stood at the helm giving orders. Maya regained herself as well, and was now working with the men on the portside to determine how much damage was done to the *Fury*.

It was a close call, Len couldn't deny it. They'd been complacent much too long. They would need to find a god-blessed to join their crew at some point. But where had the man come from? Most ships didn't sail out this far, and those who did didn't have any god-blessed either. Kayna knew the other captains well enough to know if they'd hired one of the god-blessed to join their crew.

Bodies moved around them, avoiding Len and the two as though they were rocks in a fast-moving stream. No one questioned them. No one demanded they do anything.

"Come with me," Len said.

When Deylan and Heru didn't move, having not heard his instructions as they tried to reach a logical conclusion to what happened, Len repeated his order. The two jumped, finally acknowledging the Xanan warrior.

The three wound through the busy ship, staying out of everyone's way. It wasn't difficult as the commotion was dying down. Those who had been on break before the attack were making their way below deck once more. Len considered going down with the others, but decided against it at the last minute. Instead, he took Deylan and his son to the stern. Wind still filled the sails unlike anything they'd seen for the last few days and propelling her forward. Watching the horizon, Len noticed a spot where the heavens darkened and lightning flashed. The lone mage was still there.

"What is going on?" Heru snapped. "Clearly you know something. What is it?"

Len bristled at being spoken to that way. His son should show him the utmost respect as the former Great Heart. He nearly slapped the young Xanan, but stayed his hand. He deserved it. After all, the two were nearly strangers despite being sons of Xan.

"Has your mother told you of the God Wars?"

Heru shook his head. Even Deylan lost his characteristic smile as confusion filled his face. Len wondered why his wife never told their children of his feats. The fact that such an important part of history wasn't being continued sent a spike of anger through him.

"But Pram mentioned that it was the stuff of legend," Heru said. "That even the gods feared those involved."

"In my village, it was said that this battle was beyond the gods," Deylan added. "That even higher beings fought on Corinth alongside Man."

"Pram has spoken much about this?" Len asked.

Heru shook his head once more. Len clenched his fist, but did not display his anger. Pram told him years ago that while he wouldn't speak ill of Len and would praise his legacy, he would not speak about him often. It would only give false hope to their people that he would come back, and Pram did not want to have his reign questioned.

"It's nice to know that the truth has spread outside of the united realms," Len said. "I was afraid it would only become a story in Alocar and Zanir." He paused, trying to collect his thoughts. Never one to dress up his words, Len figured it was best to be brief. "You've heard of the Faceless?"

Heru nodded.

"There are beings higher than our gods called Ancients. The Ancients tricked those who were hungry for power, too short-sighted to see that they were being manipulated, into releasing those fell beasts onto Corinth. With the help of our gods, we were able to defeat them.

"I have always had a strong connection to Freyna, youngest of Ayr. She has blessed my conquests and kept me safe all these years. Today, she has shown herself to me once again."

Deylan sucked in his breath, his eyes wide. A muffled curse escaped his lips as he gawped at the Xanan warrior. Heru, on the other hand, did not express surprise like his counterpart. The young Xanan's brow furrowed as he processed everything his father said.

"As much as I don't like relaying on others, I fear this is the last time the mighty Windstrider will bless me."

An unfamiliar emotion flooded Len. His breath caught in his throat, and a splash of red filled his vision. Both were so fleeting that the peculiarity of it all left him feeling shaken. A cold sweat slicked his palms that he couldn't attribute to adrenaline from the battle with the mage. He worried it might be a premonition. Dismissing the notion as soon as it entered his mind, Len wiped his hands and studied the two. Giving any credence to what he felt would surely influence his future. Even when he left home, the bones were always in his favor.

"Why have I never seen your goddess?" Heru asked. "Surely, as your son, I should be privileged to be blessed by her as well."

"The gods judge you by your actions," Len replied. "If your actions are not worthy, you will not be protected."

"But how do you get chosen?" Heru asked.

"I don't think now is the time to worry about this," Deylan interjected.

Len noticed that Heru's fists were balled, as though he were fighting back the urge to strike him. The fact that his son was willing to consider attacking an elite like himself caused a wave of pride to rise within. Maybe the boy was more like him than he thought.

"We need to figure out why he's attacking our ships and what he's after," Deylan continued. "There must be something he's looking for."

"I agree. The problem is, we don't know where to find him. If we could figure out his home, we could at least gain some advantage," Len agreed. "His strength lies with the sea."

"Why wouldn't Graak help us?" Heru snapped. Disgust soaked his words. "Surely, he doesn't approve of someone defiling his seas."

"I doubt Graak would get involved," Len replied. "He couldn't be bothered with the God Wars."

The young Xanan looked as though he wanted to retort, but Len silenced him with a withering look.

"We have to handle this without the gods." Len's words left no room for argument. "What we need is a god-blessed."

"And a way to find our tempestuous friend," Deylan added. "I would venture that he lives somewhere in Nem Pah or even further. Have you visited the far eastern lands?"

"I will talk with Kayna, but we haven't gone farther than Tan'quao, which is next to the coastal land of Nem Pah. Maya collects the purple flowers and sells them to a local apothecary for a princely sum. We don't go too far into Tan'quao though. Nor very often. Maybe once every five years."

"How many realms are there?" Heru asked.

Deylan looked puzzled, his brow knotting as he tried remembering some morsel of information hidden within the recesses of his mind.

"I know of six," Len said. "I will speak to Kayna tonight. Keep this information to yourself. We don't want others to talk. There are ears everywhere."

Done speaking, Len turned to head back to his bed. After all that happened, he found himself suddenly exhausted. Nothing sounded better than sinking into his hard cot on the floor and letting sleep overtake him. He didn't take more than a few steps when he heard his son call out.

"Le – Father."

Hearing Heru refer to him as such left him feeling hollow. He thought there would be some sense of pride at his son calling him father, but it had the opposite effect.

"Why did you abandon us?"

He could hear the pleading in the young Xanan's voice. The vulnerability his son was expressing only left him feeling awkward towards the young man.

"Did I do something wrong? Why don't you want to stay with us?"

"I don't know you."

Len noted how his flat tone broke his son's spirit. The empty feeling returned. Not bothering to turn back around, Len walked away. He really needed to rest.

XXXIII

DEYLAN COULDN'T BELIEVE the exchange he'd just witnessed. In the very wilds of his imagination he never thought he'd see a literal god. He hadn't even been sure that they truly existed, and now – now he saw their power before his very eyes. The sheer power the young one commanded was astonishing. Where the stories about the Eldest Brother, Graak, true as well? Just what power did he possess?

As Deylan stared at the spot where Freyna had been, the silhouette of the solitary boat long gone as the distance between the *Fury* and it grew, he heard Len and Heru share a heated exchange. The way Heru's voice broke as he entreated his father to speak with him pulled at the strings of Deylan's heart. He could hear the broken child seeking an answer. It reminded Deylan of himself.

"I don't know you."

Len's words snapped Deylan from his surveying the horizon. The ghosts of his past floated about his head and he could only imagine what went through Heru's mind. Without drawing either of their attention, Deylan shifted himself until he could see the two Xanans comfortably out of the corner of his eye. Len stalked away from the two, not bothering to turn back and speak to his son. To his benefit, Heru did not chase after his father.

Deylan wondered if he would have sought out validation after an exchange like that. Mentally shaking himself, Deylan quickly put the question aside. Of course he wouldn't. He and Heru were similar in that manner, but that was what drew them together.

Men swarmed the deck, shouting and checking the rigging, cursing the damage left in the wake of the god-blessed. No one spared them a glance. Taking a quick moment to look around him, Deylan didn't see anything nearby appeared to be too damaged. Satisfied that there was no imminent threat, he returned his attentions back to Heru. The young man stood rooted to the spot, still staring at Len's now vanished form.

Taking the few steps to close the chasm between, Deylan quietly slipped his arm around Heru's shoulder and pulled him in close. Heru didn't fight the motions, allowing Deylan to rest his head against Deylan's shoulder. He was broken; Deylan could tell. So, he held his friend just like his mother held him during the long nights after her husband spent the evening beating her. Despite how she felt, Deylan's mother always managed to focus on him and physically manifest her love. She'd done it for years. Now it was Deylan's turn to fill that void for Heru.

The two stood together for several long seconds, letting the movement of the ship pass them by. After several heartbeats, Heru broke the moment and pulled away from Deylan. Without a word, Heru walked towards the stairs and disappeared below deck.

Deylan felt a warmth on his face and lightly touched his cheek. A single tear rolled down his cheek, leaving a thin, wet streak on his face. Wiping away his pain, Deylan went for a walk around the ship.

///

Leaning against the wall beside Kayna's chamber door, Len observed the two women with crossed arms. Maya stood nonchalantly, her hip slightly jutted out as she used the small table to lean upon. Kayna sat on her bed, head down and deep in thought. Len gnashed his teeth. They couldn't wait any longer.

"We can't head back to Last Call," he said. "We need to go back to the Bone Coast and find a god-blessed."

"There's no reason to think that we'll encounter him again," Maya said cooly.

"There's been six ships gone missing in these waters in less than a fortnight. More if we include the ones missing back home. How in the hells do we account for this? He's targeting us." Len shifted on his foot as he glared at Maya.

"But why would anyone attack sailors?" Kayna said, cutting the tension between the two.

Len shook his head. He couldn't think of an answer.

"None of the big crews are out scavenging," Maya said. "Even Jylla and Hallows have pulled back and limited their search for riches to closer to home." Turning to Kayna, she added, "Maybe there's something to what he says."

Shaking her head, Kayna stood up and smoothed down the imaginary wrinkles on her front. "But what is their aim? Surely, there's something there."

"I don't know," Len admitted. "We have a lot of questions. How did a god-blessed end up in this part of the world? They rarely venture out of into Thyllasis, and I haven't seen any at Last Call. For one that powerful, with a style of magic I've never seen, to be floating on the water like that, there must be something bigger than we can possibly conceive going on.

"People don't just sail the seas by themselves like that for no reason."

The women nodded their head in agreement. Kayna pinched the bridge of her nose as she pondered the implication of his words. Maya was much more reserved.

"We head back to the Coast," Kayna said with finality. "We have enough supplies to skip Last Call. I need to talk with my father."

"He won't be home for a few more months," Maya reminded her. "The hot season is coming and he will be out with his sister. Whatever we do, we need to figure it out on our own."

Kayna dropped her head, frustration evident by the way she sighed and dropped her head.

"We also need a god-blessed," Len added once more.

"Where will we find one of those?" Kayna asked.

Giving Maya time to think, Len realized that their resources were limited. Without her father, Kayna didn't have the manpower necessary to handle this.

"I know one," he admitted. "If he's still out on the coast."

Kayna clapped her hands. "Then that's what we'll do," she said. "Upon our return, you'll find your god-blessed and bring him to us." Turning to Maya, she added, "Relay our plans to the crew. Do not mention the search for the god-blessed, however. We don't want to scare the men."

Maya pushed off of the table and exited the room, leaving Len and Kayna alone. Len wondered if he should talk to her about what his retinue knew, but decided against it. There hadn't been much more that could be added that hadn't already been said.

"Talk to your son."

Kayna's request startled Len.

"I don't know him. It would be a disservice to keep us together."

"You will talk to your son," Kayna repeated. "If this is as bad as you believe, we will need more warriors. We will need your son and his friend."

The emphasis she placed on her last sentence warned Len that it wasn't a suggestion. She planned to keep the crew together and sail out to confront this lone man. She must have taken the attack on her ship personally since no one dared to challenge her in years. Either that, or she felt the rush of blood lust that Len had twenty years ago when he first met Kayna and her crew. Len resigned himself to speak to his son, after all, Kayna's orders weren't ones to be ignored.

XXXIV

THE SUN BEAT DOWN on *Graak's Fury* with an intensity like Deylan hadn't seen. Maya's proclamation earlier that morning that they would be making their way back to the Bone Coast shocked almost everyone. The expectation that they would be returning to Last Call and spending a few days to recover had been prevalent amongst the men. Though there had been no injuries, such a powerful attack by a singular enemy shook the confidence of even the surliest. Having survived twice, Deylan wasn't sure he would again should a third ambush occur.

He also wanted time to speak with Heru. After the disastrous exchange after Freyna saved them, Deylan feared that Heru would do something reckless. So when Len approached the pair and asked to speak to his son privately, Deylan positioned himself nearby and listened closely for the sound of conflict.

"We need to talk," Heru said, an uncharacteristic humility dripping from his words.

Deylan could see that Len's statement still effected the young Xanan. Heru's usual brusque demeanor melted away. In front of Len, he was no more than a child.

"What happened to Bermet?" Len asked, cutting to the chase.

"Bermet? It's always been about Bermet! What about your son? What about me?"

Heru's voice came out strained, as though he fought back the urge to yell. Deylan considered coughing, but thought against it. The two had a lot to work out. Len didn't appear to be fazed by his son's outburst. The former Great Heart waited a beat, possibly to let Heru compose himself, before continuing.

"Bermet is my tie to Freyna," Len said at last.

The admission startled even Deylan. He made a soft gasp at the same time that Heru let out an exclamation.

"It's been twenty years, and my connection to Ayr has grown weak. When she was young, I noted how her innocence brought Freyna's good will and protection to our family. Bermet was... is my pearl. The thought of returning to her, seeing her blessed by the same god that saved my family, and our people, brought me great pride. My son was to be in line to be the next Great Heart, my youngest, a shaman, and my Bermet, a great leader in her own right.

"I am getting older. My time on the sea is coming to an end. During my last visit home, I told Pram that the next time I return, I will stay. He wasn't happy, my visits remind my people of when I ruled. Pram has worked hard to keep peace and stability in Xan. He's done a good job. But the time is coming when we remember our past and honor those who fought for our greatness. I told him that I would be getting you ready to become the Great Heart.

"Without Bermet and her divine connection, without my little girl, things may become more difficult. She will have no doubt developed her mother's calm and confident demeanor. Zaa'ni shares that with Pram. Bermet is the key to restructuring Xan's future."

The news sent Deylan reeling. His hand flew to his mouth. Deylan wanted to see how Heru reacted. The young Xanan's silence stretched on for agonizing seconds. Surely, Heru's face betrayed the swirling miasma of emotion that no doubt would be within him.

The quiet extended into minutes that dragged on.

"She disappeared about six years ago," Heru replied at last. His voice soft, almost as though he mumbled. "She helped Mother raise Arezou and disappeared while I was studying to become an elite. As an acolyte, and because of... our situation... no one told me Bermet went missing. I didn't find out until I returned home to Mother a couple years ago."

Sparing a glance at the two, Deylan noted how Len pinched the bridge of his nose. The warrior clearly struggled to keep his dismay in control, but Deylan could see the pain in Len's face by the way his eyes dropped and the corners of his mouth turned down ever so subtly.

"I looked for her, but I never found her." Heru's words came out as an apology.

Len turned from his son, resting his arms against the side of the ship.

"Father," Heru begged.

"You probably want to know why I left," Len said after a long pause. "I doubt Pram ever gave you a satisfactory answer."

"He said you wanted to follow your heart," Heru replied.

"True. Part was for selfish reasons – many would say mostly selfish – but something about the East called to me. Just as we ruled Xan with the power of our champions, the people out here ruled with their own leaders. No magic is needed to maintain order. After each battle with those accursed god-blessed, I struggled with showing the true might of the Brothers of Xan. We don't need divine power, but behind the shadow of the god-blessed, our strength is hidden. Diminished.

"So, I searched for a way to bring true power to the Brothers of Xan. I've learned new techniques and collected a sufficient number of salves containing the purple flower of Tan'quao to treat injuries. I am ready to return home and resume my mantle.

"I am ready to take back what is mine."

Deylan couldn't take any more. Len's explanation came out so casually, without any hint of apprehension, that Deylan couldn't imagine what Len had learned. Deylan had seen battle-hardened pirates, and had seen the effect of decades-long fighting. Len had lived among those men longer than Deylan. Len had seen combat in the East. His words bespoke a confidence that Deylan could only imagined would be backed up with physical action.

Turning away from the two, Deylan started to circle the deck. He needed to clear his head. He needed to talk to Heru when all of this was done.

It's always the same, Deylan thought to himself. His face became warm and he fought back tears. *All we're good for is carrying on the family name. We're just an extension of them, and once we're no longer useful, they throw us away.*

Swiping at the tears that rolled down his cheeks, Deylan took a steadying breath.

"Gods damn it," he muttered.

〜〜

Kayna requested both Deylan and Heru to remain with the ship until they'd figured out their next move. From the sound of it, both of their skills would be needed when they set sail to confront the man once more. The thought of engaging with such a monster unnerved Deylan, but he resigned himself to the eventuality.

Now, nearly five days out at sea, Deylan and the crew had drunk through all of the fine wine Kayna's men had brought aboard the ship the night before the incident. Five days. And in those five days, Deylan rarely saw the two acknowledge each other.

Leaning against the side of the ship, Deylan thanked the gods that his wide-brimmed hat had not been destroyed on this trip. The balm he'd been using to protect his body from the blistering heat never lasted long, and even though he'd been careful and used it sparingly, Deylan knew he wouldn't have much left by the time they returned home. He'd have to buy more, especially if he stayed with them and ventured back out to sea.

Sweat beaded on his arms and under the lining of the hat, matting his hair to his head. He wished that even a slight breeze would come by to chase away the heat. If the heat continued, their water supply would run out by the time they reached the Bone Coast.

Out of the corner of his eye, Deylan noticed Heru come up beside him and rest his elbows on the ledge of the ship. Keeping his gaze steady, Deylan let Heru settle in next to him. He felt the young Xanan beside him, not touching him, but the comfortable presence the two shared with each other, return. Heru no longer moved rigidly. Instead, the graceful fluidity granted to him after over a decade of dutiful training had been restored.

"It's hotter than the seven hells," Heru noted, keeping his eyes on the horizon. "How do you manage being out here for so long?"

Deylan hummed as he pondered the answer. "I suppose, I've just gotten used to it a bit." Turning to face his friend, he added, "I can't wait until we get a breeze. If this is hotter than the seven hells, I can't imagine death being all that bad."

Heru met his gaze, a darkness crossing over his face. Deylan wondered if the jest proved to be a little too dark for the Xanan.

"Are you all right?" Deylan asked, changing the topic.

"Well enough. I'll have to approach my father at some point." Heru no longer sounded enthusiastic about the prospect.

"So you'll be staying as Kayna asked?"

"As long as you."

It wasn't a question.

With a sigh, Deylan pushed some of his matted hair off his face and closed his eyes. He pictured a breeze cooling him. The water was beautiful – a glistening sapphire that sparkled under the sun. If only there was a little bit of wind.

"I suppose I'll join you," he said at last. "You'd be absolutely lost without me."

An unwonted snort escaped Heru. "Always humble."

The two stood quietly together. Gulls cried overhead, their raucous noise echoing from far away. The waves lapped softly against the hull of the ship, and a few men shouted to each other from across the deck. Most of the crew took shelter below deck. Those who remained above carried large water skins, drinking frequently from them as they strolled on the deck, the flesh of their tan, leathery skin beginning to turn a painful shade of red.

Deylan took a handful of cherries from his pocket and popped them into his mouth. The warm juices that burst with the first bite brought a smile to his face. Spitting the pits into the sea, he shoved a few more into his mouth. Holding out some for Heru, the Xanan took a few and popped them in his mouth.

"Are you going to spend more time with Kayna?" Heru asked after a long, comfortable silence.

"Perhaps. Right now I want to focus on a way to finish what I started." Deylan let his words hang ominously.

"Will that involve you telling me more of your stories?" Heru asked. "I can probably help you figure out a way to solve your problems if I know the full truth... You said you wanted us to be honest with each other."

Deylan hummed.

He did say that. It might be nice to have someone to regale with his exploits. The two could find a way to make his stories appropriate enough to tell his mother and little sisters. Perhaps he would tell Heru. Someday.

XXXV

THE LIGHT FROM TWO CANDLES FLICKERED in the otherwise darkened room. One candle sat a hair above the candletreow in a pool of fat. A thin tendril of black smoke emanated from the tip of the flame as it sputtered to death. The second candle, a fresh one Jolly picked up from Last Call on the Xanan's behalf, shone brightly, a little halo of light surrounding the entirety of the flame. Len sat on his bed, a small, silver, circular hand-mirror in his hand.

While the crew manned the ship back to the Bone Coast, Len found himself seeking the quiet solitude of his room. The day of the god-blessed attack, Len spoke to his little retinue and confirmed that there was no more information regarding the disappearance of the other ships. A few wild rumors, but nothing specific.

His conversation with his son ended on a disappointing note. The two Xanans proved to have more in common than Len realized. His stubbornness and determination had always gotten him to push past his obstacles and further his conquest. It was how he overthrew his predecessor and became the Great Heart. Yet for some reason, he didn't expect Heru to share the same qualities. Damn kid.

Turning the mirror over between his fingers, Len absentmindedly stared through the intricate engravings on the exterior of the mirror. Framed with a concentric circle, three jasmine flowers, their delicate petals pointed to perfection like little stars, formed an angled triangle design. Long ago when he was first courting Zaa'ni, Len bought the mirror for her. The jasmine flower was a symbol of beauty. He loved how she would stare at herself as she applied red paint to her lips or checked her hair, often tucking a strand behind her ear. Zaa'ni never tied her hair back before having children, letting her thick, wavy locks flow freely down her back.

Opening the mirror, he could have sworn that he saw her face flash in the reflective glass. The mirror closed with a snap. It had been too long. Len almost regretted pocketing the mirror the last time he was home. Almost.

What happened to Bermet? he asked himself for the hundredth time since he first laid eyes on Heru aboard the *Fury*. Len hated not knowing. *After this, I should take some time and return home with the boy.*

Len's mind wandered as he recalled Heru saying that he had a little sister. Arezou. Len wondered if it would be better to never meet the girl. Eight years without knowing her father, it might be kinder to let the girl think that he had died. But the questions about Bermet continued to haunt Len. Zaa'ni would be fine. She was strong. But Bermet...his pearl. He had to make sure she was okay.

Slipping the mirror into his pocket for now, Len laid back and rested his head on the pillow.

It's been a long time since I've encountered a god-blessed. This one seems stronger than the Avalanche. By the gods, I really hope Freyna hasn't forsaken me. Especially with what I'm about to face.

Len pressed his palms into his eyes until tiny stars appeared. Though he didn't want to admit it, he missed having Pram around so he could talk out his plans. Pram, being as skilled as he was, always provided a solid counterbalance to Len's aspirations – pointing out potential weaknesses that needed to be shored up. He trusted no one else but Pram.

I've never seen a Tempest or Stream who could do that. Tempests can create wind storms and Streams can manipulate water, but for someone to be able to mix the two together? And on top of it all, to somehow pull light from the heavens like that. Their power is unheard of. Do we even stand a chance against such might?

Len stared up into the ceiling as he mulled over everything.

This will be an uphill battle, he finally admitted to himself. *He has both the ability to ambush and a strong knowledge of the sea. He could sneak up on us without us even noticing him. He might even don a disguise – perhaps a merchant seeking asylum. And who knows if there are more like him? We must be prepared.*

Swallowing his pride, Len knew what he needed to do.

I need Hroth. I hope he hasn't left the Bone Coast.

About the Author

K.N. Nguyen is a fantasy author and founder of DragonScript. Growing up, she often found herself immersed in some imaginary world, conquering enemy nations, and saving the day. As time went on, her love for horrible puns and nerd culture pulled her out of these worlds and brought her back to reality.

It wasn't until she started working at her office job that she felt the itch to begin writing. Since 2015, she's been bringing her stories to life, one-by-one, and following her passion by delving into new mythologies.

A native of Sacramento, California, K.N. Nguyen spends her time singing karaoke, playing taiko, enjoying rhythm dancing games, and traveling with her friends and family when she isn't writing.

Also by K.N. Nguyen

The Fallen Series

King's Blood

Oath Blood

God's Blood

Nightmare Blood

Dragon Script

Dragon Script

Lost Chapter

Mother of the Night

Venari

Other Works

A Song of Strength

Last Chance

Kuchisake-Onna

www.ingramcontent.com/pod-product-compliance
Lightning Source LLC
Chambersburg PA
CBHW072006190726
48293CB00001B/181